MAD, BAD &
DANGEROUS
TO KNOW

Also by the author

Love, Hate & Other Filters

Internment

MAD, BAD & DANGEROUS TO KNOW

SAMIRA AHMED

Atom
An imprint of
Little, Brown Book Group
Carmelite House
50 Victoria Embankment
London EC4Y 0DZ

An Hachette UK Company
www.hachette.co.uk

www.atombooks.co.uk

ATOM

First published in the US in 2020 by Soho Teen
First published in the UK in 2020 by Atom

1 3 5 7 9 10 8 6 4 2

Copyright © 2020 by Samira Ahmed

The moral right of the author has been asserted.

A CIP catalogue record for this book
is available from the British Library.

ISBN 978-0-349-00355-9

Printed and bound in Great Britain by
Clays Ltd, Elcograf S.p.A

Papers used by Atom are from well-managed forests
and other responsible sources.

For Thomas, Lena, and Noah,
the astonishing lights of my world.

And for those whose stories are buried, hidden in the dark
corners of history, I lift up my lantern for you.

*When I want to understand what is happening today
or try to decide what will happen tomorrow, I look back.*

—OMAR KHAYYAM

KHAYYAM

I live in between spaces.

The borders between nations, the invisible hyphen between words, the wide chasm between "one of us" and me alone.

French American.

Indian American.

Muslim American.

Biracial. Interfaith. Child of immigrants.

A Parisienne for one month a year: the month when all the other Parisians flee the city.

A girl staring at her phone screen, looking for love but knowing it's not going to show up.

I didn't choose any of this. Which is not to say I wouldn't have, given the opportunity. But it's not like I ever had the option.

I don't even get a say in my diminutives. It's always "Frenchie" or "la petite Américaine."

The people who can't guess what I am think I'm "exotic." Some people say I'm lucky to be an ethnomorph—a person whose brown skin, brown hair, and brown eyes make it seem like I could be from half the countries in the world. But I'm not a passport that everyone gets to stamp with a label of their choosing. Others look at me and try to shove me into their own narrative to define who and what I am. But I'm not a blank page that everyone else gets to write on.

I have my own voice.

I have my own story.

I have my own name. It's Khayyam.

KHAYYAM

I just stepped in dog shit. Bienvenue à Paris.

Welcome to my life of constant code-switching. Witness my attempts to blend an occasional impulse for Bollywood melodramatics with my flair for complaining like a local. I shouldn't be cranky, summering in Paris. I should be an expert at dodging excrement on sidewalks and accustomed to tepid service from waiters and sardonic smiles at my fluent but slightly accented French. And I should absolutely be prepared for les grèves—the strikes that bring the Métro to a standstill every single time we're here.

I should be French about it and nonchalant.

Instead, I'm American and have no chill.

Because it *is* hot. The air-conditioning is mostly aspirational. And I'm a captive here, since my parents value family vacation tradition more than my desire to stay in Chicago, stewing in self-doubt and woe-is-me pity and the truth universally acknowledged that the forces of entropy attack you on all fronts.

This is what metaphorical multiple organ failure feels like:

My head: I have likely, most probably, almost definitely

royally screwed up my chances of getting into the School of the Art Institute of Chicago—my dream college that I've been shooting for since ninth grade. It is *the* school if you want to go into art history. Which I do. Obsessively.

My heart: Belongs to Zaid. *Still*. Zaid, my not-exactly boy-friend, but only because he never actually called himself my boyfriend, who is thousands of miles away in Chicago.

My lungs: On top of the dog crap, there's a railway strike today, somehow precisely coinciding with this heat wave and my arrival in Paris. The air is humid and so thick I'm panting.

But those are merely symptoms.

The underlying cause? An essay. Yeah, really.

The School of the Art Institute is super competitive, so I wanted to find a way to stand out from the pack. I had this brilliant idea to submit an absolutely mind-blowing essay for its Young Scholar Prize. Technically, I was ineligible because you have to be a high school grad to enter. I was only a junior, and I petitioned the judges to make an exception. I didn't want a technicality standing in the way of my dreams. Besides, my college counselor told me it would show I have "moxie" and would look great on my college applications. I was certain I had solved a centuries-old art world mystery, proving that Eugène Delacroix had secretly given a painting—one of several—from his *Giaour* series to the writer Alexandre Dumas, the *all for one, one for all* dude. Not just any painting in the series—*the* exact one on display at the Art Institute. I was going to astound the old fogey museum curators with my genius. I would unveil a secret that was hiding in plain sight. I would be the youngest prizewinner ever, an art world darling. I based my entire theory on a single sentence in a twenty-year-old article about Delacroix I found online and followed down a rabbit hole. Apparently fake news is also old news.

The thing with confidence, though, is that when you're proven wrong—and holy hell, was I proven wrong—you wither away into the smallest version of yourself. And head judge—now my lifelong nemesis—Celenia Mondego made sure of that. In her words, I had written, "*an earnest if ill-conceived attempt at unraveling a mystery of provenance that fell far short of its ambitions due to slipshod research—a catastrophic inability to grasp obvious facts. The work of a dilettante, not a future art historian.*"

The words still stab.

Maybe I could deal with it better if I didn't feel so alone, but *my* person, *my* I'll-always-be-there-for-you pseudo boyfriend, graduated from Lab High in June and is apparently so busy getting ready to leave for college that he can't even pick up the phone—his second favorite appendage. Meanwhile, I'm pleading with myself not to text him *again*. Clinging like a lifeline to the one text he did send while I was mid-flight: I'll see you when I see you. p.s. I got Ice Capades. Quoting *our* thing, *our* ridiculous thing, an inside joke from our cheesy retro first date movie. I melted. Ugh.

I keep letting myself forget that it's at least partly his fault I screwed up my prize essay. Somewhat. Probably. Indirectly. It seemed like every time I was in the library researching or trying to write, he'd sneak up behind me in the stacks and kiss me on the neck. His kisses are highly distracting.

Basically, I'm seventeen and already washed up. What do I do now?

Mom would tell me to go easier on myself and to trust my own voice to find a way out.

Papa would remind me that I'm young and in Paris, a city with pastries on every corner, and that life is still beautiful: C'est la belle vie, chérie.

Zaid, if he were acknowledging my existence and wasn't part of my problem, would probably tell me to forget about everything and suggest creative ways in which he might be able to help me with that.

And Julie, my best friend, who is currently inaccessible because she's on a Dark-Ages, technology-free family holiday at a cabin in Door County, would tell me to figure out where I want to go and do whatever it takes to get there. Easy for her to say—she's both an unstoppable force and an immovable object.

Here's the thing: I actually know where I want to go. But too many things I can't control keep getting in my way.

Sometimes literally.

With les grèves there's no Métro, and every electric scooter and bike share is taken. Normally I wouldn't mind a long, leisurely walk along the quais of the Seine River on the way to the Petit Palais—that's kind of the point of being in Paris. But I'm reminded that this is why there are no songs about August in Paris, when it's all tourists and la vie en sweat instead of the Hollywood version of Paris where it's perpetual spring, when young love and chestnut trees are always in bloom.

If I believed in fate, I'd say the universe was conspiring against me.

THE COURTYARD CAFÉ of the Petit Palais has always been my reliable refuge. I plan on photographing every inch of its meandering path, fragrant plants, blue-and-gold tiled fountains, and, of course, the perfectly pillowy macarons I'll be inhaling at a small wrought-iron table amongst the blossoms. Luckily, the place is made for Instagram, which is good because I need new content to replace all the dusty old books and archival material I posted in my "ill-conceived" attempt to impress the ultimate *we are not amused*, judgiest of judges Celenia Mondego.

Maybe meticulously cataloguing my trip will help me forget my "catastrophic inability" to do anything right.

And maybe, perhaps, Zaid will see my posts and remember I exist.

First, though, I need to scrape the remaining dog crap from my red All-Stars.

I skulk into the shadows of the sculptures of naked women flanking the alabaster staircase that leads to the doors of the Petit Palais. As soon as I bend down to inspect my left sole, I hear someone behind me attempting to stifle a laugh.

Do not look, Khayyam. Keep your head down.

"Welcome to Paris!" a honeyed French accent declares in English.

I roll my eyes. I almost decide to bite back in French, but this arrogant jerk already chose my preferred language for sparring. "How do you know I'm not from Paris?" I ask with my back still turned to him.

"I'm s-sorry," the Frenchman stammers.

I stand and whirl around, ready to go for the jugular, but see that this particular jugular leads to an extremely cute face.

He's my age. Or a little older? Brown wavy hair with hints of red. Lightly tanned skin. And when he pushes his tortoise-shell sunglasses to the top of his head, he reveals eyes that could be the inspiration for the Crayola crayon I preferred above all others for my childhood masterpieces: Raw Sienna.

"Well, then you know the adage: it's the left foot; it's happiness!" he says.

I burst out laughing. And when I try to curb it, I end up snorting. It's another childhood flashback; every time I hear the word *happiness* spoken with an even remotely French accent, it kills me.

The cute boy gives me a quizzical look.

"A-penis," I explain. "With a French accent, 'happiness' sounds like 'a penis.' I'm sorry; I know what you're saying: 'C'est du pied gauche, c'est du bonheur!'" I shrug, feeling my natural defensiveness creep up. "I guess you can chalk it up to my American immaturity?"

He grins like a true Frenchman, showing no teeth. "I think no such thing about Americans or about you," he says. Those raw sienna eyes dance. "I have heard you Americans are sometimes presumptuous, though."

"Ha, ha. Touché," I say, smiling back like an American, displaying all my gleaming, orthodontically perfected teeth.

His smile widens in return, challenging my assumptions about his aloof Frenchiness. Damn. His teeth are perfect, too.

"Tu parles français?" he asks.

"Je suis française," I answer immediately.

"Et américaine?"

I sigh. Apparently being brown means you have to be something other than European. I get the *but where are you really from from* version of this back home in America, too. "What, my accent sucks too much?" I grumble.

"No, no, not at all. I'm sorry. I didn't mean . . . I only meant because of the merde on your shoe. Living in Paris . . . Parisians have a kind of dog crap radar."

I bite my lip and look down at my All-Stars. They're mostly poop free now. My emotional pendulum has swung from rage to mortification. I think I prefer the rage. It's much less embarrassing.

"I step in actual crap, then I step in figurative crap as well," I mutter, mostly to myself.

He laughs again. "Not at all. In fact, it's my fault. It was hardly chivalrous of me to question your citizenship based on your inability to avoid crap."

I laugh again, too. I can't help it. Laughing with a hot, anonymous French boy is a more satisfying diversion than either Instagram or macarons. Plus, he actually used the word *chivalrous* without irony. Zaid knows what it means, but it's not exactly in his vocabulary.

The boy clears his throat. "Perhaps I can ask for a modification?"

I knit my eyebrows together. He's pronouncing "modification" the French way, which throws me. *"Modification?"* I repeat. "Oh, um, you mean, a do-over?"

"Oui. Oui. Yes. A do-over." He offers a soft grin, then places a hand on his chest and straightens his shoulders. I realize he's tall, taller than me, and I'm five-foot-seven or, as we say in France, 1m70. I'm not just bilingual; I speak metric, too. "Please, let me begin again. I'm Alexandre Dumas."

I burst out laughing. The universe *is* trolling me. "Alexandre Dumas? Let me guess; your best friends are three brothers named Athos, Porthos, and Aramis?"

His smile falters a little.

I can feel my face getting hot. Sometimes I speak before I think. Now I actually *hear* my dumb dad joke made at his expense. Somehow I managed to be both childish and pretentious, because duh, doesn't everyone know the names of the Three Musketeers?

"Dumas is my sixth-great-grandfather," he says.

My mouth drops open. Is he kidding me? I *know* there's no such thing as fate. Fate is coincidence. Coincidence is math. But damn, the odds of this . . . I should've bought a lottery ticket.

"Alexandre Dumas is your grand-père? No freaking way." I clear my throat and collect myself, reaching out my hand. "My name is Khayyam Maquet. It's nice to meet you."

"Enchanté," he says.

He's reluctant to extend a hand back. Our eyes meet. Shaking hands is *not* the customary French greeting between friends. But we're only strangers who engaged in witty banter, and I'm not about to kiss this dude on the cheeks. Still, I don't think he'll leave me hanging.

"This might sound weird," I say when he finally does shake, "but follow me. There's something I want to show you."

Leila

Haseki.

The favored.

That is what they are compelled to call me. All of them. Eyes cast downward in reverence. Do not aspire to this, *I want to warn the young ones. The ones whose rosy lips and cheeks have yet to be introduced to Pasha. But I do not say this. I say little, choosing my words wisely.*

This is how you survive.

Study.

Rise through the ranks.

Become irreplaceable.

Become the chosen one.

Find your power. Use it, but softly.

Haseki.

Pasha conferred this once-ancient title upon me, to fashion me after Süleyman's most beloved and trusted haseki. It is an honor, *he told me.* A gift.

In that moment, my name was erased, buried under dirt. But my spirit was not.

KHAYYAM

The Petit Palais isn't a palace at all, and it certainly isn't *petit*. It was built for the 1900 World's Fair, l'Exposition Universelle. It's a trapezoid of stone and steel with marble mosaic floors, immense columns, and a sky-grazing rotunda where I can roam the exhibition halls content in anonymous humidity-controlled solitude—as my barest self, Khayyam, unadorned and unfettered.

Except this time, I'm not alone.

I'm with a boy. A decidedly cute one. Who happens to be an Alexandre Dumas. In other words, a boy who might have answers to the questions banging around in my brain ever since my epic essay fail.

If I believed in kismet/qismat/destinée, I might trust that the universe planned this meeting. There's a kind of poetry to it. But believing in fate is magical thinking. A lot of people want to find the deeper meaning behind random circumstances. But what's the point? Extraordinary events are basically chance plus time.

So why are my palms all sweaty?

I can actually hear my friend Julie answering my question

with one of her own: *Who cares why it all happened? You're walking around a museum with a cute French guy. Stop over-thinking it.*

But she's not here to stop me from considering my clammy hands and fluttery stomach. Maybe I'm nervous because chance and time have collided and brought me to *this* place. With *this* boy. In front of *this* painting—Eugène Delacroix's *The Combat of the Giaour and the Pasha*—that I discovered a couple years ago and that inspired me to jump down an art history rabbit hole where I landed with an unceremonious thud. Maybe I shouldn't tell Alexandre that I've dedicated countless hours of my life to find a connection between his ancestor and this painting's mate—the one in the Giaour series that lives in the Art Institute of Chicago. Maybe not reveal-ing everything about my entire life in the first five minutes of knowing this stranger is a good thing. I should cultivate an air of mystery like a proper French girl.

"You love the Delacroix?" Alexandre asks. "It's one of my favorites, too."

"There's an art world legend that Dumas—that your grand-père—owned this painting," I manage, glancing shyly at him.

Alexandre arches his eyebrows.

"Well, not this exact one, but one in the Delacroix series that's in Chicago. At the Art Institute. Where I live. I mean, I live in Chicago. The city. Not the museum. Duh." I bite my lower lip to stop this embarrassing overflow of sponta-neous dork. Proper French-girl flirting involves elegance and restraint. Clearly, I lack both.

He shrugs. "Delacroix and Dumas were friends. And Dela-croix did gift him art . . ." He clears his throat. "You certainly seem to know a lot about my family."

When I try to hold his gaze, he turns back to the painting. I clam up. I'm not sure how much more I should confess. If he hadn't been the one who approached me, I'd seem like some weird stalker-y Alexandre Dumas fangirl. Or worse, a dilettante. Celenia Mondego's judgment echoes in my mind, and an awkward silence occupies the space between Alexandre and me.

"So . . ." He scrunches up his forehead, trying gallantly to fill the pause. "You think that my great-grand-père Dumas might have owned one of the Giaours by Delacroix?"

I shrug and shift my weight from one foot to the other. "Maybe?"

Alexandre nods. "There are family rumors, at least according to my uncle Gérard who researches that kind of stuff. It's definitely, um, interesting . . ."

Oh God. I *am* a *dilettante*. A bumbling, ineloquent amateur art-splainer, telling the five (or was it six?)-times-great-grandson of Alexandre Dumas all about his family. Cascading organ failure continuing. What am I on now? Spleen? Bladder? Please don't let it be bladder.

Before I can stop myself, I blurt, "Actually I wrote this entire paper on it. For a prize. That I didn't win. I thought Chicago's Art Institute Delacroix was the one Dumas owned. I thought I'd made this huge art world discovery about the line of ownership. Turns out I was totally wrong about the provenance." A nervous giggle slips out. So much for an air of sophistication. "Supposedly Delacroix created at least six in a series based on the same Lord Byron poem, *The Giaour*. I came here today to take another look at this one in case I missed something, like maybe *this* was the one Dumas owned, not the one in Chicago. But um, I guess not? I mean, I'm not sure what other clues I was looking for. Probably wishful thinking? I guess if anyone would know if Dumas owned this Delacroix, it would be . . . you. I . . . well . . . anyway . . . Two of those six paintings have been lost—maybe it's another one?"

I need to pause for air. I think I'm speaking English, but it's really a high-speed torrent of nerd. This boy could potentially help me, and I'm over here taking random stabs at history. I cover my face with my palm. *Focus, Khayyam.*

Alexandre gently pulls my hand away. "Are you embarrassed? Don't be. Your paper sounds amazing. No one seems to care about our lost family history anymore, except maybe my uncle. But to me, the past is a mystery waiting to be revealed."

I perk up. Maybe this guy speaks nerd, too. And did his hand just linger on mine? "That's why I'm obsessed with art history!" I practically yell, then quickly lower my voice to a museum-appropriate level. "It discovers life in relics of the past and brings that past forward to the future—it's like an academic time machine. Those Etruscan vases we walked by? They're echoes of people who lived over two thousand years ago. We can extrapolate a lot based on a few puzzle pieces. Sometimes it's a revelation. Though I guess other times, like with my essay . . ." I'm rambling and also too embarrassed to finish the sentence.

He gazes at me with a warm smile. "Who cares if you didn't win the prize? Qui ne tente rien n'a rien."

"No pain, no gain?" I sigh. "If only I'd gained something more than humiliation."

"I thought Americans weren't defeatist," he quips.

"That's the French part of me speaking," I deadpan.

"Well, I think all the parts of you are charmant," he replies without missing a beat.

I'm such a pushover for casual French flirting. Wait. Am I

enjoying this? I'm enjoying this. I'm supposed to be putting my life back together, but I'm flirting with a cute boy in a museum. Which sounds like the kind of thing Julie would do, not me. But being my usual cautious self hasn't been working out that great lately, so why not go for it?

And on cue my stomach twists and turns and knots up with guilt. I stare at Alexandre's rakish grin, but an image of Zaid's gorgeous smile pops into my head. I have no reason to feel guilty. Unfortunately, my thoughts and feelings aren't like a finely crafted Delacroix. They're messy and abstract— loud, confused streaks and splatters of paint on a canvas.

"Right," I mumble. "Of course. Charmant. Because what could be more charming than meeting someone who is scraping crap off their shoe?"

He grins at me. I smile back. I have to admit, it feels good. Standing here, right now, in front of the Delacroix. Smiling like I belong here. Defiant like: *You tried to kill me, but you only deeply wounded me. So there.* I think for a moment about what first drew me to *this* version of the painting in Delacroix's series, and what led me to its mate in Chicago: There's something disturbing, almost terrifying about the scene. It's immediate and entrancing; it pulls you in. Two men on horseback clashing, daggers drawn, tangled ferociously in battle. The Pasha in brooding jewel tones—emerald and garnet—blood dripping from the leg of his white horse. A sharp contrast to the Giaour, the supposed infidel in a vest and simple white robe, the sinewy muscles of his forearms flexed, ready to drive his blade into the Pasha's chest. The colors are deep and rich and striking. It's a painting, but when you turn the corner and catch your first glimpse, it's as if you've stumbled onto a real fight. The canvas isn't even that big; it's only about two feet wide and two feet tall. But it explodes with movement, as if the scene is about to burst from the frame.

I clear my throat. "So you said this was one of your favorites, too. Why?"

"It's fierce. Alive. So—" He pauses, trying to find the right word.

"Viscérale?" Visceral. Sometimes the perfect word exists in both my languages.

"Yes!" His sienna eyes sparkle as he continues. "The brushstrokes are angry. And I know it's inspired by a Byron poem, but it feels very Dumas to me. Passion. Vengeance. Beauty. Two men fighting over a woman. One loved her, the other killed her."

I kind of get what Alexandre is saying. It's not the first time a man has described Delacroix's paintings this way, but his words pinch. They're all wrong. Dismissive. Entitled. "In Byron's poem, the Giaour and the Pasha both have dialogue, but the woman is silent. I mean, the poem is, like, nine thousand words, and she's only even *mentioned* eleven or twelve times." My voice is flat, betraying my anger. "She's the whole reason the poem exists, but she never gets a chance to speak. A poet created her. A painter was inspired by her. But they both denied her a voice in her own story. She was erased."

Alexandre turns to me, puzzled. It's clear we're not flirting anymore. "But she isn't real. She's fiction."

"So are the Giaour and the Pasha."

"We agree, then?"

I scoff, pointing to the painting's title, named for fictional men created by real men whose art gets to endure.

"She had a name, too," I say. "It was Leila."

Leila

❦

I take care to remove all my jewels, especially the anklets, lest their tinkling wake the entire serai. Tiptoeing barefoot over the stone floors, I slip in and out of the darkness. The full moon could reveal me, but she's consented to hide her beauty behind passing clouds, offering me safe passage through the latticed corridor. Valide would have me killed if she knew where I was going, but Si'la has assured me that Valide sleeps through the night—lulled into a slumber by the dream spells of the ruya peri who dwells in the serai. Still, I step lightly through the Courtyard of Eunuchs. If I rouse any of them, my wiles will be useless to dampen their suspicions.

The Passage of Concubines leads to the Forty Steps . . . down, down, down to the hastanesi reserved only for the women of the serai. With no trace of the moon, I am in utter darkness. But I have passed these stones thousands of times, and my fingers follow the cool walls until they reach a door that is almost forgotten.

Tonight, it is my portal to a tiny world outside my golden cage.

I step through the door into the second courtyard. The

smallest of the courtyards, it lies abandoned. Even the gardeners have forsaken it in fear of the jinn that lurk in the trees. Though their branches arc and reach to the heavens, heavy with green leaves, the trunks of all the trees here are hollowed, carved out into perfectly smooth caverns. They say the jinn whittled away the trunks to create hiding places. In the center of the courtyard, two trees grafted together over the years stretch to the sky, branches intertwining like lovers' arms. Their hollows meet to form the heart of the courtyard.

The night smells of damask roses.

He is near.

KHAYYAM

On cue, life reminds me once again that magical thinking doesn't work. Sometimes shit is just shit. Period.

Stepping in that merde yesterday? It's not going to bring me "a-penis" after all. Sure, I inexplicably ran into a French guy who may possibly be able to help salvage my academic self-worth. Did I mention that's he's hot? Or that he is an *actual descendant* of Alexandre Dumas? Or that for one fleeting and lovely art-filled afternoon, I was tempted to believe in magic? Fate, even?

For a few brief hours, the Métro shutdown didn't seem like such a pain. I spent the dreamy walk home posting scenic Paris shots on Instagram: boats on the Seine, a lone red love lock attached to a bridge, even a Robert Doisneau–style pic of a couple kissing with a black-and-white filter. I've been posting almost nonstop since I landed, detailing every step of this trip—except for my chance encounter with the cute Frenchman—hoping to inspire Zaid to appear out of thin air.

And now he has. With Rekha in his lap.

I squirm on the sofa, glaring at Rekha's feed. Even on my phone's screen she is larger than life: heart-shaped face, golden-brown skin, impossibly long lashes, and eyes that smolder for the lens. A classic Rekha selfie—stunning. Only this time her arm is hooked around Zaid's neck. It's classic Zaid, too—mischievous grin, long coffee-brown bangs partially obscuring his beautiful dark eyes that are clearly fixated on her. And he's wearing his Chicago Brown Line 'L' T-shirt.

I gave him that shirt.

It was a memento of our first date. We took the Brown Line 'L' to the Music Box, where they were screening movies set in Chicago, and saw *While You Were Sleeping*—a classic, corny holiday rom-com that somehow takes all the clichés of mistaken identity and misunderstandings and makes them charming. Turns out that the Brown Line plays a role in the movie, too. Hours later when we shared our first kiss under the rumble of the Southport stop on that "L," I almost fooled myself into believing that maybe, just maybe, life did have magic in it.

For the one-month anniversary of that kiss, I bought Zaid a Brown Line T-shirt. Soon after, he gave me a tee emblazoned with a dorky, desperate *While You Were Sleeping* quote: I GOT ICE CAPADES. It was so silly and so *us*, romantic in a completely unromantic way. Unassuming. Comfortable.

That's why the gifts were special. Sentimental, even. Until right now.

Maybe I need to adopt Zaid's nonchalance and focus on something more rewarding. Say, the French guy who literally almost fell into *my* lap. It's infuriating that Zaid was even a stray thought yesterday. That pang of guilt I felt? Tragic. Why does my brain (my heart?) do this to me? The actual facts are right in front of my face, but still, my reason always seems to lose out to my stupid feelings.

ZAID LITERALLY INTRODUCED me as a "friend" on prom night to a new neighbor—a gorgeous college sophomore with bright hazel eyes. Half the block was on the sidewalk, an informal party since so many kids on my street were going to prom. The parent paparazzi were out in full force, snapping a million photos—group shots, couples, obligatory family formals, and a bunch of me and Julie and other kids goofing around then pinning boutonnieres on our dates. Zaid had to run back to his car because he forgot my wrist corsage. Of course he did. Julie had had to remind him to get me flowers in the first place. Another obvious sign I chose to ignore. When he finally headed back, he walked over with the new neighbor, so engrossed in conversation with her that he seemed startled when I appeared.

I want to say it was like the scene in a rom-com when the girl finally realizes that the guy she thought was *the one* is only just the one *before*:

ZAID

Oh . . . Khayyam! This
(points to lithe, gorgeous girl)
is the new neighbor.

NEW NEIGHBOR
(waves)

Hey!
(Awkward pause, feet shuffling.)

ZAID
And this is my . . . friend, Khayyam.

KHAYYAM
(gulps, pulls knife out of heart)

```
        Is that for me?
        (Points to orchid wrist corsage in
                plastic box.)


                    ZAID
            (chuckles nervously)
        Yeah. Yes. Here you go!
            (Hands Khayyam the box.)
```

Camera pans from box to Khayyam's enraged face.
She throws the box on the ground and walks away.
Zaid calls her name, but she doesn't turn back,
and he falls out of focus. Camera zooms in on
Khayyam as she walks off into the sunset, a smile
spreading across her face.

END SCENE.

But that's not how it played out.

I took the box, slipped the corsage over my wrist, and went to prom with Zaid, where we danced and laughed and I pretended I didn't feel the point of that dagger in my heart. Julie gave him the stink-eye all night long; I'm surprised she didn't sucker punch him on my behalf.

In hindsight, it all should've been obvious. Zaid and I never had a firm status agreement. We never called ourselves a couple out loud. At least, *he* didn't. It always felt like there would be more—there were intimations of things to come, like whispered plans to backpack across Europe while we held hands at the Point or suggestions of me visiting him at college while we snuggled in the hollow of Henry Moore's *Nuclear Energy*. I wanted to believe it all because we fit perfectly in the chiseled space of that sculpture, arms and legs intertwined. Because when we first kissed under the 'L' tracks, it felt like we'd invented the idea of kissing. Because sometimes we'd sit on my back porch doing physics home-work and Zaid would ask if I was Bohr'd and then smile at me, and I knew I could listen to his corny dad jokes forever.

A catastrophic inability to grasp obvious facts. Remem-ber? I was reading between the lines when there was nothing to see but blank space.

Now Zaid's off to Reed College in a few weeks, where he's going to be majoring in environmental studies and smoking pot, and I'm . . . *here*. Afraid to text him. Scared to admit what Rekha's Instagram screams at me, that the one person I thought was closer to me than anyone in the world seems to have forgotten I exist.

TO ADD SALT to the wound, Alexandre is apparently ghost-ing me, too.

When we exchanged numbers yesterday, he said he wanted to meet up again today. I swear we had a moment. *Moments.* Sparkly eyed glimpses of what *could* be. Still, I'm stuck in the moments with Zaid that *have been*. Maybe it's my fatal flaw: I'm always in the Past or the Future and never in the Now.

"That's three long sighs in a row," my mom says, peeking around her newspaper from our little balcony, the afternoon light streaming in through the floor-to-ceiling windows.

I wasn't even aware that I'd sighed out loud.

Mom is staring at me expectantly over her bright red cat-eye reading glasses, her graying brown hair unfurling from her loose bun. When I don't say anything, she puts down the paper and rises from her seat, stepping through the patio doors into the room. Every August when we're in

Paris—annual time away from her job as Professor of Medieval Islamic Civilizations at the University of Chicago—she reads an actual newspaper. Not a digital edition but real ink and paper. She says human beings are becoming too detached from the simple pleasure of tangible things in our world. It's why she adores dusty old books. It's the *musk* of history that gets her. Smell is linked to memory, she always says, and technology has no smell because it's never been alive.

Still, I dunno if I totally buy that, because Rekha and Zaid looked *very* alive on Instagram. I could almost smell the hormones pulsing off my screen.

Mom sits beside me on the couch, placing her reading glasses on the coffee table. I know what's coming next. The concerned mom look: mouth turned down at the corners, eyes focused and worried. I'm blessed with my mother's dark eyes, the color of brown glass. When I look at her, it's like a mirror into my slightly wrinklier future. I wonder if she sees me that way, too—as a looking glass to her past, a version of her younger self.

"It's nothing, Mom. Waiting for something that's not going to appear."

"That's rather existential of you."

"Well, we *are* in Paris."

My mom grins and pats my hand. "Still haven't heard from Zaid?"

Ouch. I feel that question like a static shock to my chest. It's a simple question without an easy answer. No, he hasn't texted, but it doesn't mean he hasn't sent me a message.

IF ZAID WERE some random guy, say, one I met while scraping crap off my shoe, I might be wary about sharing details, but Zaid isn't *any* guy. We know his family from school and the mosque. Like me, Zaid is Muslim and has one Indian parent.

Unlike me, he's absolutely mastered tameez, the art of appropriate desi behavior, especially around parents. He started a
tutoring program at our mosque for the younger kids, and his
Urdu kicks ass. On paper, Zaid is the perfect desi catch. In my
current Instagram-shaped reality, he's a lot less so.

As it stands, a lot of people probably side-eye my "good"
Muslim desi girl qualifications because they find them . . .
lacking. My French is fluent. My Urdu, not so much. I have
my dad's language and my mom's religion. I'm a bunch of
disparate parts that aren't enough to make a whole. But I'm
trying to stop caring about what everyone else thinks about
me. I am enough.

Even when I waffle and question my own devotion, even if
I miss Friday prayers, being Muslim is part of my identity, as
much as French or American or Chicagoan. It's in my bones
and my blood. And no one can take that away from me.

Yeah, Mom knows about Zaid. But that doesn't mean
I want to share *every* single detail. I still keep some things
tucked away in secret.

"MAYBE IT'S A technical glitch, beta," Mom suggests, gesturing toward my phone.

"Un pépin technique? Where?" My dad chooses the perfect moment for his entrance. He walks out of the bedroom
and gently places his hand on my mom's shoulder. She looks
up at him, and he smiles without showing teeth. He's lived in
America a long time, but not long enough that a toothy smile
comes naturally.

I watch them lovingly gaze at each other. In many ways they're
opposites—my dad has pale blue eyes, and his fair skin burns
every single summer, while my mom's deep brown skin defies
the sun. I'm somewhere in between. When I was a kid, I wished

I wasn't so in the middle. I wanted to look exactly like my mom because when she and I went out alone, someone would inevitably ask if she was my nanny. It made me mad, but she would wave it off, seemingly unbothered. *"I know who I am,"* she once explained. *"I don't have to prove it to anyone."* She's always been enough for herself, too.

My mom takes my dad's hand in hers. "Khayyam was hoping to hear from Zaid, but—"

I bolt from the couch and grab my purse from the table. Sure, my mom knows about me and Zaid. Papa does, too. But I'm not ready for their academic unpacking of my relationship. I'm not the subject of an undergrad seminar. Before they can protest, I grab my bag and am halfway to the door.

"I'm out of here. You guys can talk about me behind my back like regular parents. I'm going to get a goûter and then head to Place des Vosges." One good thing about being stuck in Paris for the summer is the comfort of an afternoon pastry. Or three.

They laugh a little. My mom blows me a kiss. My dad tells me to text them when I get to Place des Vosges as he settles in next to my mom on the sofa. My parents exchange another loving glance. I swear, you'd think it's their third date. I wonder what it takes to sustain that kind of adoration for over twenty years. Or even twenty weeks . . .

I push open the centuries-old wooden doors to our apartment and step into the dark hall. Maybe I *should* keep more secrets from my parents—less chance of getting trapped in an awkward conversation about my nonexistent love life. I sigh and sidestep the claustrophobia-inducing elevator—it's the size of a double-wide coffin. We're on the fifth floor, but I take the stairs up and down every time. Halfway down the wide, winding staircase, my phone buzzes.

Alexandre: Bonjour. I have spoken with the mayor of Paris, who has agreed to clear your path of merde—both real and figurative—for the rest of your stay. 💩 😃

Me: . . .

Me: . . .

Me: Who is this?

If Alexandre is the diversion the universe has presented, I might as well have fun.

Alexandre: Is that American humor?

Me: Ha! Touché.

Alexandre: I lay down my épée. Shall we meet?

Me: Place des Vosges? Thirty minutes?

Alexandre: Perfect. I will bring a surprise.

Me: A surprise?!

Alexandre: I will make it an American surprise so it comes with many exclamation marks!!!

Me: I see I'm not the first American to get a surprise from you?

Alexandre: You're by far the most beautiful.

This guy seriously knows how to turn on the charm. Sadly, some of that charm is lost on me. I don't feel completely enamored; I feel a little resigned. Because cute as it is, it's not the text I was hoping for. My memory of Zaid is the anchor weighing me down. Zaid, whose easy smile and warm embrace felt like home no matter where we were. He *was* my home, but now he's packed his bags and moved on. Why can't I do the same?

Maybe the real question is, why are my own feelings a mystery to me?

Leila

⌘

"Haseki," he whispers.

I cringe at the word. It is no title, but bondage.

"Giaour," I whisper back. Infidel.

He pulls me into the heart-hollow of the twinned trees.

I place my hand on my chest, drop my eyes, pause. Then raise them to him in a flash. "I may be Pasha's favorite, I may be confined here, but I still own my name."

He lifts my chin toward him. "Leila," he murmurs. "You think you are powerless, but I am under your command."

"Thus the world is as it should be." I smile and remove the diaphanous veil I've wrapped over my head; it wafts gently to the ground.

He smiles back. Flecks of gold dance in his hazel eyes. He traces an index finger over my lips. His touch is coarse, nothing like Pasha's, whose hands are massaged with scented oils by girls of a lower rank before they slip on his silken sleep gloves. But Pasha is not soft; I harbor no such illusions. He could slash us both down with the curve of his kilij in two deft strikes.

"Did you forget to wear your riding gloves again?" I chide.

"I'm sorry." His hand falls away. "You deserve much better."

He plucks the fuchsia rose from his vest and gently brushes the petals against my lips. They say the scent can drive men mad.

I close my eyes and lean back against the smoothed trunk in the hollowed heart of our tree. He leans his body into mine and kisses me just above the jugular notch between my neck and collarbone. The stubble of his beard grazes my skin and makes it burn with want. He unwound his sarik before I arrived, so I run my fingers through the soft dark brown waves of his hair, scented with sandalwood oil, a precious gift from an Indian merchant.

As he unbuttons my midnight-blue ferace, he kisses me along the neckline. I look up through the hollow and see the moon has come out of hiding as her beams enter the cavity of the tree, illuminating us in silver light that pools at our feet. I draw his hand down the ornately embroidered edge of my ferace to where it parts, giving way to my sleep chemise. He sucks in his breath. His hand traces circles up my thigh—his fingernails pecks of moonlight against my skin. I pull at the sash at his waist, drawing him closer, and arc my body into his.

The boughs of our twinned-trees curve down from the sky, screening the entrance to our hallowed space. Stardust shines as it cascades around us, giving rise to tiny sparks that bounce off our bodies.

"Run with me," I whisper.

"Anywhere," he says, sealing his lips over mine in a promise.

KHAYYAM

In America we bulldoze our past, build the future on the rubble, and pretend that ghosts can't haunt us. I wonder if sometimes we ignore their voices because we're scared of hearing ourselves in their echoes. Maybe that's why I love Place des Vosges. It's the oldest planned square in a very old city, and you can almost feel whispers of the past commingling with the present here. Turn away from the people scrolling on their phones and taking selfies, and you'll find the oldest graffiti in Paris on one of the stone pillars around the perimeter of the park: *1764 Nicola*. A guy who wrote a book about his observations in Paris and simply wanted the world to know that, once, he was here, too. That, once, he made his mark.

Another reason why my love for this place endures? Place des Vosges has grass you can sit on. Garden after garden in Paris forbids sitting or walking on the grass. It's like grass is this untouchable objet d'art and not a tangible childhood memory of freshly mowed lawns that spark with fireflies during games of Ghosts in the Graveyard. But at Place des Vosges, I can sink my Midwestern-raised toes into the lawn. It's a reminder that, like Nicola, I found a place here, too.

ALEXANDRE AND I didn't choose a specific meeting point. I don't see him by the seesaws, so I walk around the park. It's filled with tourists and some poor, unfortunate Parisians who apparently have to keep the city running for all the out-of-towners. I tap my phone with an itchy trigger finger—I don't want to text him and reek of eau de desperation. He's only ten minutes late. Fifteen minutes is an acceptable level of tardiness in France. Being on time is actually a bit rude, especially if you're going to someone's house. But that's nothing compared to Indian Standard Time. I don't think I've been to a single desi wedding that started less than an hour late.

This cultural one-two punch of lateness compels the contrarian in me to be punctual. Besides, I hate being late, because I always feel like I'm on the verge of missing out on something important.

"Khayyam, bonjour!"

I turn at the sound of my name. Alexandre smiles at me as he sidesteps a gaggle of tourists. He's even cuter than my memory gives him credit for: wavy reddish-brown curls and a fitted white T-shirt highlighting his tanned skin. He kisses me on both cheeks. In France, la bise—the two-cheek kiss—is perfunctory, an easy, informal greeting between friends and family. But the feather-touch of Alexandre's lips makes me catch my breath. His cheek barely brushes mine. Yet it's a whisper on my skin that feels like a promise.

Can't read into this. Shouldn't.

But the last time I felt this sensation—this effervescence—was that moment under the Southport Street 'L' stop when Zaid's lips hovered just above mine. And closing that distance with a kiss felt like capturing eternity.

Okay, well, maybe Alexandre's peck on my cheek didn't feel *quite* like my first actual kiss with Zaid. Besides I'm guessing that for Alexandre, la bise is just la bise.

"That dress looks beautiful on you," he says.

I look down at one of my summer staples: a magenta voile shift with pink embroidery around the neck. Accepting a compliment gracefully is another particularly French female characteristic that eludes me. I mumble a thank-you, then turn my eyes away, happy my skin is brown enough to hide a blush.

Before I can turn back, Alexandre places a white cardboard box in my hands and lofts a small striped cotton blanket into the air and settles it on the grass. He drops onto it with a smile and reaches a hand out for me to join him. My heart thumps as I slide my free hand into his, taking care to tuck my legs to the side as I take a seat. My knees graze his thigh. He gestures for me to open the box, and when I do, whiffs of butter and sugar and choux float out like clouds.

"L'Eclair de Génie?" I ask.

He nods. My favorite éclair shop in Paris.

"Pistachio raspberry?"

He nods again.

I'm delighted; a perfect éclair awaits. Although I was kind of hoping the surprise was going to be secret Dumas family documents. I need to be patient, or at least act like I am. Being excessively eager is not a good look in France, or anywhere for that matter.

I tap his éclair with mine and say, "Santé." To your health.

He laughs. "You didn't look me in the eyes when you toasted. How do I know you didn't poison my pastry when I looked away?"

I lean over and take a bite of his éclair, making slightly

embarrassing, yet not-so-exaggerated *mmmmmmm* sounds. "See? Poison free."

"Touché," he replies.

Our eyes meet. His spark with a knowing smile, a familiarity. A *moment*. A first step from a me-and-him into an us. Or it could all be in my imagination.

"I wish Americans did pastries like the French," I say, trying to bring my mind back to the now, away from the what-ifs.

Alexandre shrugs. "Well you might not excel at pastries, but no one does cheese in a can like Americans."

I shake my head. Cheese in a can is blasphemy. "I'm sorry that Cheez Whiz entered your life. Should I even ask how?"

Alexandre looks away and clears his throat. "A-a . . . friend . . . bought it for me," he stammers. "When we were on holiday in the States as a . . . joke gift."

"A gag gift? It's totally gag-worthy, so that makes sense."

"Ha!" He smirks as he wipes his hands on his skinny jeans. Then he points to one of the buildings that line the perimeter of the park. "Did you know that Victor Hugo used to live there?"

I nod. I guess we're done talking about the Cheez Whiz friend.

"He used to take hashish with Dumas."

I pull a cartoon double take. "What! Dumas spent his days toking up with Victor Hugo?" I laugh. "I can see it now—France's greatest artists waxing philosophic about killer bud and arguing about whose turn it is to change the bong water."

Alexandre scrunches up his eyebrows like I've annoyed him. Then he sighs like he's exasperated. Crap. Maybe I offended his family honor by mocking his ancestors or something?

"Obviously, a servant would've dumped the bong water," he says with a grin.

I breathe a small sigh of relief and laugh.

"Anyway, it probably wasn't an issue, because they didn't smoke it. The hash was a paste they'd mix into their coffee to inspire hallucinogenic visions. They called themselves the *Club des Hashischins*." The Hash Eaters Club.

"I love the name! If they were around today, they'd probably have custom logo T-shirts and a huge Twitter following with their own . . . Hash-tag." I pause, giving him the chance to appreciate how I crack myself up. "Get it?"

"Is this more American humor?" Alexandre deadpans.

I elbow him. "What? That was a quality quip."

He laughs lightly, reaching out to tuck a stray wisp of my hair behind my ear. I shiver. He appears unfazed. "They had a real clubhouse. On Île Saint-Louis."

"That's where our apartment is," I answer quickly. "Maybe I'm staying in the Hash Eaters Club headquarters right now. With the ghosts of Dumas and Hugo cringing over my inability to avoid crap and a world where cheese in a can exists." I draw my hand to my heart and open my mouth in mock horror. "Sacré bleu!"

Alexandre smirks. "Congratulations. You are the first person to utter that phrase on French soil in over two hundred years."

"I aim to please. Did Dumas do anything else, um, illicit?"

Alexandre gives me a little grin, but I catch something wistful in his eye.

"I do wonder what it must've been like back then. All those swashbuckling bon vivant adventurers Dumas wrote about? Some people say he could've been one of his own characters."

"Your family history is definitely a lot more colorful than

mine. Famous authors and their affairs, surprise children, missing paintings, a Hash Eaters Club . . ."

Maybe I'm being unfair. It's true that my family is a little boring comparatively, but then again, I'm a child and grandchild of immigrants—and uprooting yourself and seeking out a new home in a foreign land is pretty damn brave, if you think about it.

"I'm sure there are many exciting secrets in your family's history. Perhaps even in your life?" Alexandre gently nudges me.

I wish I could come up with a duly flirty response, but the only secret I have is concealing a broken heart over Zaid, and there's nothing clever or coy about a fresh wound. I pivot the conversation back to Alexandre. "Is it awkward, people knowing things about your family that you haven't told them? Or having a name that everybody knows?"

"And by people, do you mean you?" He flashes a rakish grin. "Everyone knows Dumas. Everyone studies him in school. The teasing and dumb questions I got in lycée—ridiculous. People actually ask me if *The Count of Monte Cristo* is based on a true story and if we have some hidden stash of gold on the old Dumas estate. No one believes me when I say I have no idea because the place isn't even ours anymore. It's a museum."

"Really?" My eyes widen. "That sucks."

I feel a pinch of guilt because when I say that, it's not only because I feel bad for him. It's because I wonder if it's another missed academic opportunity for me, too.

"There's no family treasure trove, sadly. At least none that we know of. But truthfully, I don't know if my parents would even—" Alexandre stops short, like he's said something he shouldn't. Although it sounded like he was going to complain about his parents, which seems, I don't know, normal? Then he shrugs. I can't tell if the gesture is meant for me or for his hidden thoughts. "Besides, it could hardly be based on a true story. Dumas's main character, Dantès, survived being thrown into the sea in a tied-up sack."

"Another Giaour connection! I'm not sure how popular sack deaths were during the literature of the 1800s, but Leila, the woman in Byron's poem that inspired Delacroix's painting, was drowned in a tied-up sack." I shudder. If two different authors were writing about that, it must have happened to real people, too.

"Except Dantès planned his as a means to escape a prison fortress and went on to find his fortune hidden in a cave. Dumas had this way of enchanting people, of making them believe in things—romance, passion, adventure—that couldn't possibly be real. Have you read the book?"

I shake my head. "Dude. It's, like, a thousand pages. I know the basic story, though."

"My parents made me read it when I was twelve."

"Ouch. As a kid of two professors, I feel your pain."

"It's obligatoire in our family to know about our most famous ancestor. My dad goes on and on about how it's our duty to honor the family name. Preserve the cultural legacy of France . . ." His voice hardens. "But it's all talk. Flowery pronouncements about honor don't save anything, you know? We've already lost so much."

I blink. "That's hard-core."

He relaxes his shoulders. "I love these American idioms. Isn't that word supposed to be used for pornography?"

My mouth drops open, my cheeks suddenly on fire. The French are direct about sex and nudity. But some cultural norms don't transfer. They aren't imprinted on DNA. "I . . . uh . . . I meant that it seems like an intense family burden," I sputter.

"Ahhh. It's not that bad. It's how I learned about the Hash Eaters. From my uncle. He's the reservoir of family knowledge—the only one trying to salvage what we have left of Dumas. He would probably love to read your essay."

I ignore his comment because it was devastating enough when Celenia Mondego ripped my essay to shreds, and if an actual Dumas read it . . . Well, I might be the first person to die of impostor syndrome. Still, I can't deny that it would be amazing to interview his uncle if I manage to come up with a new thesis for my essay—hello, expert source. But I'm not there yet. So I ask, "Who else was in this cannabis club besides your many-greats-grandpa and Victor Hugo?"

"Many renowned artists and writers of the time, including our friend Delacroix. They got the hash from Morocco and apparently wore some kind of vaguely Arabian dress when they met for their hash-inspired hallucinations."

"Of course they did. It's a classic colonizer tale: steal or appropriate the interesting stuff; oppress or kill the people who created it."

Alexandre nods, his face serious. "My sixth-great-grandfather should've known better. Dumas's grandmother was an enslaved woman. He might have been partly, begrudgingly accepted into French society because of noble birth, but he was still subject to ferocious racism. There are incredible stories about Dumas tearing people apart when they insulted his African ancestry. He even wrote a novel called *Georges* about racism and colonialism. I guess he didn't think that applied to him and his friends."

Studying Delacroix's Giaour series, I came across a lot of writing about the role of Orientalism in his paintings—the prejudiced outsider lens through which the West sees and depicts the East. And especially because of Mom's academic specialty, we've had lots of long dinner conversations and debates about how that worldview still colors how the West sees Islam and the East in general. My mom can draw a road map from Napoleon's attempt to conquer Egypt to the recent crop of authoritarians who use the rhetoric of Islamophobia and racism to bolster their campaigns. But even though Papa is French, I haven't thought of my own ancestors in that light; it must feel weird for Alexandre to investigate his family that way. Maybe we all should because the past is complicated, and what is history but the everyday lives of our families?

"It's Orientalism, right? The idea that any culture that's not Western is somehow savage and inferior and needs to be conquered and saved." I glance at Alexandre, who seems both fascinated and bewildered. "In both the Byron poem and the Delacroix paintings, the Giaour, he's written as Christian—an infidel in a Muslim country, and he's the noble hero, the savior—and the Pasha is the cartoonishly evil villain. I mean, sure, he *could've* been a villain, but there's never any nuance. Leila, the harem girl, is the one who needs to be saved. She's the currency between two men. She's voiceless and objectified—it's sexism and racism in one fell swoop." My body hums with anger. I take a deep breath. "Sorry. I didn't mean to go off. It's the curse of being a child of two professors—I found a rumor, a little thread connecting that Delacroix painting to Dumas, and I had to unravel it."

While I'm trying to calm myself down, trying to figure out why this rage came on suddenly, I remember that I gave Zaid nearly this exact same lecture when I first took him to see the Delacroix at the Art Institute. I wasn't as angry, not like this, but, then again, I was only starting to peel back all the layers to this painting, to the poem, to the history it came out of. And I hadn't crashed and burned yet.

And Zaid, in that moment when I was going off on the Orientalism of the painting, about how it was rooted in a centuries-old Islamophobia . . . Zaid held my hand, looked into my eyes, and said, "I know." He understood. He got it. He lives under the shadow of America's casual prejudice every day. Just like me.

ALEXANDRE BEGINS ABSENTMINDEDLY picking the white clover flowers that dot the grass of Place des Vosges. "Remember those family rumors I mentioned about a possible gift from Delacroix? There might be more to them than legend—"

Before he can finish his sentence, I blurt, "Has your family ever tried to find that Delacroix? Wait—do you think the Nazis stole it? Some scholars think a few Delacroix paintings might have gone missing during World War II."

Alexandre sighs but doesn't look up from his flower gathering. "The Nazis did steal a lot of art, so it's possible. But we do know that Delacroix gave Dumas at least one sketch." He hesitates for a second before continuing, "Also, my uncle and I recently came across some old letters that hinted at the possibility of lost things, and we couldn't figure it out. Honestly, he didn't even quite believe it. Would you like to see them?"

My heart pounds in my ears. Am I hearing this right? I can't get ahead of myself. Can't get too excited. But what if those old letters prove that maybe my thesis wasn't totally wrong? What if there is a missing Delacroix? What if Alexandre's family documents help me solve the mystery or even give me another clue? If there is something, any new information, I could rewrite my paper for the Art Institute. I could prove

I'm not a failure. I could show everyone—especially Celenia Mondego—that I'm a badass art historian. This could change everything for me.

Calm down, Khayyam. Stop fangirling over this dude's tragic family history. I take a deep breath. "That would be amazing," I say in as even-toned a voice as I can muster.

Alexandre gives me a wan smile. "We've lost so much of Dumas's work—a lot of his archives aren't in our possession or even in France anymore. It's a family tragedy. There are lots of rumors, family lore, about my illustrious ancestor and his various escapades. Maybe you can help us find the truth." His voice falters. He seems worried. Maybe he's nervous about what truth he'll find. Maybe he's wondering if the past should stay in the past.

I've thought about that a lot. Wondered whether I should move on, bury all my failures—with the Art Institute essay and with Zaid—and try to forget about it all. A clean slate. But I'm figuring out that neither life nor history work that way.

"You were right," I say softly. "He does sound like a character in one of his own books."

Alexandre pauses his flower gathering and looks at me. "Yes. Exactly. Fact and fiction blur together in his life. What is the truth? Who was this man?"

"Who are any of us, really?"

"That is awfully Sartre of you," Alexandre says and begins knotting the flowers together, stem to bud. His fingers move deftly around the delicate, petite blooms.

"That's the second time I've been called existential today. It must be like how my French gets more colloquial every summer in Paris . . ."

"Ah, geography is destiny."

"I don't know if I believe in destiny."

"What about us meeting?" he asks, still weaving his daisy chain.

A tiny flutter rises in my chest. "I'll admit it feels odd. You know, like a fluke."

"If only the French had a word for coïncidence." Alexandre pronounces it the French way and chuckles at his own joke.

"Coincidences feel like magic, but they're just math." Even as I'm saying the words, there's still a tiny part of me that wants to believe that magic could be real, like our meeting was written in the stars.

Alexandre inches closer to me, holding up his creation. "May I?" he asks.

I nod and dip my head so he can place the white clover flower crown on my hair. His thumb grazes my cheek as he pulls his hands away. "You are the queen of your own fate."

I smile. Maybe I am. Maybe I'm going to find a way to erase all this pain and confusion swirling around me. Maybe the Alexandre Dumas of the past is the one who got me into this mess, but the present-day Alexandre Dumas—this handsome, charming boy—is the one meant to help me find my way out of it. And there may even be kissing.

He leans back and says with a smile, "C'est parfait."

I beam back at him. Yes, my sentiments exactly.

Leila

❧

I enter the solitary Room of Ablution. I have barely slept, but I am awake, alert. The blue-tiled mosaic on the floor and walls is soothing, mesmerizing as I take care to wash away my Giaour's touch. Pasha's senses are sharp, like his vengeance. But, like all men, he has weaknesses—his unfettered devotion and unusual trust in me that I have earned, painstakingly and at a cost.

I take the cloth and scrub off the sandalwood and musk of my Giaour. I massage rose oils onto every inch of my skin and run my scented fingers through the loosened black tresses that fall down my back, which Pasha loves to twist and coil around his fingers.

"You must be careful. Even my protection has limits." Si'la appears before me, impeccably dressed and dry despite the wet floor. Nothing can touch her. Not even me.

The otherworldly beauty of the jiniri might be too much for most human beings to bear, but she has been with me since I first remember gazing out of my cradle, since the accident that left me orphaned and destined for this palace prison. They say I arrived clutching the opal that now hangs from my neck. Some of the other girls say it is cursed. Even Pasha doesn't dare touch it, too afraid that the rumors of my jiniri are true. I hold the opal between my fingers, watch its fire blazing within. The same fire burns in Si'la's eyes.

"I am ever watchful," I say. "Vigilant. I am biding my time until I can escape this place."

"The time will come," she agrees, "but I am afraid it will not be as you wish."

"Nothing in this world is as I wish."

"Nothing but your beloved."

"Nothing but my beloved."

"At your father's dying breath," she reminds me, "I swore on my love for him to shelter you, but this world offers few protections to abandoned baby girls. Even fewer to women cast out from the serai by their pashas. Fewer still to those who betray their masters. For them, there are only watery graves."

"Better a grave than this living death," I counter. "I cannot grow old here. I can no longer wear the mask of love for another when love has shown me its true face."

Si'la smiles enigmatically. The flames in her eyes diminish, and she disappears.

KHAYYAM

I'm a creature of habit. Painful ones. Yesterday I spent what can only be described as a romantic afternoon with Alexandre, but even as I'm on the way to meet this charming French boy, I can't stop myself from checking Instagram. Of course, I find *more* shots of Zaid getting friendly with Rekha.

What did I expect? I swear, I'm going to unfriend him on everything. Tomorrow.

I slip my phone into my bag as I turn the corner. I spot Alexandre sitting at the corner table of Café de Flore. He doesn't see me yet, so I take a moment to study him. His sienna eyes are hidden behind the same tortoiseshell sunglasses he wore when we first met. He's oozing a kind of French languor—he's slouched back, legs in skinny khakis stretched out in front of him, crossed at the bare ankle as he drinks a cup of coffee and watches the world pass by. There's a hint of stubble along his chin and jaw. He's at ease. Content with himself. Zaid is the same way, always comfortable wherever he is because he carries that sense of self with him. I guess I have a type—the opposite of me.

As I walk up, he grins demurely, then stands to kiss me on both cheeks.

"Salut."

"I was surprised you picked here to meet," I say.

He gives me a quizzical look as we settle into our seats.

"Café de Flore? It's a little touristy and cliché, don't you think?"

"It's August in Paris. Everything is touristy and cliché," he says with a smirk.

The waiter comes by, and I order an Orangina and grenadine.

Alexandre bursts out laughing. "You're drinking l'indien?"

"What? I love the drink, but I refuse to say the name because it's ridiculous and, like, racist."

"Orientalist, even?"

"Oh, so you *were* paying attention to me yesterday?" I gently nudge him in the arm.

"It was the best part of my afternoon." He smiles that rakish smile I saw at the museum. He pauses. "Can I ask . . . Is it difficult being so aware of yourself all the time?"

Maybe he only means to tease me. But I look at his face and realize he's genuinely curious, which might actually annoy me more. I take a breath. "You don't understand. It's different here. Not that France doesn't have prejudices. I mean, being Muslim here isn't exactly a picnic, especially if you're hijabi. Or Black and poor and living in the banlieue. But in the United States, you're forced to be aware of the color of your skin and constantly reminded of your supposed otherness."

My words linger in the air. It's hard to explain to people who aren't American sometimes how I'm always conscious of being othered but also want to make sure I'm aware of my own privilege. "Look, it's not like almost all the white people get off the Métro before reaching a specific neighborhood in Paris, not like they do in Chicago."

He hasn't taken his gaze off my face. It's intense, but his eyes soften. "I see. But I guess I can never totally understand? I hope I'm trying, though. One of my ancestors was an African woman enslaved in Haiti. I can't ignore my family's past."

I nod.

Alexandre continues. "She's actually the one who gave us our family name."

"Wait. What?" This is totally new info to me. The waiter brings my drink. It looks like sunset in a glass. I take a long sip, letting what Alexandre said sink in. Even though my essay was about finding a Dumas-Delacroix connection, I didn't exactly do a deep research dive into Dumas's personal life. Here I am going off on racism and sexism, and I totally missed this part of Dumas's identity. Maybe Celenia Mondego was right. I'm a crap historian. I look at Alexandre, unsure how to respond.

"I'm a descendant of slaveholders," he says, "with at least one rapist in the family who was also nobility, about seven generations back. That was Alexandre Dumas's grandfather. Dumas's father was biracial and was one of the highest-ranking Black men in any European army—ever. He served under Napoleon."

"Whoa. That's, like, major." God, I sound like an idiot, but I'm blown away. "Napoleon had a biracial general leading the entire French army. Wow."

"And he's still one of the highest-ranking Black generals ever in Europe. *Still.*" A scowl crosses Alexandre's face. "Trust me. We don't exactly live in some perfect post-racial world here, either."

I take a breath and lean back.

Alexandre puts his empty coffee cup down with a thud. "Dumas is one of France's greatest writers, and he wasn't even permitted burial in the Pantheon until 2002. Because he was Black. They reinterred his ashes there so he could be buried with the other great artists of France. He should've been there from the beginning."

I nod. "Totally. But there's another lost story here, too, see? The highest-ranking Black general in France's history *and* one of your greatest writers both bore the name of a woman who was enslaved. The same name you have." I wonder if there's some angle here I could use in my essay reboot, connecting Delacroix and Dumas and lost women. Then I catch myself. Maybe not everything has to be about my essay and me. "How did you end up with her name, anyway? How are you a Dumas?"

"The story goes that when Dumas's father wanted to enlist in the army, Dumas's grandfather, who was French nobility, pushed his son to take a nom de guerre because he didn't want to be embarrassed by his half-Black son, who was only a private. Even though he *should've* been an officer due to his ancestry. But French race laws made it impossible for him to claim his nobility because he was mixed race." Alexandre's jaw tenses. I can hear the anger rising in his voice. "Instead of Alexandre Antoine Davy de la Pailleterie, he joined the Dragoons as Alexandre Dumas."

I shake my head. "Thus begins the line of Alexandre Dumas. But what happened to Dumas's grandmother? Do you even know her name?" I find myself getting agitated, too, not at Alexandre, exactly, but at the circumstances—at the entire world dehumanizing and erasing this woman who had a life, who mattered.

"Marie-Cessette Dumas. We think. Sometimes she's referred to as Louise. Dumas might have just been a descriptor given to a slave. Du mas means—"

"'Of the farm'? She didn't even get her own name. That's awful."

He sighs. "It's like you said, another lost story. Dumas's grandfather sold her and two other children he had with her to another owner. And when Dumas's grandfather came to France, he brought his son, who was still technically a slave."

"What a monster. It's so cruel and unfair." I stop talking, feeling a little sick about this whole story. About the stories that are right in front of us, that we disregard and refuse to see. We see history through a tiny peephole and fool ourselves into believing it's the big picture.

Alexandre is quiet.

I am, too.

I've never met this woman, but I feel like she deserves this moment of silence because I can't give her anything else. God. I can't imagine how inexplicably awful life must have been for her. Humans can be horrifically evil to one other. I blink away a few tears. It's not at all the same, but I can't help but think of my own family in India and the stories Mom and Nani told me; we lost touch with some of our family during Partition—the crappy British mandate that divided India in 1947. We think some of them were killed. I have distant cousins somewhere in Pakistan that I'll probably never know. It's infuriating how few people get to take center stage—mostly men in power, who hog the spotlight while billions more live life in the darkness of the wings. Maybe I can help change that.

Alexandre grazes the back of my hand with his thumb.

"You want to hear something ridiculous? I let myself believe that taking the Dumas name instead of de la Pailleterie was a small, rebellious way Dumas and his father kept Marie-Cessette's spirit alive. She was the legacy they chose. And the one they gave me."

A lump wells in my throat. "It's sad that she never knew the Dumas impact on French history and culture. Even American culture. I mean, hello, the Three Musketeers. And when I say that, I'm specifically referring to the candy bar."

His face lights up with a smile. "I'm happy my family could make this important contribution to your life."

I laugh. "Hey, it was my favorite Halloween score from second through sixth grade. My friend Julie used to help me hoard them when we trick-or-treated, and she even got me a bag of minis for the plane ride over here. My love endures."

"Good to know you're not fickle." Alexandre tosses a few euros onto the table before standing up and reaching for my hand, an impish glint in his eye. "Come on. I want to show you something."

It doesn't escape me that those are the exact words I said to him that led us to this moment. I don't think it escapes him, either. Show-and-tell is how every relationship starts. My mind drifts to Zaid and all the things hidden and revealed even though we're not speaking at all. I guess that's how Instagram works—you only choose to show certain parts of yourself, but sometimes you end up telling more than you realized or intended. And people say social media isn't the real world.

WE HURRY UP Rue Bonaparte and onto Rue de l'Abbaye. A quick left, and we find ourselves in an adorable, barely trafficked little square. I love these little hidden nooks you can discover in Paris. You can be smack-dab in the midst of a throng of people, and you take a turn and then another, and boom, you have a small corner of Paris all to yourself. Alexandre grabs my hand and pulls me across the street. He doesn't let go. I'm pretending it's no big deal while secretly pleading with my palms not to get clammy.

"Where are you dragging me to?" I ask.

"We're here," he says and stops in front of an unassuming set of brown wooden doors. He finally lets go of my hand and points to a plaque above the door: LE MUSÉE NATIONAL EUGÈNE DELACROIX.

I know of this museum—it was Delacroix's home and studio once. I wanted to visit when I was working on my essay, but my parents weren't about to let me make a special trip to Paris by myself at their expense, even for research. I tried to talk to the archivist on the phone, but it was like smashing my head against the brick wall of French bureaucracy: a lot of *no, it's not possible* and *sorry, the archive is not yet fully digitized*, and *why can't you do your research here during our ridiculously limited hours?* Please let there be some treasure trove.

At the entry kiosk, Alexandre flashes an ID, and the woman at the desk gives him a tight-lipped smile and nods us through.

"What's that, your all-access Paris badge?" I ask.

"I wish," he says. "It's my school ID. I've been doing some archival research here."

"What school do you go to?" It occurs to me now that I haven't bothered to ask where he goes to school or even how old he is. I'm not sure if it's my weak attempt at keeping my distance, if I'm desperately focused on how to salvage my potential post–high school academic life, or if my brain has been too wrapped up in the Zaid situation to gather intel about the guy who's actually available and whom I'm feeling a little bit fluttery about. Probably all those things.

"I'm starting my second year at university in September. École du Louvre. I want to specialize in nineteenth-century French art."

He's older. That is a bit unexpected. I was thinking maybe last year at lycée, the French equivalent of high school. But he's probably at least nineteen. Does he know I'm only seventeen—almost eighteen? He must know. I told him I was starting senior year. I guess he doesn't mind hanging with someone younger, because it's not like I'm forcing him to do banal high school things like . . . prom. French kids don't even have prom. But I let myself imagine them dancing along the banks of the Seine as the magic light of summer descends on a Paris night, the Eiffel Tower twinkling in the background. I may be Franco-American, but the American part of me still indulges in the occasional romantic, filmic Franco-fantasies.

It *is* summer in Paris, after all.

THE MUSEUM'S LIBRARY is empty except for a pale-faced woman sitting at a desk, ash-blonde hair pulled into a tight bun. She's wearing a turtleneck. In August. From the looks of her nearly translucent skin, I don't think she's seen daylight for some time. She raises her eyes from her book to take us in. She's probably the one who couldn't be bothered to help me and chided me for making too many demands on her time. The Archival Knight, sworn to protect dusty piles of paper and old books from the unworthy, sacrificing her social life and access to vitamin D.

Alexandre marches up to her and flashes a smile. They exchange a few hushed words. She nods—grins, even—pushes her creaky chair away from her desk, and breezes past the wall of packed shelves that reach to the top of the high ceilings, disappearing into a back room. If she's the same archivist who blew me off, and I'm sure she is, she seems far more agreeable to Alexandre's requests than mine. Gee, wonder why.

While we're waiting for her to return, I snap a photo of the library for Instagram—it's not a perfectly color-coordinated shelfie, but I could explore this place for hours. There are probably endless secrets hidden between the pages of these forgotten books. And I love that you need one of those old-timey rolling ladders to reach the highest shelves. Even with my back to him, I can feel the weight of Alexandre's stare as he watches me. I turn to catch his eye and smile as the woman reemerges and silently hands him an archival box before returning to her work.

Alexandre motions for me to join him at a small table next to the only window in the room, overlooking a perfect little garden in full bloom. He gingerly takes the lid off the box. I know he's been digging through these archives, but judging from some of the dust that remains undisturbed, he's likely the only person who's touched this box in ages. Alexandre sucks in his breath as he carefully draws out a thin, manila file folder, which I'm assuming is lignin- and acid-free. Wow. I'm standing close to a cute guy and my mind immediately goes to safe storage for archival documents. Hot. He opens the folder that contains a single sheet of paper—aged, yellowed at its edges, written in grayish-black ink. A fountain pen, judging from the blots.

I squint at the date scrawled at the top: *August 18, 1844.* "A letter to Dumas? That's pretty cool."

Alexandre nods but doesn't lift his eyes from the page. He's obviously seen it before, but he's staring so intently, it's like he's hoping for a new clue to magically appear. I understand the feeling.

"I discovered this and a couple other letters when I began to focus on my specialization," he says, nodding at the letter. "My uncle nearly lost his mind when I showed him. This is where I learned about the Hash Eaters Club. Here and the archives we still have at home and my uncle's research. It's amazing to hold this in my hands."

He's nerding out over history. It's kind of adorable.

"You have letters like this between Dumas and Delacroix and—"

"Other Hash Eaters, too. Baudelaire. Hugo. Balzac."

My heart stops for a moment at this revelation. At these names. They're a who's who of nineteenth-century artists. Our world is so small, interconnected. Tangled, even. On a road trip once, my mom tried to get us to play this game called Six Degrees of Kevin Bacon. She fake-cried when I admitted I had no idea who that was. But then she explained it was a Hollywood riff on this old idea that any two people can be connected by six links or fewer. I was terrible at the game because apparently the pre-phone ancient rules say you can't google anyone. But the theory stuck with me. It's comforting in a way. We don't have to rely on something as arbitrary as destiny in life. We're connected. It's like Alexandre and I would cross paths eventually. And now I'm one degree away from Dumas's family. It's math, but it doesn't make it any less wild.

Alexandre whistles to get my attention. "Khayyam? Where'd you go?"

"Oh, sorry. Just mind blown that these dudes had a hash-ish coffee klatch. Total reality show." I look up at Alexandre and smile. I don't feel like a dilettante right now at all; I feel like a bona fide art history sleuthing badass.

He laughs. "I think this is one of three documents that you'll find interesting. At least, I hope you do."

My ears perk up. My stomach somersaults. I'm trying not to appear too eager. *Breathe.* "Let me see."

He points to the slightly slanted, curled French cursive of Delacroix. "Right here he says, *'Tonight you shall meet the lady with the raven tresses. And see the dream of the poet come to life.'*"

"The lady with raven braids? Or does he mean hair? Is it the French or English? And a dream of a poet? What poet?"

"That's what's strange about it—it's Franglais. And he's using it with the English construction, the adjective before the noun. Then it's the English, I guess? Hair? And as for the poet, I have no idea. I was thinking it was like a metaphor—a woman so beautiful she was like the dream of a poet, maybe?"

Alexandre pauses and locks eyes with me. I think this is for dramatic effect. It totally works. "But the lady, I think she's real. Important. Dumas was notorious for affairs, but this lady intrigues me. My uncle says that this is one of the only references to a woman that we've found in Dumas's let-ters—"

"But if he had all those affairs, there must be love letters somewhere."

"Probably New Zealand or Texas. If letters like that even exist."

My eyebrows knit together. "What?" It's fair to say that New Zealand and Texas were the last places I thought Alexandre would mention.

"Ridiculous, right? A collector from New Zealand owns the largest private collection of Dumas archives. We don't have direct access to them. Some are at a university in Texas—they're not even all properly catalogued or available." Alexandre sighs and runs his hands through his wavy hair.

"That sucks."

"Tell me about it. We've been terrible stewards of the Dumas archives. Even his own children sold off whatever they could after his death."

"Damn. Gold diggers."

"In their defense, Dumas made a fortune in his life but wasted it all on lavish parties. Plus, he totally had a weakness for the ladies and showed his interest with extravagant gifts." Alexandre sighs at this.

"So, um, does the apple fall far from the tree?" Oh God. Did I actually say that?

"What does that mean?" Alexandre asks, and it's hard to tell if he's annoyed or genuinely confused.

And now I have to explain myself. Idioms never translate well. Dammit. "I mean, perhaps you take after your ancestor?"

Without missing a beat, he looks into my eyes and says, "If you mean do I find beautiful, clever, dark-haired women irresistible, then yes, I am like my grand-père. But I believe there will be only one woman for me."

Ugh. So perfect. So French. I ignore him, which I'm learning is the best way to deal with a charming Frenchman. "Tell me more about the raven-haired lady."

"Look at this." Alexandre begins leafing through the other folders. He delicately draws out a plastic sleeve that protects a few torn scraps of thick paper the size of Post-its with doodles of faces. No, it's a single face. I look closer at the woman in profile with long, dark hair accented with a few scattered flowers. There are two drawings of this woman on these roughly hewn slips of paper—one sketch the size of a quarter, the other a bit bigger. The ink is a little smudged, but, especially in the larger one, I can clearly make out the pen strokes of the woman's hair, curled lines that start wide and thin out past her undrawn shoulders as she looks off somewhere in the distance.

With our heads bent over the table, I steal a glance at Alexandre and realize how close we are. A slight warmth creeps from my chest up my neck to my cheeks. "Is that her?" I whisper. "The raven-tressed lady? And are these Delacroix doodles?"

Alexandre leans in closer still. "I think so, but there's no signature. I have . . . What's that word you Americans use? A hunch?"

"The pencil strokes, the look on her face . . ."

Alexandre's eyes widen. "There's something else."

He straightens and removes another file folder with no particular flourish. But I find myself holding my breath, waiting for the fireworks to explode from a humble paper sleeve. Another letter. This time to Dumas's son—Alexandre Dumas, fils. The edges are ripped, whole paragraphs are unreadable, dried traces of ink stain the page, and there's a tear through the center that someone seemed to have tried to fix years ago with tape. *Tape.* An archivist's nightmare. But some sentences remain, traveling through time to find us here.

1870

Mon cher fils,

I have kept guarded this priceless treasure with my life—and my soul. But in the waning light, I believe the time has come at last for the world to see what, for these many years, has been reserved for my eyes only. An entire generation has passed, so I bequeath it to you now, with further instructions enclosed. Cherchez la femme, trouvez le trésor.

Je t'embrasse,

Papa

It's dated 1870. The year Dumas died.

"Holy crap," I say, too loudly. The archivist shushes me. We're the only other ones in here, and she shushes me. No wonder she didn't want to help me.

Alexandre flashes her a warm smile in apology before he answers me. "The words in the letter, cherchez la femme. It's one of his most famous lines, part of it anyway, from *Les Mohicans de Paris*. Cherchez la femme. Seek the woman. But the treasure line isn't from the book, so what does it mean?"

My heart skips a beat. What if the treasure is the lost Delacroix? What if it's something even bigger? What could be bigger than that? This could be everything. "And that's your directive? *Seek the woman, find the treasure?*"

"I want the truth. There are so many family rumors about Dumas and his various affairs, but this . . . Even his use of that phrase, cherchez la femme. Did this mystery woman inspire the phrase or even the story itself? It rouses my curiosity, you know?"

Yes, so aroused, I think. Wow. At least I didn't say that out loud. I nod but try not to look at him—it's the only way to calm my rapid breathing. "Where are the instructions? And why is a letter from Dumas to his son in a Delacroix archive?"

"My questions exactly. I asked her"—Alexandre nods toward the archivist—"and she suggested that the Dumas family sold some of the letters between Dumas and Delacroix to the Delacroix estate. This letter got mixed up in the files."

"But maybe it wasn't a mistake? Maybe the treasure is related to Delacroix after all? But then the instructions would have to be here, too, right?" I can't disguise the urgency in my voice, the panic.

Alexandre shakes his head. "I've looked in every Delacroix file they have from those years, and . . . nothing. My uncle couldn't find anything even remotely resembling directions to any possible treasure in any other archive, either. He'd never even heard of it. That note was sitting here, ignored, all this time."

"Another dead end." I bury my face in my hands. I'm scared to be hopeful, maybe even afraid to try. I don't know if I can take slamming into a brick wall again.

Alexandre places a hand on my shoulder. "Khayyam, finding this treasure would mean a lot to my family—more than I can say. I'm not giving up. I'm taking it as a challenge, not a dead end. Would you like to join me in my quest?"

I bite my lower lip. I'm getting ahead of myself. There are almost no actual facts or clues to go on. But this could be a chance to fix everything I've screwed up in my life this last year. I imagine myself walking into the head judge's office, throwing my paper onto her desk after I've discovered a missing Delacroix. I'll be the toast of the art world. And Zaid—the beautiful boy, my problematic fave, whose ghost simply refuses to stay locked in the remembering closet of my mind—will fade away into the past instead of floating around us, all afternoon, every time I look into Alexandre's sparkling sienna eyes. Maybe I'll be able to leave Zaid in the dust like the artifacts in these archives. Maybe Dumas has unwittingly reached forward into the future to give me this directive so I can save myself from myself. I don't believe in fate or things happening for *a reason*, and I'm trying hard to not view everything through romantic rose-colored lenses.

But none of that matters because I'm here right now. And I have nothing left to lose.

I nod at Alexandre. "Cherchez la femme."

Leila

⁂

The door to the Room of Ablution creaks open. Valide steps in, clacking her carved ebony cane against the tile, the single ruby in its center shining a beam of purple-red as the morning light streams and bends through it.

She scowls at me. "What are you doing at this hour?"

I turn to her, naked. "As you see, I am preparing myself for the Pasha. He has summoned me."

Valide harrumphs. "God knows what he sees in you, feckless girl. Girl who has failed to bear him an heir."

"Perhaps you should ask him."

"You may be the favorite for now, but there is treachery in your velvet eyes, and one day he will discover it." She glowers at me.

"But that day is not today. Today I am called to serve Pasha, and I do so humbly. But I must first finish my ablutions and ready myself, as he prefers. I wouldn't think you'd want to interfere in that."

She narrows her eyes at me and cackles. "Shameless barren girl. I suppose you think my son honors you with the *ancient title of haseki, that like Süleyman the Magnificent, he would elevate you to wife. I'm afraid you may find your confidence is woefully misplaced. You're merely an expendable object of desire. One that is easily replaced."*

KHAYYAM

Alexandre gave me his key.

Well, his key code, anyway.

In Paris, most apartment buildings have exterior doors that lead into a courtyard where you can access the main doors for the actual building. It's common practice to give visitors your building code since a lot of the doors facing the street don't have buzzers. But knowing this doesn't prevent my heart from racing or my fingers from hesitating. To steel my nerves, I picture the imaginary high five Julie would give me for not chickening out. I enter the four digits with shaky fingers and wait for the mechanical *click* that tells me I can push the door open.

I take a breath. I'm two flights of stairs away from meeting Alexandre's parents. And I've only just met *him*. I've never faced a meet-the-parents-of-a-guy-I-like scenario. I already knew Zaid's parents from before we hooked up. I don't even know Alexandre's parents' names, and I guess they'll expect la bise? Because a handshake would be weird. What is the protocol for meeting the parents of a cute French boy who you have not kissed—*yet*—and who could maybe help course-correct your entire life? That's not in any guidebook or handbook for understanding French culture. I'd say my desire to puke is several orders of magnitude greater than any moment I had going to Zaid's place. I should've limited myself to one pain au chocolat this morning.

As I climb the winding stairs, I distract myself in the way of a true nerd—remembering a lecture my dad gave me about Paris city planning. I love random historical facts because facts don't betray you. Alexandre's building is classic Haussmannian—grand in scale with an ornate stone façade. Haussmann was an urban planner hired by Napoleon III to give Paris a serious make-over—redesigning the buildings for greater uniformity and creating the wide boulevards and leafy parks that transformed overcrowded, cholera-infested, dirty, nineteenth-century Paris into the City of Light we know today. All those facts are true. Also true? Thinking about Parisian city planning is absolutely not a distraction from the sparkling-eyed, wavy-haired boy who is waiting for me in his open doorway.

"Ça va?" Alexandre asks and gently wraps his fingers around my upper arm as he bends down to kiss my cheeks. They warm instantly. I don't think he understands the pulse-pounding power of his la bise.

"I'm good." I step into his foyer, waiting for the rest of his family to greet me. Alexandre shuts the door. It's just the two of us. I shift my weight from one foot to the other. I clear my throat and whisper, "Um, how do I address your parents? Monsieur and Madame Dumas? Or—"

"Oh. Sorry. Didn't I mention my parents are with my younger brother near Arles? Papa is meeting with my uncle—some, um, family business needed their attention." Alexandre looks down and rubs the back of his neck.

I open my mouth to say something, but nothing comes out.

Because here we are, alone. Not that it's bad. It's less pressure than trying to make a good impression on the parents, but also weird and anxiety inducing? I scratch an imaginary itch on my forehead. "Oh. You mean, your dad and uncle are mixing work with vacation? Doesn't that violate French holiday regulations?"

Alexandre meets my gaze. "I'll join them in Biarritz in a few weeks. But I also had some, uh, matters to attend to in Paris."

"You're working in August, too? Stuck in Paris with the strike, the sweltering heat, and the tourist onslaught? Bummer." A proper holiday is sacred in France. We come to Paris in August every year because of my parents' work schedules, but I am not a tourist. My dad would prefer visiting in June or September—his favorite months when the light is even more glorious and the actual Parisians haven't escaped to the beaches of Brittany or Côte d'Azur or some charming countryside gîte.

A grin spreads across Alexandre's face. "I was dreading my tasks, but August in Paris is turning out to be beautiful."

I try to curb my smile without success. "Ahh, that's why you invited me to your apartment, your empty, lacking parental supervision apartment?"

"I-I . . ." he stumbles. "I'm sorry. I wasn't intending . . ."

I start laughing. It's kind of fun to see someone else a little disarmed for once. Alexandre's face relaxes into a smile.

He clears his throat and continues, "Perhaps my great-grandfather would've invited you up to see his estampes japonaises. But I assure you my intentions are far more honorable."

Now I'm the one who's confused. What would Dumas owning Japanese prints have to do with any—"Wait, wait, is that like the ancient French version of 'Netflix and chill'?" I place my hand on my chest in mock surprise.

"Like I said, Alexandre Dumas, père, never lacked for, um,

company," Alexandre says as his open smile shifts to something more serious. "But I'm not him." I only nod in response because I'm not sure why the sudden turn. "Anyway, let me fetch those papers I wanted to show you. Make yourself at home," he says, waving me toward the living room before disappearing down a long hall.

Make myself at home? If only that were ever easy for me.

I STEP TOWARD the main room. It's light and airy; gauzy white curtains frame the windows and billow with the warm breeze. The wide gray couch is strewn with embroidered and mirrored pillows. The shabby chic sofa—emphasis on the shabby—is inviting, but I'm too nervous and fidgety to sit.

I turn back toward the foyer and start to take off my shoes. We are a strictly shoeless household, in Chicago and in Paris, but there is no pile of discarded shoes in the entryway, and Alexandre had sneakers on. As I'm having my ridiculous internal debate about wearing shoes (I mean, I stepped in dog crap with these shoes!), my eye is drawn to a small sketch. I move closer. It's a woman, the inky folds of her dress falling off her shoulders to reveal her breasts. She's holding a flag in one hand, a bayonet in the other. She's looking over her right shoulder at the flag she's holding aloft as it flutters behind her. The woman is alone, but she's clearly waiting for the scene to be filled in around her. It suddenly strikes me that I know exactly who she is.

It's a Delacroix. They have a Delacroix sketch in their damn entryway.

"It's a study for *Liberty Leading the People*," Alexandre's honeyed voice whispers by my ear. "I'm guessing you know that?" I was lost in the drawing and didn't notice he had come up behind me until his breath tickled my skin.

I nod. "See? You did want to show me one of your *etchings*, and it just happens to be a sketch of the most famous Delacroix ever? Well played." I elbow Alexandre, and he clutches his stomach with one hand, pretending to be wounded. He's holding a large manila folder in the other.

He laughs and steps past me. "Remember when I said you were right about Delacroix giving art to Dumas? This is the one gift we are certain he gave him. It's been in the family since the 1830s or 1840s—we're not sure if it was given before or after he finished the actual painting."

That *actual painting* is displayed against a dark red wall along a huge hall in the Louvre. Alexandre has a Delacroix character study of a painting that's in the Louvre. No big French deal, right?

I restrain myself from an *in your face, Celenia* fist pump, because it would be weird, even if the pettiness would make me feel good for a second. But this proves that my thesis for the Art Institute essay was *plausible*, if not quite probable yet. I was only wrong about which Delacroix Dumas owned. Okay, understatement. I was spectacularly wrong, and since my supernova-sized crash and burn, I pretty much doubt myself all the time. But my art historian Spidey sense is tingling—and not only because I can feel Alexandre's arm brushing against mine.

"My father almost sold it, but I begged him not to." Alexandre's shoulders slump as he tells me this.

"What! Why would he even consider it?" It's impossible for me to imagine owning a Delacroix drawing, so it's unthinkable anyone would consider selling one gifted to their family by the artist himself.

"I . . . oh . . . well . . . my father . . . We don't always see eye-to-eye on our heritage. He's much more practical, and I'm—"

"Sentimental?"

Alexandre's eyes twinkle at me. "Yes, that's one way to put it."

"So your dad is blasé about the whole being related to a famous writer and having art from his famous friends on your wall."

"He's French; of course he's blasé. It's a requirement for nationality." He gives me his easy, whole-rogue half-grin. But for the first time, it strikes me that his smile is disarming enough to easily hide the truth.

I laugh. "Well, I'm French also, and you don't see me being all blasé about the Delacroix in my house. Besides, being sentimental is pretty damn French, too."

"It's possible to be both at the same time, I guess? About the same thing? Perhaps there is something or someone in your life like that, no?"

I swear, Alexandre's been reading my diary. If I had one. I wish I could be blasé about Zaid's friendly cameos in various Instagram feeds. It's a scandal, but only in my mind, because it's not exactly shocking that a cute, single eighteen-year-old boy is snapping selfies with gorgeous girls the summer before he leaves for college. A bitter taste coats my tongue as I imagine the pictures, which I absolutely should not have been looking for. I'm a glutton for punishment. This would be the exact right moment for me to be as French and c'est la vie as possible. But the emotional side of me, the one I try to hide, won't let me let go.

Clearing my throat, I nod to the thick folder in his hand. "What did you want to show me?"

Alexandre guides me over to the sofa and places the folder on the coffee table, then pops into the kitchen. I allow myself to relax into the pillows. A million thoughts race through my mind, but this stunning, perfect light streams across my body in wide slants. I let my eyes close for a second. I sink deeper into the couch. I feel like a cat stretching out, ready for a delicious nap.

"You look like a painting." Alexandre stands above me with two bottles of Orangina that he places on the table. No coasters. Water rings be damned. Maybe that's why all the furniture feels worn. Alexandre's dad is blasé about being a Dumas, and Alexandre is blasé about wrecking old furniture.

I straighten, and our arms and thighs brush while he settles in next to me, the temperature on the couch rising as the heat pours off me in waves. Alexandre grazes my knee as he reaches over to grab the folder from the table. I suck in my breath. *Focus, Khayyam. There's a reason you're here. And it's research, not romance.*

Alexandre leans into me as he fingers the file. I feel a little flutter in my stomach, only it's not the kind indicating several orders of magnitude of vomiting. It's worse. It's the kind that suggests I'm about to make things extremely complicated for myself. I let Zaid distract me to the point of failure when I was researching my paper for the Art Institute. I can't make that same mistake again. No matter how much I may want to.

Alexandre unsheathes a letter and reads to me: "Chère Madame aux cheveux raven." He stops and looks at me.

"I'm listening," I assure him.

"Have you noticed he uses the English word *raven*? Like Delacroix did."

"He should say, 'cheveux noirs.' Black hair. Right? Or 'corbeau,' if he wanted to use *ravenlike* as a more poetic descriptor." It's odd. Odd is good. Odd can mean a clue.

"Absolutely. It could mean he heard that somewhere or—"

"Or that the raven-haired lady could be English. Read the rest of it." I'm intrigued, impatient. A teensy part of me wants to forget the letter so I can kiss this swoony boy *right now*. But I can't let that distract me from what I need. Digging up old buried secrets might be the one way I can fix my life.

But the way Alexandre keeps glancing up at me through the tousled brown hair that falls over his eyes isn't helping me focus.

He continues:

October 3, 1844

Chère Madame aux cheveux raven,
I am in agony.
Please relieve me from this despair and grace me with
a private interview, that you may teach me a small part of
what you know. I am eternally working, all hours of the day.
But you need only raise your hand in summons, and I shall
abandon pen and paper for a mere moment in your presence.

All the wisdom I have known as a man is summed up
in the words with which I leave you: I wait and hope.

Ever yours,

My fingers curl into my palms. I can't tell if I'm breathing anymore. *I am in agony.* Same, Alexandre Dumas, père, same. I'm trying not to stare at my Alexandre's perfectly pillowy bottom lip.

"Khayyam? What do you think?" Alexandre's voice pulls me back into the moment. Crap. Did he notice me staring at his lips? At least he can't read my thoughts.

I sigh and give my head a little shake. "That is some seriously eloquent begging."

Alexandre chuckles. "Yeah, from a man who could have any woman."

I tilt my head and raise an eyebrow. "That's presumptuous, don't you think? Even if he is your family."

"I'm sorry, but he was extremely popular with the ladies. Lucky man."

I'm sure my voice betrays a hint of annoyance. "You sound jealous of his, what, entourage? Harem?"

"Jealous? Not at all." Alexandre locks eyes with me. "I told you I'm not like him. I prefer to focus my attentions on only one woman."

I look away for a second, my cheeks burning. When I swivel my head back, he's still smiling at me. "Um"—I clear my throat—"is that the only clue? A letter from 1844?"

"And the notes from the Delacroix archives."

"Since we're not Sherlock Holmes, we're going to need more than a couple letters and some doodles to solve the great mystery of who the raven-haired lady is, if she even existed. For all we know, that letter could've been a draft for part of a novel."

"She's definitely real. I feel it in my gut. Dumas was a man with strong desires who could get what he wanted."

"Maybe this woman didn't want him or didn't want to be

another one of his conquests." As the words come out of my mouth, I realize I'm being defensive on behalf of an unnamed, possibly fictional, woman from the nineteenth century. But someone has to defend her honor, and it might as well be me.

"That would make this mystery even more intriguing. The woman who says no to the man who always heard yes."

Alexandre's words cut through me. Whoever this raven-haired woman was, I kind of hope she was the woman who said no to Dumas but yes to herself. I feel a sudden urgency to know more about her right now. "There have to be more traces of her in the historical record. She couldn't have just vanished."

"People are lost in history all the time." Alexandre shrugs. "C'est la vie."

I IMAGINE A life that completely falls through the cracks. A person no one remembers. Unloved. Forgotten. Expendable. Like Alexandre Dumas's grandmother. Like my own grand-mère. Once I'm dead, no one will have a living memory of her. I think of this raven-haired woman who inspired Dumas's passion. A woman who doesn't even get a name of her own. There are literally centuries of women who never got to tell their stories. An invisible hand squeezes my heart for the nameless women history brushed aside. I thought before that maybe Dumas was reaching through time to help me, but it's not him. It's this forgotten woman who's holding her hand out, and I'm not going to let her stay lost. She was a real, live person who walked these streets, and she must've left her mark somewhere, even if it's hidden. Maybe no one else cared enough about her to write her name into history books, but I do.

I take a deep breath and look at Alexandre. "Cherchez la

femme, trouvez le trésor. If we find her, we find the treasure. We're going to raise the dead."

He smiles. "Les nécromanciens."

"Dude, I don't mean black magic. Indians do not play with that."

This inspires a head-thrown-back laugh from Alexandre. That act is startlingly un-French. I raise my palm, twisting my fingers upward in my desi-fied WTF gesture.

"You are such an unusual combination of American, French, and Indian. It's fascinating," he says.

"Ugh. You sound like a nineteenth-century anthropologist discovering a 'lost' tribe."

He stops grinning and takes my hand.

I'm annoyed, but I let him. And my skin feels like it's cupped around a lit sparkler.

"I'm sorry. That's not what I was trying to convey. At all. What I meant to say, and failed at, was that I've never met anyone like you. You're so . . . unexpected." Alexandre looks at me with those hazel-y eyes and presses my hand. Bending his head lower, closer to mine, he whispers, "You are singular."

His face hovers inches from mine.

"As opposed to plural?"

Dammit. We were about to have a moment. And I come up with a dad joke? He's right. There is no one like me. I explain the singular-plural play on words. He laughs politely and releases my hand.

I would like to be the girl in the Instagram picture, like Rekha, all big smiles and confidence and expectations that are always met. But I'm the self-sabotaging dork who falls for physics jokes and snorts sometimes. What's the opposite of je ne sais quoi? Because that's me. Despite my Frenchiness. Whenever I need it most, I have no chill.

An extremely pregnant pause passes between us. Apparently, I'm the human form of an electricity dampener. I open my mouth a couple times, searching for something to say. "So . . . you said there were no other references to the raven-haired woman, right?" At least I'm on topic.

Alexandre looks down and touches the file with his fingertips. His voice now is all business. "There's nothing else in the Delacroix library, but I haven't searched through all the Dumas archives. These are only some of the letters and documents we have from the 1840s. There're probably more stuffed away in storage boxes."

When they speak, the French end their sentences with a period. Americans seem to end all our sentences with exclamation marks. The French talk with a flat intonation—an almost totally unaccented language. And there are instants, even knowing the language, even being French, when the neutral accent sounds harsh to my ear. Like I've done something wrong, but have no idea what.

This is one of those moments.

I try to breathe through it. I know Alexandre felt that charge between us. He's the one that took my hand. Was I wrong about that, too, about him leaning in? Maybe he's being nonchalant, friendly, French. Or maybe I'm overreacting, and our entire interaction only feels totally awkward to me.

I'm still mentally grasping for something to say when Alexandre turns back to me. "Can I interest you in a little more detective work?" When he smiles, the color of his eyes shifts a little toward amber, like the eyes of this old stray cat in my neighborhood. Hyde Park has a weirdly large number of strays. And one, a fluffy cinnamon cat, used to hang out by the front porch a lot. There were times when she seemed to understand what I was saying—even if I wasn't speaking to her. She was well fed, everyone on the block saw to that, but this cat took a particular pride in her appearance. I have no idea how she managed to have fur that never looked matted. And sometimes when she looked at me with those amber eyes, it would make me think of the old jinn stories my nani would tell me from when she was a girl in India. About how some jinn might protect you. About how you can sense it.

As far as I know, there are no corporeal French-speaking jinn, but I could be wrong, because Alexandre certainly has the enigmatic eyes for it.

Alexandre's phone buzzes and snaps me out of my daydreaming. He glances at it, frowns, and then quickly puts it away. "What do you say?"

"Sorry. Sure. I mean, yes, definitely." I reach for the file.

He places his fingers on mine, staying my hand. "Perhaps tomorrow or the day after? I have some things I have to attend to this evening."

"Oh . . . I . . . Of course." Am I getting the boot? That's what it feels like. I stumble over my feet as I get up from the couch and head to the door, my head in a fog. He follows.

"I'll text you in the morning," he says and leans down to give me a kiss on each cheek. "Ciao." This time, la bise is cursory. His lips don't linger; they barely touch my cheek.

"À demain." I walk out and watch him shut the door behind me.

What the hell just happened?

Apparently, I've stepped out of a time machine, because I'm right where I was a few days ago: wondering why a cute boy has closed a door on me. Agonizing over whether he's opening another door for someone else, someone he has to *attend* to. I'm not a single step closer to fixing my academic failures. I thought I was resuscitating my life, but multiple organ failure strikes again.

Leila

Few see Pasha's inner apartments. The bedroom, of course—all the girls called at night are privy to that chamber. But the Terrace Kiosk is reserved for those in his counsel. The large windows of the Kiosk look onto the tulip garden aflame in yellow-orange-red blooms. Silk rugs line the floor. Pasha leans back against a red brocade settee. I sit at his feet. He rests his hand on my head, stroking my hair and gathering my braid. I am the perfect pet.

To all who see him, Pasha cuts a fine figure. His dark almond eyes pierce as easily as they laugh, ready to respond according to the moment and his mood. His beard and mustache are always neatly trimmed, thanks to the expert groomers who live in fear that their straight blades will nick his skin. When he stands, his sinewy body and broad shoulders reveal his training in combat and in self-assurance.

"Be happy," another woman in the serai told me when I had come of age three years ago, almost still a child. Childhood here is painfully short. As a child you learn, too soon, that time is a luxury you are not afforded. "Our Pasha is handsome and still youthful. There are many less appealing masters

to whom you could succumb." Though my body has borne his
weight, my mind and my heart will never yield to my captor.

A servant arrives to bring us our tea and pours it in steam-
ing arcs into our filigreed-glass cups of green and crimson.
Mint and cardamom scent the air between us. Pasha draws
me up to sit next to him.

"You know I have accorded you a place few others, men
or women, have occupied." He sips his tea in dainty drams,
lest his tongue burn.

"Yes, Pasha," I say and cast my face downward, feigning
humility and gratitude.

"I have given you the finest clothes and jewels and my
time. I have employed tutors to teach you as if you were a
man, because your acumen called for it. Because like Süleyman's haseki, I thought you worthy of elevation, of one day
ruling by my side. Thus, you have lived a life of leisure that
most orphans could only dream of. And now the time has
come for you to repay my favor."

I tense but keep smiling, always wearing the mask. "Yes,
Pasha. Your kindness toward me has been immeasurable."

He smiles, too. "Very good. The tutor tells me your English
has advanced, more than anyone's in the court. And now you
must use it to my advantage in places where I myself cannot."

"Pasha?"

"We are to have visitors tomorrow. A lord from England.
A poet-traveler who they say is entranced with our customs,
adopting traditional dress in his travels. But I am interested
in the real reason for his visit. It is said he is a confidant of his
King George who has taken an increased fascination in our
part of the world. I must know to what end."

A spy. He wants me to be a spy.

There are many things the Pasha could ask me to do.

Indeed, I could not refuse even the vilest without forfeiting my life. But I could not have imagined this.

"You will serve as his translator and show him the grounds. Determine his mission here. Use your wiles and arts as needed."

And now I see his true course. The haseki is not shared. To be shared—to be given to another man—is to be cast out, to lose favor. Before I can stop it, a tear springs to my eye. Pasha wipes it away as it drips down my cheek.

"Don't be scared. I have no doubt you will succeed."

"But Pasha, am I no longer to . . . to be beckoned to your chamber?" I try to ask with as much pain and humility I can muster.

"You possess a beauty beyond beauty. Raven hair and ruby lips like no other woman I've known. But Valide reminds me that you have borne me no heirs. That your womb is barren. It has been two years since my poor wife passed in child-birth, taking my son with her. I must marry another. And as beautiful and wise as you are, my dear Leila, I cannot wed a woman who is both an unfruitful concubine and an orphan. Like Süleyman, I might have married my haseki. It was my intention. But now, no noble woman will marry even a pasha with a favorite such as you. You, whose beauty and charm and wit makes poets weep."

"Pasha, I—"

"My mind is made up. But you will not be cast out from the serai. Valide has promised to take you under her wing and counsel. There are still many ways in which you might prove yourself useful to me."

"Yes, Pasha." A vise grips my heart. Life under the thumb of Valide will be unbearable without my protected status as favorite.

Pasha leans over me, pushing me down on the settee. He kisses me hard on the mouth. The Valide enters. He turns to her, unbothered.

"Son, your chamber is ready."

So he already seeks my replacement.

"I will be there momentarily. Thank you, Valide." He dismisses his mother. Before she leaves, she sneers at me over her shoulder.

Pasha rises. "Leila, you have served me well. I will not forget you. Take rest now. Prepare yourself for tomorrow. I know you will not fail me."

I watch him exit the room.

I am out of time.

KHAYYAM

I keep looking at the one text Zaid sent me after I left for Paris: I'll see you when I see you. p.s. I got Ice Capades, as if there must be more to it. Twelve tiny words that hold an infinity of smiles and kisses and a longing for a home that doesn't exist in the same way anymore. Twelve words that really mean one word: goodbye.

Obviously Zaid hasn't exactly fallen off the face of the earth, because he keeps popping up for star turns on Instagram. At least I know he's not dead. I'm serious, because before I saw him on my feed, I had this stray thought that maybe he got hit by a driver while he was riding his bike. He doesn't wear a helmet. Who doesn't wear a helmet while bicycling in Chicago? The same guy whose infectious carpe diem-ing is showing up not only on Rekha's feed now, but also on Claire's and Alia's. It's not like he's kissing them. *In the shot*. But if my anxiety can imagine his brains splattered across 57th Street, then obviously my stomach is tied up in knots with invented scenes of what's happening outside of the frame.

"**YOU'VE BARELY TOUCHED** your couscous," Papa says.

"I thought you loved the merguez here. Are you feeling okay?" Mom adds as she and my dad exchange worried glances.

The lamb sausage at the restaurant of the Grand Mosque in Paris is one of my favorite things, and I look forward to it each summer. Since I was little, one of my beloved family traditions has been coming to the Grand Mosque for Friday prayers with my mom and then meeting my dad in this adjoining restaurant after. Because as my dad says, and I heartily second, outside of Morocco or Algeria or Tunisia, Paris has the best couscous, because, well, colonialism.

"It's nothing," I say as I add a little harissa paste to my couscous and scoop up a mouthful. "A little distracted, is all."

"Have you heard from Zaid?" My mom takes a sip of her sparkling water, trying to act casual.

"Way to be subtle, Mom."

My dad laughs. "Chérie, adults lose all ability to be subtle once they become parents." My mom grazes my father's forearm with her palm and smiles at him.

I shake my head. "It's not like I was expecting it. He's leaving for Reed soon, and I'm here in Paris with you, my beloved parentals." I give them a cheesy grin that's been in my arsenal since sarcasm entered my bloodstream in middle school.

"Maybe you weren't expecting but hoping?" my mom gently muses.

My dad nods and pats the back of my hand. This is usually the time one of them busts out with a line from an old movie or some book that only four people on earth have ever read. This is the fate you resign yourself to when you're the child of professors. I settle back into the crimson brocade banquette. The best way to get my parents off old news is by revealing the new news I've been keeping to myself.

"So this is kind of funny . . . I met the great-great-great- or some number of greats- grandson of Alexandre Dumas."

My dad puts his fork down. "Pardon? You met a Dumas? From *the* Dumas family? How? Where?"

"I, um, literally bumped into him at the Petit Palais. He's named Alexandre Dumas. Apparently the great literary families of France are terrible at coming up with unique names." Both my parents laugh. They are such easy marks.

"And to think you were initially skeptical about the theory of six degrees of separation. Will we get to meet this young man who has now connected us all to Dumas?" my mom asks a little pointedly.

"Absolutely not," I sputter, trying not to choke on my couscous. "Because you guys will try to embarrass me."

My father wrinkles his brow, then laughs, trying to decipher if I'm actually mad or just joking. I'm still trying to figure that out, too. "I might have a few questions," he admits. "That family is a French cultural institution. The father of Alexandre Dumas, père, was one of our greatest generals. He served Napoleon. And Dumas's son, Alexandre Dumas, fils, was a playwright. He wrote plays for Sarah Bernhardt. And—"

"Okay," I say, interrupting my dad's academic fanboying. "Maybe I'll bring him around."

And when I say "maybe" to my parents, I mean "no."

My parents were always nice to Zaid—almost too nice, and as a result he never felt uncomfortable around them. He'd come in, plop right down on the couch, and make himself at home. I would've been happier if Zaid felt a little less familiar with my family. I'd have preferred a little distance.

I guess I have that now. A whole ocean's worth, and then some.

I'M IN BED by 10 P.M. I can hear my parents out on our little balcony, softly chatting, their voices carrying through my window. A notebook lies across my lap, open to a blank page. I'm trying to come up with a new thesis for my Art Institute essay redo, or, as Alexandre might call it, a *modification* to rewrite my entire life. No big deal. Something about that phrase—cherchez la femme, trouvez le trésor—and the dialogue between art and literature, the relationship between Dumas and Delacroix. But none of that seems right. My mind keeps spinning back to the mysterious lady with the raven tresses. Who was she? Why was she erased from history? How did she shape the stories of these men?

If I could figure this out, if I could find her, I wouldn't just get a kickass, possibly prizewinning college essay. I could get published. Or at least get interviewed in *Art News*. More importantly, I could be petty as hell about that judge who called me a dilettante.

My phone buzzes. I lurch for it.

Alexandre: Ready for some detective work tomorrow?
Me: I'm not sure.

I don't know why I'm saying this. It's not like I have other plans. I feel a familiar pinch—maybe conscience creeping up on me for dragging him into my own agenda? First I felt bad because of Zaid, and now Alexandre? Ugh. This is supposed to be a vacation, but at every turn, it feels like a guilt trip.

Alexandre: Do you have other plans?

Me: Maybe.

Alexandre: Are you doing the American play-hard-to-get thing?

Me: I didn't realize you were trying to get me in the first place.

A tiny white lie, but that is the art of French coquetry—concealing a little truth to build an irresistible mystery. Maybe I have some flirting skills after all—at least when I'm screen-to-screen with a boy, if not face-to-face.

Alexandre: Oui, naturellement.

Dammit. He's way better at text flirting than me. Probably because he's direct and honest and not shifty. Crap.

Me: . . .

Me: . . .

Alexandre: Khayyam? Still there? BTW, what does your name mean?

He's throwing me a softball. I'm both irritated and thankful.

Me: My parents named me after Omar Khayyam—a Persian poet, philosopher & astronomer from about a thousand years ago.

Alexandre: That's beautiful. Did he write anything famous?

Me: The Rubaiyat? Heard of it?

Alexandre: Sadly, no.

Me: "A jug of wine, a loaf of bread—and thou, beside me singing in the wilderness. And oh, wilderness is paradise enow." Enow is an old way of saying enough.

Alexandre: A perfect plan. Tomorrow?

Yeah, he's good. How is it even a contest between him and Zaid? *Is* it a contest? Of course it is. I've made it one, which is asinine, because the only competition I should be thinking about is the one that leads to my redemption. I need to focus on this missing woman and my essay and my future. I should've learned my lesson about letting a boy distract me, but here I am again.

> Me: There is no real wilderness in Paris.
> Alexandre: Leave that to me.

Every text from Alexandre makes me want to spend more time with him. He's swoony in print *and* in person. And I'm imagining the kissing. I could write a whole story about the kiss that has not yet happened. But even with the blow-my-mind kissing fantasy and the in-real-life swooniness, my life feels a little off-kilter—like I've stepped off a boat and am walking wobbly. I don't do well with uncertainty. I prefer the familiar to the unknown. Maybe that's why I'm clinging to the memory of Zaid. Why I can't let go, even when what I'm trying to hold on to is a puff of smoke.

Leila

"Checkmate, dear." The door to my chamber is open, and Valide stands under its arch. "You thought your wiles ensnared my son, but all the while, it was I running the board. You play checkers. I play chess."

Growing up in the serai, I learned to steel myself, to make my skin armor, but Valide is a master at the game of disarming people.

But I have learned also.

I turn to her and smile. I finger my opal. "Has the ruya peri brought you sweet dreams? Remembering your youth, perhaps? When your skin was smooth and your body ripe?" I watch as Valide blanches. "You should take care. They say the peri partner with jinn."

She snorts, trying to regain her composure. "Good luck with your British lord tonight. I've heard he has quite the reputation, that his hungers are insatiable. I've heard what the ladies call him. His nom de guerre, as it were. These British treat us as if we are savages beneath them. Who knows your fate if you do not satisfy his needs? I shouldn't be surprised if perhaps you didn't return from your evening's sojourn. But rest assured I shall make certain you are not missed."

Her laugh echoes down the hall.

I slip gold bangles over my wrists. She means for her words to bury me, but she doesn't know they planted a seed.

KHAYYAM

I walk up Avenue Franklin Delano Roosevelt. In Paris there are a surprising number of streets named after Americans. A lot of times I get this question about why the French hate Americans. They don't. They only hate Americans who are xenophobic, isolationist assholes, but who doesn't?

Alexandre stands casually at the foot of the steps of the Palais de la Découverte—not far from the Petit Palais where we first met—a black messenger bag with a baguette peeking out strapped across his body. He doesn't look bored; he's not anxiously tapping his foot. He's standing there, comfortable with himself. I envy that. He catches my eye and smiles, hops off the step, and walks up to meet me. Two kisses on the cheeks. This time, I make sure to kiss his cheeks back in case I was sending mixed signals the other day at his apartment, when things ended a little weirdly.

"The science museum? Going to try and carbon-date the letters?" I sound chipper and American. It's an easy go-to for me to ease my lingering anxiety. Fake it till you make it.

"No, but I am curious about this idea of a 'date,' as you Americans call it." He grins.

I smile back. No need to fake it. "So . . ."

He tilts his head in the direction of the Seine, beckoning me to follow. A few short steps, and he cuts left, stepping over a short single-railed wooden fence into a grassy corner.

"You're stepping on the grass. That's interdit, you scofflaw," I joke.

"There are no rules, only suggestions." He reaches out with his hand. I slip mine into his and join him on the forbidden lawn.

We're standing in front of an expansive white marble sculpture that I've walked right by multiple times, including moments ago, but have somehow never noticed. Alexandre draws me nearer to it. There's a small pool of water surrounded by small shrubs and flowering plants. Different scenes are carved into the marble, some fading away, like the stone is trying to recapture them.

"It's called *The Poet's Dream*," Alexandre explains. I told him about being named after a poet, and voilà. Well played, Alexandre.

It's not exactly beautiful, this massive stone block. The cream-colored marble is grayed with soot and worn. There are probably hundreds of more interesting public sculptures in Paris. But there is one scene, a man kneeling at the feet of a woman who is bending over to embrace him, hidden in plain sight amidst the other figures. It reminds me a little of the *Fountain of Time* sculpture in my Hyde Park neighborhood in Chicago—once finely chiseled faces and bodies weathered by storms and receding back into the stone, fading in time. My heart cracks a little. You'd think dreams etched in stone would be permanent, but an object remains unchanged unless acted upon by an outside force. I don't know; maybe the laws of physics are more powerful than art. Maybe they're two forces in conversation and balance.

"This way." Alexandre tugs on my hand, and we leave the enclosed grassy corner. I'm trying not to notice that he's still holding my hand. I'm also trying to will myself not to sweat. It's gross to feel a clammy palm against yours. And I don't want that to be the indelible image of me in Alexandre's mind: the girl with sweaty hands who can't avoid shit.

A few short strides and we come to a set of winding, uneven stone stairs. They are almost completely hidden by trees and shrubs. My heart pounds as we take our first step, then another, hand in hand. Alexandre smiles and inches a little closer to me as we descend through a crooked stone arch that looks like it's straight out of Middle Earth. Large stones are piled high on top of one another, but the old stone is almost completely covered by ivy, and I'm certain it's a portal to a fantasy realm.

We walk into a secret garden. A pocket park hidden in the center of Paris. A cement path leads us into a postage stamp–sized garden valley. There's literally a babbling brook with koi and lily pads. A little farther down the path, and a spectacular colossus of a weeping beech tree shelters a little waterfall that drowns out the traffic noise. I'm not sure how the planners carved this lush dreamscape into such a small space—you could speed through the entire garden in a minute or two—but that is Paris: unexpected, beautiful spaces tucked away from a bustling city. No one else is in the garden.

"This is unreal," I whisper. Alexandre simply squeezes my hand. Quietly, we find a bench set back into a pond-facing nook surrounded by bamboo, ferns, and lilacs and grab a seat. Alexandre unbuckles his bag, hands me the baguette and pulls out a scarf, spreading it on the bench between us. Then he produces a hunk of Comté cheese, a small glass jar of duck rillettes, a green pint-sized basket of perfectly plump raspberries, and two small glass bottles of Orangina. Finally, he takes out a plastic grocery bag from which he draws napkins and a small knife. He's thought of everything.

"Wow. This is quite the spread."

"What was the line you quoted to me? 'A jug of wine, a loaf of bread . . . and wilderness is paradise . . . enough?' I assumed you don't drink?" I nod. Alexandre gestures toward the garden. "Here's your city paradise. Would your namesake approve?"

I don't know how to respond besides blurting out, *It's perfect!* Searching for my French coolness, I look into his eyes. "Not sure, but I certainly do."

Alexandre's face lights up as he gives me his eye-smile. There's no hint of the awkwardness from the other day at his apartment. Maybe it was just me. He seems pleased with himself. As he should be. He slices some cheese, and I tear off a couple chunks of bread for each of us. He hands me the knife so I can spread some of the duck rillettes, a pâté brined with spices and absolutely delicious on a crusty baguette. We devour our picnic, barely talking, just enjoying the midday sun and calm of this place.

When we finish eating, Alexandre clears the remains into the plastic bag. I take another swig of my Orangina and set it on the ground next to me. Now that there's no picnic separating us, he inches closer and puts his arm on the back of the bench.

I lean into him until my leg brushes against his. I breathe

deeply, trying to tamp down the flutters in my stomach. "How exactly has this place been hidden away from the tourist throngs?"

"Paris is full of surprises, no?"

I tilt my head to look at him, the uneven patches of stubble on his jawline golden against the light. "Definitely. So . . ."

"So . . ."

"Um . . ." I giggle a little. Oh God, I giggled. "Did—did you find anything more about our mysterious raven-haired lady?" Research is a place where I'm comfortable. It's where my head *should* be, but dammit, do I have to be my own buzzkill?

"Actually, I did find something." He reaches back into his bag. "Remember when I told you I hadn't looked through some boxes that were stored away? Well, I found one with a bunch of old stuff from my papa's family— some of Dumas's loan papers, a debt collector notice, and this note."

"Don't tell me you stuffed some original document from the 1800s in your bag."

"Of course not. It's a copy. The ghost of Dumas would probably haunt me if I got duck fat on his old letters." He hands me a slip of paper. It's another letter from Dumas to our mystery lady.

I read out loud: "Chère Madame." I look up from the note. "He's abbreviating the greeting now. No more *my dear lady of the raven hair*. Maybe she didn't like it? Still not on a first-name basis, though?" I raise my eyebrows at Alexandre and start again.

October 12, 1845

Chère Madame,

In you I have found a kindred spirit. At once part of society, yet separate. Ever an Other. Never an Us.

The tale you have related to our salon pierces my soul. That such a tender spirit could have known, nay, does know such pain— I long to provide succor to your gentle heart. Will you not allow it? Can such an offer, true and pure, be an imposition? If it be so, then let me beg your forgiveness. For I confess, the intricacies of a woman's heart are as like a tangled skein of silk to me.

As ever, I am in your service.

I cast my eyes up. "Desperation is not a good look."

"At all," Alexandre says. "This letter is dated a year after he wrote the other one. That is a long time to woo a woman."

"It feels creepy. He's telling her what she needs. Mansplaining, nineteenth-century style. Hello, learn consent, dude." That defensiveness for our mystery woman swells in me again. Reading these letters feels sort of intrusive in a way, but also like this is what I'm supposed to be doing—helping someone who is lost, maybe because I'm a little lost and trying to find my way, too.

"I think he believes he's asking for consent. And actually, it's still probably better than some men today." Alexandre shrugs. I'm not sure if maybe he feels defensive, too, *for* his ancestor.

"Don't *well, actually* this. Anyway, that's a depressingly low bar. What do you think happened in the year between these letters?"

Alexandre shakes his head.

"In the earlier note," I say, "he was trying to get an audience with her, and now they obviously have some type of relationship. Gah. I'm dying to figure out who this lady is." What I don't add—what I'm maybe only just realizing—is that I'm counting on the raven-haired lady to rescue me. To redeem me. But it feels too pathetic to say it out loud. "The Hash Eaters Club is where Delacroix told Dumas he would meet her. Maybe we should dig into them a little more? See what secrets *they* might reveal."

"Come to my house after breakfast tomorrow. We can go through whatever Dumas files I haven't looked at. Maybe the past will expose itself."

I tap my toe on the ground in front of the bench. I don't even know this lady's name, but I'm reaching back into the past to ask a stranger to help me. A stranger who's nothing but dust between the pages of history books. I feel a pang of melancholy for this lost lady who has been waiting patiently all these years for me to find her. But there's also something undeniably romantic about all of this—following the breadcrumbs of a literary mystery in Paris with a beautiful French boy who somehow knows the right things to say to me, while the boy I still at least partly love is an ocean away and silent.

Alexandre stands up, momentarily blocking my sun, the light blazing in a halo around him. He reaches for my hand and pulls me up, close to him, then closer. Time slows around me. I can hear the splashes of the waterfall as it hits the pool, the distant and muffled drone of the traffic beyond this hobbit-sized park. The leaves on the lilac bush behind us flutter ever so gently. Above it all, my heart pounds in my ears. Alexandre brushes my cheek with the back of his index finger. I tilt my head up toward his—

"Can you please take our picture?" a loud, nasally American voice asks from behind me.

I snap my head back and pivot to see a middle-aged white couple in coordinated khaki shorts and polos. *Of course.* There should be some kind of unwritten rule that tourists—or really anyone for that matter—cannot interrupt an almost kiss.

"Pas de problème," I hear myself say. No problem.

I half smile and take her phone while she explains to me using exaggerated gestures how to take a photo. I can see Alexandre smirking in my peripheral vision. I'm so irritated at these interlopers that I almost take a bad picture on purpose, but they're only trying to enjoy their vacation. I hand the camera back to the woman, who thanks me with a huge smile. Her husband nods and says, "Merci." His accent is like nails on a chalkboard, but at least he's trying.

When they walk out of earshot, Alexandre asks, "Why didn't you speak in English so they would've realized you're American, too?"

"Because I didn't want to end up talking to them for half an hour about how we are all American and *where do you live* and *oh, you live in Chicago, we went to Chicago once and loved it. What's the shiny sculpture called, the one in the park? The Bean. The Bean. That's it. Everybody there is so nice. Way nicer than the people in Paris. Sometimes they're awfully rude here. They don't even have English menus in all the restaurants. Why, last night . . ."* I trail off and roll my eyes.

"Quand même. They weren't that bad."

I shrug.

We start walking back down the path, the air between us rippling with *another* lost moment. As we pass under a faux jungle-esque bridge, covered with vines, bits of fake tree trunks showing through, I slow down and take a look around at this utterly Instagram-worthy spot—a beautiful garden in the company of a beautiful boy. I grab my phone, reaching my cheek up close to Alexandre's for a selfie—and put on a huge American smile, showing all my teeth. I take a dozen quick snaps, then draw back to flip through the photos. The first is perfect: I'm beaming; he's gazing at me with his signature grin.

I'm posting this on Instagram the second we part. I don't know why it didn't occur to me before. If Zaid wants to rub his summer escapades in my face, so be it. Two can play that game. And one of us is in Paris with a hot French guy—

"Khayyam?"

I look up. We're already at street level. I turn back and realize I was so focused on upping my Instagram game to get Zaid's attention that I didn't notice the walk up another winding storybook staircase with the gorgeous boy who is actually with me right now.

"Sorry. Zoned out."

"Everything okay?"

"Sure." Distracted, I give Alexandre two quick pecks on his cheeks. "Tomorrow at your place. Like 10 A.M.?"

He scrunches the corners of his eyes for the briefest second
and nods. "Ciao," he says and walks away.

"The picnic was amazing!" I call after him, but my mind
is elsewhere. I scurry across Pont Alexandre and take a few
obligatory shots of the Eiffel Tower. Then I turn toward the
Louvre and snap a picture of the Ferris wheel in the Tuileries
as it peeks over the green treetops. The light is perfect right
now. Paris is stunning, and I have a feeling the city approves
of my little plan. Paris may be the capital of love, but it's also
the city of scorned lovers.

Scorn isn't the right word. That's not what I feel for Zaid
anyway, more like confusion and heartache, the echoes of
love. But I'm not above being petty, and I think this little
Paris collage will snare him. It might be a little mean girl
of me to get Alexandre involved, but it's not like I'm faking
wanting to be around him. I like him. I *want* to kiss him.
And I *need* to find the raven-haired lady *and* whatever secret
treasure she holds the key to. Why not try to get everything I
want in the process?

I hurry and tag the photo #parisisforlovers before guilt or
my better judgment makes me change my mind. I don't care
if anyone else likes it. For this post, I have an audience of one.

Leila

❦

The poet is nothing like I expect. He is baby-faced with deep-set brown eyes, small hands, and hair that curls at his nape. The dark circles under his eyes age him, though I doubt he could be much older than one-and-twenty, only a few years older than me. Perhaps he is in the service of his king, but I doubt the service could be of any state consequence, as the poet seems to be only in service to himself.

When Pasha at last grew tired of his British audience, he dismissed everyone from the room save the poet. He then beckoned me forth, offering me as a guide and a gift, like a basket of deep red pomegranates ready to be eaten.

When Pasha exited the room, he could not look me in the eye. Good. If he feels a pang of guilt or regret, it is most likely the first time he has experienced such feelings. May he know true suffering in this life and the hereafter.

I pass the afternoon with the poet, offering him tea and sugared sherbets, fruits, and sweets. I tell him tales of the serai and Pasha's prowess in battle, but he is most interested in jinn stories, so I weave the tales for an Englishman's ears. He listens and watches me intently.

"You are a storyteller," he says.

"Thank you, my lord. I am simply trained in the ways of the serai, like all the other girls. The sun is setting. Shall I take you to the second courtyard? The courtyard of hollowed trees and jinn?"

He rises and offers me his hand; I take it.

"In my travels, I have heard many stories of jinn, but yours are told with, dare I say, affection and awe. Do you not fear them?"

I shake my head. "I have much more to fear from men than jinn, my lord."

KHAYYAM

I've gotten a bunch of likes on my Instagram photo of Alexandre and me from yesterday afternoon.

But *if* Zaid saw my feed and *if* it made him even a tiny bit jealous, he's certainly not admitting it to me, because his silent treatment continues. At some point I'm going to have to deal with the possibility that maybe he doesn't care. But right now, I have other plans.

I'M STANDING IN front of the peeling red wooden door to Alexandre's apartment. I buzzed myself in again but texted from the street. The door is cracked open. I put my hand on the knob and hesitate. I know it's normal to give friends the key code to your building in Paris, but it still feels, I don't know, too new? Too full of possibilities? Too weird knowing we'll be alone again?

I've been alone with Zaid a million times—but being alone with him, even after our first kiss, never felt awkward or new the way this does with Alexandre. My romantic relationship with Zaid felt like a continuation. With Alexandre, it feels like a beginning.

I raise the large brass ring knocker and tap it against the door. It might be open, but I still have some tameez.

"Entrez." Alexandre's velvet voice floats out the door that creaks as I push it farther open and step in, shutting it behind me. "I'm in the study," he calls.

I walk by the Delacroix sketch in the entry foyer, pass the large front room where we sat last time I was here, and enter the central hall of the apartment. It's dark and not helped by the overcast day. The air outside is humid and charged, like thunderstorms are approaching. It's a little charged in here, too. I pass two closed doors and then come to a third on the right that opens into an expansive room.

The study (do they call it the library?) faces the street like the front room, but instead of wispy white curtains, heavy dark blue drapes are pulled back from the tall windows to let in what little light there is. The other three walls are all bookshelves, floor to ceiling. There are so many books, some of the smaller ones are stacked horizontally on top of the larger ones.

Looking around, I feel like I've stepped through a portal into the past. I know Dumas never lived in this apartment, but it's easy to picture him smoking on the beat-up leather sofa that looks two centuries old or shuffling through piles of paper on the worn wooden coffee table that's piled high with books. Alexandre sits cross-legged on the nearly threadbare scarlet dhurrie rug. He's deep into a book, and I have to clear my throat to get his attention. He pops up to kiss me hello—on the cheeks.

A distinct old library smell wafts over me. "Are all these books, like, two hundred years old?" I ask.

Alexandre gently shakes his head, and his smile is a mile wide. I notice this uncharacteristically large smile gives him the slightest dimple in the lower half of his right cheek. He's wearing a T-shirt that has a picture of John Lennon wearing a T-shirt that says *New York City* on it. He might be the hottest dork ever.

"That shirt is really meta," I say.

"I got it on the street in SoHo when I was in New York last year."

"The famous cheese-in-a-can discovery trip?" I ask.

Alexandre nods. "I want to live there one day." He absolutely beams when he says this.

"I've been a couple times with my parents. It's a great city, even though the pizza is totally weak."

"I thought the pizza was quite good." It's cute how he's defensive about New York. He's totally wrong, but still cute.

"That's because you've never tried deep dish from Chicago. I know the perfect spot to take you. It will blow your mind."

"Are you asking me on a proper American date?"

My cheeks flush. I open my mouth to say something but clamp it shut and rub my forehead like it has a streak of marker I'm trying to erase.

"Um, does your family go to New York often?" I'm trying to change the subject to allow my body temperature to return to normal. I didn't come here to flirt, even if it's a definite bonus.

"I didn't go with my family. I went with a . . . friend." He looks away for a moment. "And you didn't answer my question."

I take a breath. "Fine. If you ever make it to Chicago, consider it a date. I'll even pay."

"You're inviting me to visit you in Chicago?" A sly grin spreads across his face.

"Oh my God. How forward. Don't push your luck."

"I can see my French charm has no power over you."

"Does it work with the other Americans?"

"Oui, bien sûr." Alexandre's roguish smile appears, accompanied by the little dimple.

"I'm immune to your charm—and to your ego as well."

He laughs and moves closer to me. "Touché," he whispers.

I look down at my sneakers. I smile. Wide. Too wide. With too many teeth. Totally American. Alexandre hooks my chin with his finger, and I look up to meet his gaze. He bends his head closer to mine and kisses me on the cheek, allowing his lips to linger. I take the final step that closes the distance between us and run my fingers slowly down his arm. I hear him catch his breath, which means at least one of us is breathing. Then he slowly moves his lips to my jawline and kisses me there, and then lower to my neck. Goosebumps pop up all over my skin, which is odd, because I feel like I'm on fire. He raises his head and looks into my eyes. I tilt my chin toward him. He cups my cheek with his palm.

We kiss.

It's slow and warm and tastes like old books and Orangina and promises.

It is perfect.

I don't understand the saying *time flies when you're having fun*, because I'm pretty sure this kiss has stopped all the clocks in Paris.

I COULD LIVE in this suspended animation forever. But I stop before I completely lose myself in a frenzy of kisses, because I know why I'm here. That would be déjà vu all over again.

I clear my throat. "You wanted to show me something?"

He smirks. "I thought I just did." I elbow him. "Okay, yes.

You're very businesslike for a French girl in August. But I do have some books and papers for us to look at."

Alexandre walks to the desk while I take a seat cross-legged on the rug. The wool is tatty, and when I run my fingertips over it, there's still a slight roughness to the fibers. The texture feels weirdly comforting against my palms. Alexandre grabs two beat-up volumes from a tall pile of books and hands them to me. The covers are stained and scarred, the spines mostly faded. But I can still make out the embossed titles: *Revue des Deux Mondes 1844–1846. Revue des Deux Mondes 1847–1849.*

I glance up at him. "Around the same time as our letters."

He nods. "They're bound volumes of a magazine. My uncle dropped a dozen books off earlier this morning—he thinks they may be helpful. He's been busy with other family stuff and hasn't had time to look through them."

"I thought he lived in Arles? Aren't your parents there, visiting?"

"Oh, um, yes. My uncle had to make a quick unexpected trip here for the day. Some boring real estate stuff."

"Do I get to meet him?" I'm still nervous about meeting the real Dumas scholar of Alexandre's family, but I also can't let this opportunity slip by.

Alexandre squints at me. "Sorry. He's terribly busy this trip, but he does want to meet you. You'd like him. In some ways I'm more like him—closer to him than I am to my dad. Like me, he believes we should preserve our family legacy. Aggressively."

I'm not sure what it means to aggressively preserve your family's heritage—it's not like there are duels involved in archival maintenance. I'm starting to believe that Alexandre's uncle is either massively introverted or a figment of his imagination. "I'll skim through these *Revues*, and you . . ." I lose my train of thought because I'm staring at Alexandre's lips, which are even redder than usual, and I suppose it's from all the kissing. I bite my lip wondering if I'm sporting the just-kissed look, too.

Alexandre picks up where I left off. "I'll try to see if I can find one of Dumas's old journals."

"You have his old journals?"

"Apparently my dad thinks we might have one that wasn't destroyed or scooped up at auction by other collectors." Alexandre winces as he says this. I can see how it's almost physically painful for him to acknowledge the history his family has lost. "I couldn't find it in storage, but Papa thinks it might be in there." Alexandre points to a large cupboard with a glass door.

"It could've been sitting in this library for years without anyone knowing?" All along, I've been curious how people and ideas fall through the cracks of time, and this is one of them—the quotidian acceptance of the extraordinary as commonplace. Taking what you have for granted or just not caring. I guess Alexandre's dad is a perfect example—it's probably why Alexandre seems frustrated with him and closer to his uncle.

Alexandre touches my cheek, then walks to the shelf and opens the door with a creak. That old sweet-musty book smell I noticed when I walked in doubles in strength. I wonder how long it's been since someone has opened that cupboard.

I run my fingers over the spine of the book I'm holding. A light brown dust rubs off on my skin—I can almost taste the rusty oxidation on my teeth and tongue. I flip open the heavy book, and a cloud of dust puffs out of it, making me cough. Alexandre turns to me to ask if I'm okay. I wave him off, not wanting to open my mouth and suck in any more of the pungent past of this book, but I like that he was worried about me.

The table of contents only lists the *Revue* issues by date, but when I flip to the back, there's an index. Bless. The first volume turns up nothing that seems relevant. I pick up the second, heading straight to the index and trailing my finger down the two-columned page. The print is tiny, and some of it slightly smudged; I kind of want reading glasses, and I'm only seventeen. I stop at a name. *The* name:

> DUMAS, ALEXANDRE
> Fils, naissance . . .
> Hashischins, Club des . . .
> Scribe de duc d'Orléans . . .

I turn to the Hash Eaters page. It's an article; I quickly scan down the lines. Honestly, it's not that quick. My French reading is only half the speed of my English. My heart is actually thumping a little—from a passage in a two-hundred-year-old book. Fine, it's not *only* finding a possible clue that's giving me palpitations. The incredibly hot, charming boy a few steps away from me, the one I've just kissed, he has a little something to do with this elevated heart rate, too. Probably. Maybe. Seriously, though, I'm such a nerd. I could've spent the next hour making out with Alexandre, but I stopped to heed the siren call of research in a musty old book. May the gods of academe favor me for this sacrifice.

"Boom." I beckon Alexandre with a finger hook. He takes four giant strides over and takes a seat next to me. His shoulder grazes mine, and our knees touch as he peers at the page. The thud of my heart grows stronger; it's the discovery. And the boy.

"There's an entire article on the Hash Eaters Club by

Théophile Gautier." I glance up at Alexandre, whose eyes narrow in focus.

He taps his finger on his lips. And now I'm staring at his lips again. "Gautier was some kind of writer then, too, I think. Maybe a poet?"

I force my eyes off his lips and onto the page. "Anyway, look." I point to a line and give him a little nod so he'll read it. He obliges.

"*I arrived in a remote quarter in the middle of Paris, a kind of solitary oasis which the river encircles in its arms on both sides as though to defend it against the encroachments of civilization. It was in an old house on the Île Saint-Louis, the Pimodan hotel built by Lauzun . . .*"

"Our apartment is, like, right around the corner from where they used to meet. Isn't that weird?"

"Destiny, perhaps?" Alexandre grins. "But you don't believe in that, do you?"

"Keep reading," I urge and move his finger down a couple paragraphs on the page. He turns his hand around, pulls my fingers into his palm, and then flips it back over so his hand rests on mine as we follow the words on the page. I suck in my breath. It feels . . . intimate. Is that possible, when all we're doing is reading?

"*Delacroix spooned a morsel of the greenish paste from a small crystal bowl, and placed it next to the silver spoon on my saucer that I then added to my strong coffee with moderation.* He's describing how they got stoned. Here it says the paste was a mix of the hash plus cinnamon, cloves, nutmeg, orange juice, butter—"

"Orange juice and butter? Disgusting. I wonder why they didn't smoke it."

"Hash wasn't exactly the same as weed now. Definitely not

like what you have in the States. Here it's almost like a resin. Most of the time we crumble it and mix it with tobacco." I raise an eyebrow at him. He grins. "It was research."

I nudge him a little; he nudges back. He's still holding my hand.

"Keep reading," I say. "We haven't gotten to the good part yet."

"I disagree," he says while grazing the back of my hand with his thumb.

I smile, then tip my head up to kiss his neck.

He keeps reading. *"Slowly, our soirée was joined by the most extraordinary figures, a disarray of fantastical beastly and human shapes in rags and tatters. All seemed aware, moved by the phantoms, save Dumas. He had thoughts only for her, the dark-haired beauty with melancholy eyes, the high priestess of our séances. Dumas would retreat into the shadows, a corner, wholly unto himself, allowing quiet to reign over him. Besotted by she, who though with us, was always apart. La belle dame aux cheveux raven, he would call her, using, always, the English word."*

Besotted.

Alexandre slips a piece of paper between the pages and puts the book down. Then he leans his body into mine, bright eyes twinkling. "You found her."

"She wasn't even that hard to find. She's literally right here. Who knows how many people read this and didn't even give her a second thought? She's just some random, unimportant woman—window dressing in the life of important men."

Alexandre knits his fingers through mine. "Maybe it was your destiny to find her. La belle dame aux cheveux raven," he says and takes a few strands of my hair between his fingers.

"I still think it's weird how Dumas uses an English word in that phrase to describe her. 'The beautiful woman with raven hair.' It's romantic, though."

Alexandre grazes my cheek with his thumb. "This time I'm the Dumas using that endearment, and I'm talking about you."

Leila

❦

We step into the courtyard at the magic hour. The golden rays of sun descend onto the trees, setting the hollowed trunks aglow like they are lit with fire from within. The poet's eyes fill with the wonder of this place. He walks between the trees, running his hands across the trunks and stepping into their carved spaces.

"A garden of hollow trees. It is poetry," he says.

"Yes, my lord."

"Please call me Byron," he asks, nay, commands. It does not escape me that my own name does not pass his lips. He turns to face me. "May I be so bold as to ask you to detach the veil from your hair?"

So it begins.

I raise my fingers to my head, but the poet stays my hand and instead plucks the pins from my hair himself. Gently, he unwinds the chiffon scarf from my hair, revealing my braid that I've plaited with a golden tassel. He wraps my pale blue scarf around his own neck. Then begins to unbraid my hair.

I step away, startled at the intimacy of the gesture. He smiles like a schoolboy. I nod at him; anything else is death.

He begins again, slowly, slowly unweaving one section of hair from another. I softly shake my head, and my hair unravels down my back.

"You smell like roses," he says and then walks around to face me. "But the rose envies the color of your lips and the night your raven hair."

"Is it true what they say about you?" I ask. He raises an eyebrow. "You are mad, bad, and dangerous to know."

He throws his head back and laughs. "I see my reputation precedes me. My misfortune."

I am emboldened, because for most of my life in the serai, my only choices were bravery or fear. "They say you have appetites."

"Your beauty and your self-assurance demand my candor, and thus I willingly give it. Yes, I have certain passions, as a poet and as a man. My faults are many, but I am determined that if I am to be alive, then I must live and live fully. Taste all the fruit life offers, in all the ways it offers them. To some, I am stern and artful. To you, I hope I am more, as your charm and exquisite loveliness and, indeed, your courage compel it of me. I present myself to you, then, merely as a man humbly at your service." With his words, the poet sweeps his hand to his heart and bows before me.

I take his offered hand in mine, and he brings it to his lips. He wraps his arm around my waist and bends to kiss my cheek, then hooks a finger under my chin, brushing his lips over mine. His is the first clean-shaven face I have felt against my own, and his skin is smooth, supple, like a woman's. He tastes of tobacco and coffee.

I flinch. He pulls his head back. Pasha could lash me for this.

"My lord, forgive me. I . . . I . . . Pasha has bid me to avail

myself to you. To make you comfortable and answer your needs . . . your desires—"

"But you cannot. Your heart belongs to him."

"No, my lord. Not to him."

"To another, then?" The poet's eyes widen.

"To another," I whisper.

"And this is why your Pasha offers you to me? Your punishment for a clandestine lover?"

I laugh. "If my deception were exposed, it would be death. To lie with Pasha means you can be with no other."

The poet's face turns paler than it already is. "And yet he gives you to me? What awaits you on the 'morrow, then?"

"I was the favorite, the haseki, but I have borne no children, and so . . ."

"You are to be employed in this manner as a price for being barren?"

"I am not barren. A jinn's curse protects me from being with child. As I have asked. As I have prayed. I will not bring a child into a world such as this." I instinctively bring my finger to my opal. Si'la slips out of one of the tree hollows. I raise my hand to stay her. I need no intervention.

The poet shivers and glances around but sees nothing.

I clutch his hand. "I must escape with you when you leave. There is nothing left for me here. My life is forfeit."

"And your lover?"

"I will see to him."

"And how do you propose I remove you from here without notice?"

"I will travel in disguise as part of your caravan if my lord agrees to allow me—us—passage beyond Pasha's lands."

"And if your treachery is discovered?"

"A sack of stones as a shroud. Water my grave. But fear

not for your own life. An English nobleman would not fall at the hand of Pasha. Indeed, perfidy is almost expected of Europeans."

"Perhaps as it should be." The poet chuckles. "You are truly a singular woman. By my troth, I am at your service."

"Thank you, my lord. A thousand thanks."

He kisses my hand again. "What a tale I will have to tell. An elegy offered to me on a damask rose–scented night. The dream of a poet, come to life."

KHAYYAM

When I got home yesterday afternoon, after researching at Alexandre's house—and by research, I mean kissing, the kind of kissing that put a swoony, if temporary, halt on looking through archives—I posted more pictures on Instagram. Macarons and artfully angled Paris shots and me and Alexandre amidst piles of books in his library. He and his library are Insta-perfect. They also might be insta-solving a lot of my problems. And are prime Zaid clickbait—if only he would fall for it.

I kind of feel like I should tell Alexandre about Zaid. I can hear my mom's voice right now: *Honesty is the best policy, beta.* But it's also absurdly complicated. I already told Alexandre about my art history prize essay fail; does he also need to know about my love life fail and about how he is, unwittingly, charmingly, maybe, helping me fix both? Sigh. I want *something* to be simple and easy, even if it means I have to deny reality—or push it to the sidelines for now.

But messy and complex is how my life usually is. I reach for my phone, and on cue, I see a missed message. I may have deleted Zaid's number, but I still recognize it. He texted at 3 A.M. Paris time: Miss you 😘

Of course he texted when I was asleep. He knows the time difference. But still. I check Instagram and see that he liked a selfie of me making a kissy face in front of the Stravinsky Fountain at Pompidou with the giant red lips sticking out of the water in the background. He didn't like the pics I posted with Alexandre at the secret garden or in his library, but now he knows the truth: another boy exists. My heart leaps.

Et voilà, I'm suddenly back in Zaid's viewfinder. Competition in absentia. The distance. Paris. Alexandre's undeniable, factual hotness. It all adds to the challenge. Zaid seems chill, but in class he's super competitive. Like, he wouldn't even share notes with other kids. He wasn't valedictorian, but close, and I know it burned him when his B in English lit cost him the top spot.

Zaid likes the chase. Right now, I'm the quarry that's out of reach.

I don't know why I didn't realize this sooner about Zaid. If I had . . . honestly . . . I don't know what I would've done differently. I'm still attracted to him. And at the same time, I want to clobber myself for being a dunce. Ugh. I *want* him to want me and miss me.

I was never good at playing hard to get. I hate stupid games. But maybe sometimes they're necessary. Didn't I say the art of French flirting is knowing what to conceal? Maybe being back in Paris actually *is* upping my dating game.

The thing is, I want Alexandre to want me, too. There's a fluttery feeling in my stomach, and I can't figure out if it's good or not. I pause. The flutters turn into queasiness. I run my fingers over my lips. I can still feel Alexandre's kiss against them. I'm seeing him later this afternoon. And I want that, too. None of this makes sense, exactly, but I'm not sure how to ignore everything I desire.

I TURN MY phone over. I need to text Zaid back. But if I want to keep up that façade of hard-to-get, aloof but alluring French girl, I can't. But how do I make that me if it's not? Fake it till I make it, American style? I think of what Julie would say to me if she saw me pining away: *Get out of bed. Brush your teeth. Read. Do something. Anything. Don't text.* I put the phone back on the nightstand and get up to draw back the curtains. I can do this.

I pull on the old metal bolt that holds the windows closed and push them out toward the street. I can smell the baguettes baking at the boulangerie on the corner. The air feels good. Not too hot. Not too humid. Fresh.

I walk over to the red upholstered lounge-y chair in my room that mainly serves as a closet. I pull on my jeans and grab a faded gray *Nevertheless, She Persisted* T-shirt and shimmy it over my tank. I slide into a pair of electric-blue jutti flats with silver flowers embroidered across the top. I don't hear my parents, so I figure I'll go get breakfast.

I look back at my phone and pause.

And pause.

Then I take three determined strides toward the door.

I stop. I turn.

I rush over to my phone and text Zaid: 😊 😊 😊

I hit SEND before I can stop myself. I slink to the bed, my bad decision immediately pressing on me. So much for my unparalleled display of willpower.

My phone dings almost immediately. It's 1:30 A.M. in Chicago.

Zaid: There you are.

Me: You expected someone else at my number?

Zaid: Awww, I've missed your snark.

Me: Plenty where that came from.

Zaid: That's what I love about you.

I stare at the screen. *Love*. He never uses that word. We never use that word. Maybe all the pictures of him with other girls on Instagram were a ruse to get *my* attention.

It worked.

Dammit.

Zaid: Still there? Did some French guy whisk you away?

He has noticed.

Me: . . .

Hold on, Khayyam. Wait, one second longer.

Me: Maybe.

Zaid: Is that a baguette in your text, or are you just happy to see me?

Me: Funny. I thought we were talking about the French guy.

Zaid: So there is one.

This is a lot easier than I thought. I need to learn to give myself more credit.

Me: My dad's knocking at my door—gotta go.

Zaid: Maybe FaceTime later?

Me: 😕

I turn my phone off and put it on my nightstand before I text anything that might wreck this tiny moment of triumph.

PARIS IS LANDLOCKED, and yet here I am, standing on a faux beach on the banks of the Seine. Somewhere in there is a witty joke, but my brain is a jumble. And my stomach somersaults. Nerves. Also, I'm wearing a swimsuit. A ratty old maillot because I didn't buy a new one for this trip. True, a gauzy, long-sleeved pink kurti with white embroidery at the neck is covering my skin from my neck to below my knee, but I'm still feeling totally self-conscious. Alexandre and I have already made out, so I shouldn't be suddenly struck by the desi modesty complex, but I am. I wonder if there are cultural identity genes that express themselves only at the most awkward moment possible. Like Murphy's Law, but for DNA.

Alexandre's snagged one of the highly sought-after blue umbrellas, and I slip out of my flip-flops onto the coarse, warm sand and walk over to him.

"Bienvenue à Paris-Plages," he says and stands to faire la bise. I wasn't sure if it was going to be a two-cheek kiss or an on-the-lips kiss since we've already kiss-kissed. Two cheeks it is. I'm fine with it. Because there are, like, a million people on this tiny strip of fake beach next to the Seine, and even if no one in Paris casts a second glance at two people kissing, I feel too exposed.

We take a seat on the large blanket he's spread out on the sand under the cover of his front-row umbrella. "How'd you manage this coveted spot?"

"I slept here overnight."

"Ha! And they say chivalry is dead."

"Chevalerie is French, you know. A way of life and love."

"Mildly sexist, yet poetic."

"See, you *do* recognize the poetry of life."

"I'm not a poet. Just named after one. I'm too practical to see life that way."

"Don't you see this as poetic?"

"The Paris-Plages? It's sand dumped on the road by the Seine and paid for by a corporate sponsor."

"No," he says and then waves his hand between us. "Us. Meeting. Stumbling onto this romantic mystery?"

I laugh. "We don't know if the mystery is romantic or not. And I told you, people believe in the magic of coincidence because they're lacking the necessary information to think of it as anything else."

A shadow passes over Alexandre's face. But he quickly smiles, pretending to stab himself in the heart and then leans forward as I draw back onto the blanket. He inches closer until his lips hover above mine. I smile, immediately and unfortunately aware of the tiny beads of sweat on my forehead and upper lip. We're surrounded by chattering sunbathers and kids yelling and cars honking on the streets above the river, but the sounds fade until I can only hear the beating of my heart in my ears. And all I feel is the thrum of Alexandre's heartbeat against my chest.

A brown curl droops down onto his forehead. I gently nudge it away. He grins, then kisses me. It's as good as last night. Better. And less bookish tasting and more salty and a little like coconut sunblock. This kiss is like summer.

He gently retreats back to his own space on the blanket. "Don't tell me you don't believe that moments of life are poetry."

I draw myself up and pull my legs to my chest. I rest my cheek on my knees and look at him. Like, ninety-five percent of the time, I talk excessively when I'm nervous or excited.

But there are rare times like this when I allow the moment to exist, unadorned, because embellishment would ruin it.

Alexandre runs his thumb down my cheek and lies back down, slipping his tortoiseshell sunglasses over his eyes. I stretch out next to him. He intertwines his fingers with mine, our arms forming a V between our bodies. As I stare up at the sun through the filter of the blue umbrella, an inkling of guilt runs through me.

But I don't think I have anything to feel guilty about. It's not like Alexandre and I are exclusive. We haven't even talked about it. I wonder how that conversation goes in French? Maybe it's an unspoken agreement? Anyway, technically, it was only one kiss. Well, an afternoon of kissing. Plus, the one right now.

And those texts with Zaid were only texts. He's not even in the same country. Besides, he's not technically my boyfriend— current or ex—because he never deigned to use that word.

God. I can't decide if I'm dumb or really clever.

I nudge Alexandre and sit back up. "I think we should go to the Hôtel." This is uncharacteristically bold of me. But I have a mission, and August isn't going to last forever.

Alexandre pulls down his glasses and sits up. "You want to go to a hotel with me? Now?" A large grin spreads across his face. He's even showing teeth. He's playing on the French and English word for *hotel*. In this case, the French use the term hôtel particulier for a grand townhouse—a mansion in the city—that is not, in fact, a hotel at all. I kinda love that he can make these little bilingual jokes and that I can understand them. It's like we're the only two members of a highly exclusive club. I probably could have this secret linguistic society with Zaid, too, if only my Urdu were better.

"I mean *the* Hôtel. The Hash Eater–séance-creepy hôtel particulier."

Alexandre props himself up on his elbows. "Well, that is disappointing."

"Whatever." I nudge his knees while I roll my eyes. "I read a little more about our friends the Hash Eaters online and found one line on our mysterious raven-tressed lady. Here, look." I reach into my bag and pull out my phone.

There's a missed text. From Zaid. I want to see you before I leave. I let out a little gasp and try to cover it with a cough.

"Are you okay?" Alexandre sits up and puts his hand on the small of my back.

I put the phone down to hide the screen from him. "I'm fine. Something in my throat, is all."

"Hold on." Alexandre leans over, and while he fishes through his backpack, I flip my phone back over and read Zaid's message again. Not sure what he means, FaceTime? That's not like him. But he's leaving for Reed in a few weeks, so what else could it be?

Alexandre hands me a bottle of water. "Here."

I take a few gulps and remind myself to breathe. My heart beats wildly. I'm certain Alexandre can hear it. He seems inordinately concerned about my little fake cough. Damn, this is uncomfortable. Does this count as lying to him? I am concealing the truth. But is a lie of omission as bad as a lie-lie?

"What did you want me to look at?"

"Huh? Oh, the Hash Eaters. Right." I flip through windows on my phone until I get to a page I saved from a site on the occult in Europe. It has a small paragraph about the Hash Eaters. And a line about the woman: "The *Club des Hashischins* experimented with the drug to heighten their awareness, believing the high provided a portal to deeper artistic expression. It is said they employed a woman of possibly Turkish or Middle Eastern descent to lead séances that allowed them to communicate with spirits of great artists and writers of the past. The woman is rumored to have been a writer herself, though there is scant evidence of her existence."

"Ahh, the raven-haired lady might've been a writer, too, perhaps. Lovely," Alexandre says.

"But thanks to misogyny, her writing is lost and her name is unknown. And she's totally erased. How quaint," I reply tersely.

"You're quite the feminist, aren't you?"

It's an offhand remark, but my hands curl into fists. I try to respond calmly through gritted teeth. "You obviously don't understand that word at all. It's not a pejorative."

"It was merely an observation. I—"

"Being a feminist means you believe that a woman's life and her choices are her own. It means you believe in equality and that you'll fight for it."

Alexandre nods. "Well, then I'm a feminist," he says. "It's simple, I guess. Anyone who doesn't believe in that is an ignorant asshole."

I look into his eyes. He smiles at me. I smile back. He hears me. He listens. He course-corrects. I don't think he should get cookies for realizing the obvious, but maybe there are some good guys, after all. "So you'll help me get into the Hôtel de Lauzun in case there's something sitting there, waiting to be found?"

"You want to break in? Like a thief?" he asks with mock surprise.

"Well, it's not open to the public, and I have a feeling that—" I stop. I'm not sure what I'm saying. I've completely made this plan up on the fly, and it's not like me at all. I'm pretty much always the model child, but my normal way to operate landed me in dog crap, and stepping out of my comfort zone seems to be paying off, at least a little. And honestly, I don't see how this could make anything worse. I blame it on some kind of surge in my French genes. The French seem to have a more casual relationship with rules—especially ones that seem unnecessary. It's not only the constant jaywalking and cutting in line; it's the sense that the rules exist but don't always apply to you. Now here I am, American compulsion to follow rules and desi tameez cast aside, the French girl emerging.

Alexandre kisses me on the cheek. "I'm in."

"Really?" I can't help but be incredulous at both of us.

"Oui, bien sûr. Summer is the time for adventure. Why not make one of our own? Dumas would approve."

Excitement surges through me. Also terror. We could get in a lot of trouble if we get busted. Breaking and entering is an actual crime, and I'm not exactly an experienced trespasser. But a part of me is pulled to this. Drawn into it by a nameless woman who is asking me to find her. If I'm being honest, this added intrigue will make for a kickass essay, too.

And it's not lost on me that this is the first evening that Alexandre seems to be available and not enigmatically busy. I've never had a first date that involved burglary before. Truth is, I've only had one other first date. Chances for an epic fail are high.

"Tomorrow night," I say to Alexandre as I lie back down and face the sun.

Nothing ventured, nothing gained.

Leila

Pasha summons me in the afternoon.

To fool him is no easy task. The kind eyes he reserves for me have daggers behind them, always at the ready to cut. And he is watching, always observing, even when he turns his gaze from you. He will notice the smallest shift in voice or posture. And he will slit a throat based on no evidence but his instinct.

Yet I am practiced at deception—meeting as I have been with the Giaour all this time, here under Pasha's roof, in the courtyard of jinn, without detection. But now, as the taste of freedom hovers like a drop of honey above my lips, I can ill-afford a mistake or an ounce of Pasha's suspicion.

"And what have you learned from the poet?" he asks as he stirs his tea with a studied indifference.

"He seems a fool. With little wit or knowledge politic. He spoke of poetry and his conquests in England and abroad. He speaks mainly of himself and is, of course, in awe of your grounds and court and your achievements in battle."

I look at Pasha, hoping I have given the right answer.

He slowly sips from his cup, taking care to set it down

before answering. He means for the pause to fill me with fear; he does not understand that fear has been my constant companion all my years.

He meets my gaze. "Valide tells me this poet is a man of specific desires. Perhaps the poet needs your further attention before he reveals his true purpose in our lands. Give him the comfort he needs. The connection he craves. I am certain deception lurks here. And as you know, I am never wrong."

"Yes, Pasha." I bow my head and walk away, bile in my throat, a cold dread whispering in my ear, but that drop of honey tantalizingly close to my lips.

KHAYYAM

"You're quiet," my dad says as we walk down the street toward our apartment.

"Hmm." I nod. "Pondering that caramel au beurre salé I had on that crêpe—I think it's the best I've ever tasted."

Truth is, there is more on my mind than caramel tonight. Still, the crêpes are absolutely worthy of sustained contemplation. Every summer my parents and I hit up Le Sarrassin et le Froment—a crêperie that is always busy with tourists, but also always delicious and, conveniently, a stone's throw from the apartment. Their savory buckwheat galettes have perfect crispy thinner-than-paper browned edges that I love. And the buttery dessert crêpes—topped with crème Chantilly or caramel or chocolate sauce and caramelized bananas or strawberries—are a moment of life's perfection.

"Are you saying the caramel crêpes are even better than your papa's? Because those are fighting words." My mom looks from me to my father and grins.

"Absolutely. Sorry, Papa. You've been replaced."

"The words every father dreads hearing," my dad responds

with a smile. "I knew this moment would come, but I thought it would be your wedding day."

I roll my eyes. "Presumptuous much, Papa?"

My father smiles and strokes my hair, then takes my mom's hand as he kisses her. I swear, his eyes glisten with tears.

LATELY, I'VE NOTICED my parents are growing more sentimental around me. I asked my mom about this earlier in the summer, and she said it was because I'd be out of the house soon. And I guess this summer is a little taste of that. This is the first time in seventeen family Augusts in Paris that I haven't been around all the time because I've been away exploring the city with a boy. As I've said before, my parents love me, but I've always believed that their love for me came after their love for each other. And they've always given me my freedom, so her answer kind of surprised me. But I suppose it makes sense, too. When I go to college, it will be the two of them again, as it was for all the years before me, but there will be a Khayyam-shaped empty space, too.

It must be a strange feeling to love a child and all the while be raising them to leave you. My mom told me that was always their parental mission—to give me the skills I need to be successful without them. That's why they give me so much freedom and trust me implicitly. It was different for my mom when she was growing up—she had stricter Indian immigrant parents, but that experience influenced everything she is and does. My grandparents had to be hard-asses, though. Everyone always talks about America as this immigrants' dream: Lady Liberty beckoning the huddled masses yearning to breathe free. Pretty words. Hollow words. My nani and nana didn't always find it welcoming—not for brown Muslims, anyway. It's not lost on me that my dad—an immigrant, too, but a white European guy—gets a completely different reception than desis with accents when passing through airport security.

My mom says Nani and Nana parented out of fear because of the world they lived in then. Sadly, that's still the world we live in now.

Growing up in France, my dad's childhood was practically the opposite of my mom's. French parenting is strict when kids are little but morphs into something more laissez-faire. Like, my dad was not allowed to be a picky eater. He had to be seen and not heard a lot. But then he was backpacking throughout Europe with his friends starting at sixteen. There are so many things that are completely different about my parents, and yet here they are, decades later, devoted and inseparable. Maybe it's not such a rare thing, but it feels that way to me.

"SEEING ALEXANDRE AGAIN soon?" my mom nudges on our walk home.

"Tonight," I mumble. Best to leave out the part about breaking and entering.

"Is it a date?" she asks. "Should we meet this young man?"

"Ugh. No. We're hanging out. Maybe getting ice cream. That's all. He's not coming to the house with a wrist corsage and shiny polished shoes to court me like it's a 1950s movie."

Both my parents laugh. I catch them exchanging an inscrutable glance.

"I don't think that's exactly how it went back in the day," my mom says.

"We're solving a mystery, anyway," I blurt.

"A murder or a heist?" my dad jokes.

"Neither." I desperately need to get out of this conversation. My flirty texting might be improving, but my neutral parent banter needs serious work.

"Tell us," my mom says as we continue our leisurely walk. I sigh. Why do I do this to myself? I didn't mean to tell them all of this, not yet, but now I can't get out of it.

"You know how Alexandre is a Dumas?" My parents both nod. "Okay, duh, I told you that already. Anyway, I showed him the Delacroix that inspired my essay for, um . . ."

"The Art Institute Young Scholar Prize." My mom interrupts matter-of-factly like I've simply forgotten. As if the biggest failure of my life could slip my mind. As if it's not a gut punch every time I have to say the words.

I take a breath. "Yeah, that. Seeing that he *is* a Dumas and all, I filled him in on my so-called theory and how I wished there was a way I could, you know, redeem myself. Do it over. Turn back time or something." My parents both nod again, and from the corner of my eye, I see these wistful looks on their faces. I have to keep my eyes on the ground because there's a lump welling in my throat, and I can't stand it.

I cough and continue. "The thing is, Delacroix *did* give Dumas a sketch that the family still has. And Alexandre showed me this letter from Dumas to his son where he wrote: Cherchez la femme, trouvez le trésor."

"Wait. Hold on." My dad stops abruptly. His eyes widen, and he and my mother exchange looks. "That is truly incredible."

"For real. Then there's this letter between Delacroix and Dumas referencing a mysterious raven-tressed woman. We're trying to figure out if all these pieces are connected. Maybe there is an actual treasure, and maybe it's a Delacroix painting. And somehow this mystery woman is the key to finding it.

Then, well, maybe I could write a whole new essay that could win the prize . . ." *And thus rewrite my entire future*, I think. "But if this is all really real—this woman, these letters—how come no one else has found her? Made the connection? All these clues have been lying there waiting to be found." I look to my mom.

My mom shakes her head. "I think you probably already know the answer to that. It's a story we've seen over and over. For too long women's contributions have been disregarded. Forgotten. Barely footnotes in the stories and *histories* of men with power. And that's something *you* could help rectify. It would be truly amazing if you could connect these bits and pieces and find this woman. And a missing painting!" I can tell how excited my mom is when she starts gesticulating as she speaks—right now she's at peak academic giddiness. "If you figure this out, it could mean a lot more than an award. Art history and literary journals would eat it up."

I give my mom a little side hug and mouth a thank-you. I know it's her job, but it still feels good to know she believes in me.

"And I'm sorry for giving you a hard time about your intentions with Alexandre."

I step aside, confused. "What are you talking about?"

"I mean Papa and I were thinking that you were spending time with him because you *felt* a . . . connection. Not *because* of his connections."

My face flames with anger. "I'm not using him or anything. How could you say that?" I snap.

Now it's my parents who look confused. Excellent. I've stepped in figurative crap again and have another mess to clean up. Not sure why I feel defensive anyway. I mean, I do actually like Alexandre.

"Mon chat, we don't think that," my dad says. "That's not who you are. We were surprised that you two shared an academic interest, that's all."

I shrug. "Alexandre goes to the École du Louvre. Maybe he will want to write a paper, too, if we find something interesting, especially because Alexandre Dumas is his actual ancestor." I start walking again with my shoulders drawn to my ears. My parents hurry after me.

My mom touches my shoulder. "Khayyam, it's critical that you not let him take credit for your work. It's like I was saying—you have to make sure your voice, your contribution, isn't silenced. It might be the twenty-first century, but as women of color, we still have to fight for our worth. All marginalized folks do. It's more important than ever. If you've hit on something, the findings are part of your intellectual property, too."

"Mom, Alexandre wouldn't do that," I say, anger edging into my voice again.

My dad jumps in. "All the same, perhaps you should bring him around so we can discuss it with him."

"Mom. Papa. You're making a huge deal out of nothing. We're having fun. Besides, *girl saves herself from academic purgatory* isn't exactly *Le Monde* headline worthy."

My mom takes my hand in hers, her voice softening. "Beta, don't sell yourself short. I know how much losing that contest stung you. But please don't ever think you're a failure. I wish you could see yourself as we do—bright, brilliant, hardworking."

I wish I could imagine myself like that, but it doesn't feel real. Since my catastrophic failure, I don't hear their words. All I hear are the judge's: *a dilettante, not a future art historian*. I don't feel brilliant or bright at all. I feel like a light bulb that sparks and pops right before it fades out.

I WALK UP the wide, winding staircase to our apartment alone.

My parents went for a stroll along the Seine. I swear to God, as I watched them walk off hand in hand, the golden light of Parisian summer afternoons illuminated their path.

My phone beeps as I reach our landing.

It's another text from Zaid:

Miss you 🖤 🖤

I slip the phone back into my purse and reach for my keys with shaky fingers. Part of me knows that Zaid is texting me again because he's jealous, so I'm not sure why I'm both annoyed and nervous.

Lately I think Zaid is at war with himself. The lovable, charming nerd versus the dude bordering on bro. And it's been pretty clear which part is winning. Almost inexplicably, I still want to be in his life. Also, it's hardly fair for me to call out *other* people for their internal contradictions.

Here we are, playing games. I put out a little trap, and he took the bait. He still has feelings for me. I still have feelings for him, too, even if they aren't the clearest or smartest feelings I've ever had. But Alexandre is creeping into my thoughts. And into my heart. And into an abandoned old building with me tonight.

Alexandre is *here*, in Paris. Present.

Zaid is thousands of miles away. And we're not even together anymore.

I need to be present, too. But the past still has its claws in me.

Leila

I step into the night, veils secured tightly around my hair and mouth. Pasha's banal cruelty has provided me the opportunity for escape. But before I go to the poet, I go to my Giaour. Down the steps, winding, through the darkness, I clutch my opal while a prayer rises from my lips: "Thee alone I worship. Thee alone I seek for help. I fall upon your mercy to save me. To free me from this bondage."

Si'la glides along the final steps with me as I approach the courtyard of the hollow trees. "I will pray for you, too, but I fear for you on this journey. I fear you will not escape wholly as yourself. I saw to it your message was delivered. He awaits you."

"Si'la, your protection has kept me alive all these years, but there is no life for me here. I am cast out even as I remain in the serai."

"This I know. We all know. And the Valide Sultan will face my wrath. But understand I am beholden by borders in the promise I made to your father. For there are limits even I cannot breach. Never could he, nor I, have anticipated the passage you would undertake. I cannot accompany you."

"Your love for my father was boundless, wasn't it?"

"As was his love for your mother."

I smile, touched by the sadness in Si'la's eyes. I place my hand on my heart. "As is your love for me. I will carry you with me, always, the only protector I have known." My opal blazes from its setting in my necklace.

"God has made you humans out of clay. Your form is too easily shaped and bent to the will of others. And you can break. Crumble back into the dust from which you came. There is little of perfection in humankind; indeed you are the one creation that destroys the very world created for you. But more than any other being, you are capable of a love perfect and pure, and in honor of that do I freely give you my troth to protect you in all the ways I am able. To watch over you. To bear witness to your courage. Peace be with you, child. Always."

I watch as Si'la fades from sight, my eyes blurring. What the future holds is not for mere mortals to discern, but what I do know, what I grasp with my entire being, is that in this palace prison, I can know no peace in a life that is not my own. I must endeavor to do what I can, to risk this life, so that I may live another.

If we succeed, escaping into the night, into the dark seas with the poet, my beloved and I will be strangers in a foreign land, without home or nation. But of that prospect I am not afraid. I have been an orphan all my life. And I have survived.

KHAYYAM

"Are you nervous?" Alexandre whispers.

His breath warms my skin as he leans in and kisses my temple. Even though it's hot and humid outside, I shiver. He pulls away, but I grab him and kiss him on the lips. Tonight, he tastes like pistachio ice cream.

A scooter honks as it passes by. I immediately step back like I'm busted.

Alexandre laughs. "Don't worry. No one in Paris gets arrested for kissing on the street."

"But they do for breaking into government buildings," I mutter.

"It's owned by the City of Paris, but it's not technically a government building."

I roll my eyes. "Semantics. And whoever owns this building, it's still trespassing. This is the most illegal thing I've ever done in my life—ever even *thought* about doing. I don't even download stuff without paying." I don't add that my nerves are also due to the fact that we're only a couple blocks from my apartment. My parents know I'm out sleuthing with Alexandre. But I told them it was over ice cream and musty old books, like Nancy Drew, the old-school version. Obviously, I left out the whole criminal activity part. It's not like they'd be worried—it's 9:30 P.M. and not even totally dark yet—and I doubt they could even imagine me doing what I'm about to.

I gaze nervously down the street at the Pont Marie as the fading sun paints the underside of the bridge's arches with a yellow-orange-dipped brush. I sigh. At this magic hour in the summer you can understand why this place inspired so many artists chasing the light.

"Khayyam?"

I swivel my head back toward Alexandre. "Sorry. Distracted by the late evening light of summer. I want to bottle it and keep it on my shelf and hold it in my hands during the dreary Chicago winters."

Alexandre smiles at me. "See. I was right. You don't only have the name of a poet; you have the soul of one."

I look away to hide my embarrassment. Alexandre hooks a finger under my chin and turns me back toward him. "Why are you timide about compliments?"

I manage an awkward chuckle. "I-I don't know. I guess I'm not used to it. You give a lot of compliments."

"You say that as if it's a bad thing. If I see beauty, I recognize it. Why hide that? Don't tell me the boys at your school don't compliment you."

My mind drifts to Zaid. I shrug. "It hasn't exactly been my experience."

"That's about to change." He flashes an impish grin. "Are you ready for this Frenchman to draw you into a life of crime?"

"Oui, bien sûr," I answer before I can even form a thought. I can't think about it too much; if I do, I'm afraid I'll say no.

WHEN I HATCHED this ridiculous idea, it was because of

a *feeling*. I had no clue how to pull it off. Breaking into a townhouse built in the mid-1600s isn't exactly in my skill set. Alexandre claims that he has it figured out, but he still hasn't shared the actual details with me except to say that we have "a thirty percent chance of success." I wish Parisians exaggerated, because the odds aren't exactly in our favor, and a little false confidence would go a long way right now, but the French aren't the fake-it-till-you-make-it type.

The heavy wooden doors of 17 Quai d'Anjou, the Hôtel de Lauzun, are adorned with carved rosettes and look utterly impenetrable. After the French Revolution, the upper floors were divided up into apartments; one was rented out to the poet Charles Baudelaire and another to the guy who wrote the article I found, Théophile Gautier. At some point one of them must've forgotten his keys and had to find a way to sneak in, right?

But the place looks empty and deserted now; there isn't a single light on upstairs. A lone third-floor balcony is decorated with chipped gold paint over black wrought-iron curlicue rails. It's all fading into the darkness. There are no tours of this building, private or public, so I have no idea what we'll find. We don't even know how long it's been since *anyone* has been inside, illegally or not.

I rub my clammy palms against my jeans, hoping it will help me calm down. We're doing this. Apparently, I'm becoming the girl who takes risks. I wish it came from bravery or even bravado, but it's more likely desperation. I close my eyes and take a deep breath. This is actually happening.

"KEEP AN EYE out," Alexandre says.

I have no idea what he's thinking because the windows closest to the ground are covered with iron bars; no way we're getting through those. I glance up and down the street. We're alone. That's the thing with Île Saint-Louis. There aren't that many apartments on it, and all the tourists who come here are usually straggling over from Île de la Cité after paying their respects and taking in the almost miraculous rebuilding of Notre-Dame after the fire that destroyed her roof and left giant holes in her.

I stare with my mouth agape as Alexandre steps onto the ledge of the lowest window. He stands on one of the horizontal iron bars and reaches up to the next window.

"Don't tell me we're going to parkour our way in," I whisper.

"Not you, just me. You get to come through the front door," Alexandre says as he grabs the windowsill. He's tall, so it's not much of a stretch, and he deftly pulls himself up onto the stone ledge. There, he crouches down and begins to pry open the windowpanes. In Paris, especially in the older buildings, a lot of the windows open out like shutters. Alexandre takes out a pocketknife and slides it between the two tall glass panes. Little chips of paint fall to the ground at my feet. He grunts and manages to get his fingers between the windows and gives a yank. For a terrifying moment, he teeters on the ledge. I cover my mouth so I don't gasp out loud.

"Yes." He laughs. "Like I was hoping. No lock."

And apparently no alarm system, either. Which is not that unusual in Paris.

Alexandre slides one leg through the window, then the other, and hops into the room. He peeks out before closing the window and stage-whispers, "I'll be right down," then vanishes into the darkness.

RUN, A PART of me screams at myself. Like, really run.

But I'm not going to desert Alexandre. Or the raven-haired lady. This may be the dumbest thing I've ever done, but I *have* to find her. To save her, even. And if there is any trace of her or Dumas or Delacroix here, I'm going to uncover it. This is really unlike me, and I'm terrified, but I'm also buzzing with the possibilities of tonight. I'm with Alexandre. On an adventure. In Paris. And this would make an excellent intro to my future prize-winning essay.

I reposition the strap of my shoulder bag across my body. I check the inner pocket to make sure my phone is in there and silenced. I close the flap. Then check again.

Seconds tick by. A minute.

Is that too long? It feels long. A few cars pass, and a couple walks along the sidewalk across the street. But no one notices me. Here I am, heart pounding, stomach in knots, about to break into an old stone building on a dark street in Paris. For once, I'm happy I'm invisible.

I startle as the door to the courtyard creaks open. Alexandre appears, a huge smile on his face. "Please enter, mademoiselle." He holds the door open, and I slip by him into the first small arched entry. He quietly shuts it behind us.

"You're awfully good at breaking in," I whisper. "Should I be suspicious?" I take a couple steps toward Alexandre until our bodies are almost touching.

"Let's keep the mystery in the relationship a little longer, shall we?" He raises his eyebrows. "C'mon. You have to see this place."

We walk into a large central courtyard. There is a high stone wall in front of us, and to our left, the adjacent apartment building—the only light in the courtyard coming from a few lit rooms. Alexandre puts his finger to his lips and shows me the side door of the hôtel.

ONCE WE'RE INSIDE, Alexandre turns on his phone's flashlight, and a bright beam makes a narrow path down the hallway and falls upon a central staircase. We tiptoe toward it, ushering past the various closed doors on our left and right. Clearly, too much to explore in one evening.

"Let's start with the salons on the next floor?" Alexandre whispers.

I put my hand on his arm and nod. I don't know why we're whispering, but this lonely place demands our reverence, and we give it.

The floor is laid out in black-and-white marble tiles angled to look like a pattern of diamonds. Some tiles are chipped and cracked. The white marble stair winds its way up to the top. The banisters are cool against my palm, and the fine layer of dust that coats everything clogs my pores almost immediately. I shine my phone's light up and down the walls. Every spot the light touches is carved and painted, mirrored and gilded, but also fractured. Murals and paintings set into the walls are in desperate need of cleaning and restoration. Clearly the people who built this place put their hearts and talents into it. It's a magnificent baroque-lover's dream, and it makes me sad that something this beautiful could simply sit abandoned and forgotten in the middle of this city brimming with life.

I take pictures as we climb the stairs. It's dark, but the flash helps.

"You're not going to post those on Instagram, are you?" Alexandre asks, catching me a bit by surprise.

"No. Obviously I'm not going to advertise my crimes. These are for me. Anyway, how do you even know I have an Instagram account?"

"Oh, I, um . . . assumed?" Alexandre usually doesn't

stumble over his words—he's probably as nervous as I am.
I'm actually a little relieved.

We get off at the first landing, and Alexandre pulls me
through a door into what must have been a ballroom. The
four walls have golden columns that reach toward the domed
ceiling. It's entirely covered in a huge mural. I can make out
angel wings, some celestial scene, clouds and strings of flowers. To the left, opposite the windows, are two balconies.
Inside balconies.

"It's stunning," I whisper.

"Imagine the parties they must have had here," Alexandre
whispers back.

I close my eyes and let the room come to life. Brightly lit by
hundreds of candles. Women swishing around in huge skirts,
their corsets crushing their ribs but pushing their breasts up
perfectly. Some sort of orchestra playing in the corner. And
wigs, lots of powdery white wigs.

"I suppose it was a 'let them eat cake' kind of crowd that
partied here," I say.

"Definitely. Until the revolution and the guillotine."

I shudder. "Vive la France."

"Without the French Revolution, our friends like Baudelaire
would never have been able to take apartments here and—"

"No raven-haired lady. At least, not in this place. But no
more talk of the guillotine, okay? This place is beautiful but
also creepy."

He takes my hand. "Scared of ghosts?"

"Not until tonight, when we broke into an old mansion
with cracked mirrors and cobwebs. This place is asleep, and
I don't know what we're going to stir up."

Alexandre bends his head closer to mine, then closer until
his lips graze my neck.

He peppers my neck with little kisses. I reach up and cradle his head, then turn into him. He puts an arm around my waist and pulls me closer until I feel the joint of his hipbone press against me. We kiss as he runs his fingers along the nape of my neck. Tiny flames ignite everywhere in my body. When we kiss, I can taste the grime from this place on our lips, and it occurs to me that a lot of our kisses are sprinkled with the dust of centuries past. I step back, nuzzling my head against his chest. He wraps his arms around me.

"Are we going to try and find this woman with raven tresses or just make out amongst the ghosts?" I ask.

"She's been lost for a long time. A little longer won't bother her," he says and lifts my chin to kiss me again.

I sneeze. Stupid dust. Luckily, I avoid sneezing directly into his face. "Crap. I'm sorry." I turn my face away, horrified, but Alexandre laughs. I let out a small chuckle and a louder one until our laughs echo in the empty space.

"Clearly that's a sign we should get out of this room." I produce my phone again and skim through the Gautier article—the closest thing we have to Dantès's treasure map. I read out loud, *"I arrived at the designated floor. A worn and shiny velvet tapestry . . . whose yellow borders and bruised threads bespoke long service, showed me the door."*

"That's not here. Next floor?" Alexandre suggests, gesturing toward the door.

We wind our way up the stairs to an even grungier hall than the one below. It's smaller and less ornate. I catch my breath and point to a hanging on the wall. Is it possible?

We step closer. Alexandre focuses his light on the border of the cloth. I squint. It's dull, but yellow enough.

"No way." I elbow him. "This is it. It has to be. Holy crap."

ALEXANDRE OPENS THE door beside the tapestry. We step inside; he shines his light across the room. The beam passes over a large oval dining table and then lands on a buffet table against the wall. I read more of Gautier's account out loud: *"I found myself in a huge room lit at the end by several lamps. To enter here was to step backward into a shadowy past. Indeed, time seems to pass strangely in this house, as if it exists outside of time entirely. Delacroix, his eyes ever intent on the minutiae, stood by the side of a buffet examining a platter filled with small Japanese saucers."*

"A buffet," Alexandre repeats slowly.

"This is it!" I say, trying not to yell. I'm nerding out over a hundred-and-fifty-year-old article about hash-eating artists. "My heart is racing. I had no idea breaking and entering was going to be this fun." I give him a peck on the cheek and walk toward the buffet. Dust is everywhere. And spiderwebs. Presumably spiders, too. Luckily, spiders have never freaked me out.

The marble top of the buffet must have a half-inch of dust on it. It's cool to the touch, like the banister on the stairs. Like a tomb. I wipe my fingers on my jeans. I wish I had a roll of paper towels and spray cleaner, but cleaning supplies didn't seem like burglar necessities. Next time, I'll remember.

Alexandre and I shine our phone lights on the buffet table. It's not large—maybe six feet across and about hip-high. The light reveals two narrow drawers below the marble. There are flowery carvings in the wood and something, maybe lion heads, with brass rings running through the noses. Beneath the drawers is a long cabinet. Intricate scenes I can't quite distinguish cover the cupboard doors. The sides of the buffet are rounded like columns. Carved into each column is a woman with her breasts exposed. I try to get as many close-up shots as possible. The flash overexposes some of the photos, but I can try and fix that later. Right now, I want to make sure to document every moment.

"These guys were pervs," I mutter.

"In France there are no perverts, only prudes."

I laugh. "Whatever makes you feel better about your countrymen, dude." I tug at the brass pull on one of the drawers. It sticks. I tug a little harder. It gives with a loud creak.

"Oh no. No. No. I think I cracked a French heirloom."

Alexandre shines his light on the side of the drawer. Sure enough, there is a three-inch-long fissure running parallel to the top. I raise a hand to my mouth, forgetting how dusty it is. I cough, then grimace at Alexandre, who wears his classic mischievous grin.

"Why are you smiling?" I ask him. "I damaged an antique."

"Okay, but it's not exactly the *Mona Lisa*. And I believe you could convince a judge it was a crime of passion."

"In America, crimes of passion are murders."

"Of course they are. In France, crimes of passion are about being overcome by desire."

I roll my eyes. "Do you ever listen to yourself?"

"Sometimes I think it's better not to." He smirks at me. I don't think he can help it.

"Oh my God." I shake my head at him. "Anyway, since I cracked this valuable French antique, might as well see what's inside it. Give me some light."

I open the drawer a little more. Gently. Gently. No more cracking. There's a long red silky scarf. When I pull it out of the drawer, a little spider jumps out and lands on Alexandre's jeans. He yells and jumps back, swatting at his pants.

I bite my lip to stop myself from laughing, then grab the scarf and give it a good shake to make sure no other creatures are going to surprise us. I hand it to Alexandre, who gently folds it and places it on top of the buffet.

Beneath the scarf are two cards about twice the size of regular playing cards. I take them out and flip them over. Alexandre blows away some of the dust and shines a light on them.

The first is a crowned figure that looks like it's sitting on a wheel. The colors are faded. Alexandre reads the words at the bottom, "La Roue de Fortune." Wheel of fortune. Then he looks at the second card. It's a crude drawing of a man with what looks like a skeleton head. There's some kind of stick or handle in his hands. Maybe a shovel. Alexandre doesn't need to read the words at the bottom, because they're clear. La Mort. Death. I shudder. I'd prefer spiders to death cards.

"Tarot de Marseille," Alexandre says.

"I get the tarot part, but why Marseille?"

He shrugs. "That's the name. Tarot is played as a card game in France, not only for fortune-telling. My grand-mère used to play a lot with her friends."

"I'm guessing if they were doing séances here while taking hash, the fortune part was what they were interested in." I start to put the cards back in the drawer, but Alexandre stops my hand.

"We should keep those," he says. "Maybe they're clues?"

"Sure. We've already broken in. Why not steal stuff, too?"

"Borrow. And why not? We're trying to unravel a cultural mystery, after all."

"Absolutely," I say. "We're *borrowing* them for the good of the country. We're such patriots . . . Justification is how a life of crime begins, isn't it?"

"If you suggest stealing a diamond necklace from Cartier for the good of the proletariat, then we'll know."

I laugh. Then sneeze. And sneeze again. Then snort. God, I'm the subtlest thief in the world.

"Ssshhh."

I'm about to unleash my annoyance on Alexandre, because I do not like being shushed. Then I hear it.

A siren.

It's close. And getting closer.

Leila

❦

The tips of the trees in the second courtyard glow as if on fire, but they do not burn. All around the jinn perch on branches, looking down at me. Si'la rises on a limb of the tree that is the heart of the courtyard. My Giaour steps out from its hollow, a smile on his face, the deepest pink rose in his hands.

I close the distance between us, removing the veil from my face. He clasps an arm around my waist and pulls me to him, folding me into a deep kiss. Is there a way for the world to end right now, in this moment of life's perfection? Can the heavens fall, crushing us in this knotted embrace forever, until we are stardust? So that the light of our love spreads across the darkness, perfuming the firmament with sandalwood and rose petals?

He steps back and places his palm against my cheek. "The skiff waits for us at the port. My man will meet us there and row us to the vessel Salsette. But I must ask you again: You trust this poet, this British lord?"

"He will not betray us. Perhaps he is a rake and selfish, but he will do this for me—and the Romantic tales he may tell from it."

"He will do this for you, as would anyone."

"We will be free, my beloved," I whisper.

"Inshallah," he says, brushing my cheek with his thumb.

I kiss him again. My heart catches in my throat. Perhaps I may not escape whole, but I need only escape with him in any manner for this tale to have a happy ending.

"Leila. If the fates and time conspire against us, remember I love you. Remember I would suffer a thousand deaths for even a fleeting taste of freedom with you. Know that you must continue the journey without me, if it comes to that. And take this." He hands me a yataghan. It is smaller than most I have seen. The word gülüm is engraved in its ivory handle. My love. My rose. "I had it made especially for you. May it be a talisman for you against harm. May your courage find you, should you need to use it. May you never have to."

I clasp the handle and pull the blade from its hard leather scabbard. The metal gleams in the night like the moon's rays have anointed it.

I look into the eyes of the one man who has known me as I am, truth bared. Who has loved me fully and without judgment. I cup his cheek in my hand. "My love. May our separation be brief. May our paths join again at the water's edge. May God keep you always in his care."

Ameen.

We kiss.

I have no more words.

KHAYYAM

On our tiny Parisian island of Île Saint-Louis, it's rare to hear a siren—*any* siren. Across the Seine, sure, but on the island this late in the evening?

I don't breathe.

I don't think Alexandre is breathing, either. We're motionless, waiting for the siren to pass.

"The flashlight on your phone," I whisper to Alexandre.

He fumbles with his screen, trying to kill the light. I can tell he's nervous, because his palms are as clammy as mine when I wrap my fingers around his free hand.

The siren doesn't pass. It stops right outside the building.

It's completely dark in here save for the faint lamplight filtering in through the dirty windows. My mouth has gone as dry as sawdust. My pulse pounds. All those flashes, the beams from our phones lighting up the darkness in an abandoned old house. God. We've been stupidly careless.

What's the punishment for breaking and entering in France for a first-time offender? I have no idea. But I definitely don't want to find out. I tug on Alexandre's hand and head for a door in the back corner of the room, past the dining table and next to a small settee. I feel my way forward in the low light until my hand can grab the knob.

The siren goes silent.

We hear a car door open and shut outside. My heart stops. Crap. Gently, I turn the knob and open the door. Like I hoped, it's a closet. A narrow one. We slip in. All I can think about is how I don't take the double-wide coffin-sized elevator at the apartment. Now here I am in a closet crypt. Possibly about to be arrested. Oh God. I try to take a calming breath while Alexandre and I shimmy ourselves into the cramped space. As I maneuver myself into the closet, I get a face full of spiderwebs. Spiders might not bother me, but I don't want my hair to be a nest for them, and they're a lot less unnerving when they're in the full light of my bathroom than in a tiny closet in an eerie abandoned mansion.

Alexandre jiggles his left arm, trying to shake off some of the sticky filaments of broken webs, and inadvertently elbows me in the boob.

"Ow!"

"Ssshhhh."

"If you want me to be quiet, how about watching your elbows?" I hiss.

"I'm sorry. It was an accident. Shall I kiss it and make it better?"

"Shut up," I whisper. I can't help but snicker.

In the filmic scenario of this situation, this is the moment we'd begin making out madly. And as much as part of me is enjoying being smashed up against Alexandre, and as much as I notice how the heat of his hands on my hips sears through my jeans, I am straining against the feeling of the walls closing in on me. My parents might be pretty low-key about discipline, but getting arrested in Paris is not something they will chalk up to teenage indiscretion.

And I don't know what would come after. Trial? Prison? Probation? Do they have probation in France? Oh my God. I'm going to miss senior year. This will probably go on my permanent record. Is that even a real thing?

I don't think I can feel my limbs anymore. I didn't think this through. Suddenly, breaking the law in hopes of winning an art history essay contest sounds extraordinarily stupid. I absolutely do not want to suffer for my art. Or anyone else's.

Alexandre presses his ear to the door. He gives his head a little shake. No sounds. I nod. He opens the door, and we step out. Then I realize that we're on the third floor behind solid stone walls in a room with a thick wooden door, so we might not hear anyone enter from the courtyard on the ground level.

I sneak over to one of the tall windows, crouching down as low as I can. I peek over the sill. The police car is still there. Dammit. I motion for Alexandre to duck. He crouches on his tiptoes, not able to do the desi squat, and works his way over to me.

"The cop is still out there," I whisper. Every muscle in my body goes taut. My rib cage tightens around my chest; I can't breathe.

"Better than in here," he whispers back. We watch the policeman walk the length of the building. He taps his baton against the iron bars on the lower windows. He pauses by the first set of building windows—the ones closest to the entry. The window we're looking out of is the second set over, so I can catch an angled glimpse of his movements. He bends down and looks intently at the sidewalk.

"What's he doing?" Alexandre asks.

I watch the cop pick up something off the ground and then tilt his head up. I draw back from the window. I'm hoping it's too dark for him to see inside, especially from his angle.

"The paint," I say, sucking in my breath. It's suspicious. I don't know what I'll say or do if he comes in here. It's France, though, so I probably don't have to worry about getting shot.

"Huh?"

"When you used your knife to jimmy open the window, paint chips or, maybe, bits of plaster fell to the ground," I whisper.

"Merde," Alexandre mutters.

"You shut the window completely, though, right? Tell me it's not cracked open."

"No. No. I closed it. Definitely."

We glance back out. The cop is at the door to the court-yard. It looks like he's trying to open it, but no luck. He pushes against it with both palms. It's secure. Right then, the door opens, and a woman steps out. She's startled by the presence of the policeman. He apologizes, but I can't make out the rest of the conversation. It looks like he's asking her some questions. She shakes her head. He smiles and says something to make her laugh. After a brief conversation, he hands her his card. She takes it and says, "Bonne soirée" with a giggle. He watches her walk away and shakes his head. He pauses for a moment and shuts the hefty wooden door to the court-yard with a loud thud.

We watch as he climbs back into his car and speeds away.

I think we were saved by the art of French flirting.

I let out a breath. Alexandre takes my hand and we stand up. I'm dizzy. We look at each other. My face is probably pale from fear, and my fingers are cold as ice, but I burst out laughing. So does he.

"I wonder who called him?" I whisper as I get my nervous laugh under control.

"Probably someone with nothing better to do. Come on, I think we should get out of here in case he returns to do a more thorough job."

"Hang on." Before Alexandre or common sense can stop me, I stumble back to the buffet table. We only searched one drawer. I want to check the other one. This is probably totally stupid, but you know how the safest time to fly is right after a plane crash? That's the logic I'm going with right now. We need to get out of here, but I also *need* to know if there's anything else.

This drawer opens easier than its mate. There's another silk scarf. I place it on the top. I shine my light into the drawer and see something wedged in the back. It's paper.

"Hold this light for me," I say. Alexandre walks over and takes my phone, angling its beam of light into the drawer.

"It's an envelope." I tug at it, but lightly; I don't want to rip it. I jiggle the drawer with one hand, hoping to loosen it. It works; I pull out the envelope with trembling fingers. It's a letter. It's in faded, curly script, but the name on the envelope is clear. It's addressed to Monsieur Alexandre Dumas.

Leila

❧ ❧

I shed no tears as I step back through the doorway. There is no time for sorrow or goodbyes or regrets.

There is barely time to move forward.

"Haseki. I have brought you a eunuch's uniform as you have asked." A young man shuffles forward with a small satchel.

"Kemal. Thank you for your kindness," I say. "And your discretion."

"I am at your service, haseki."

"I know you are, Kemal. And I am in gratitude." I sweep my hand to my heart and bow my head. Kemal's eyes grow wide. "I have trusted you with this secret and with my life. And now I offer you passage with me away from here. I cannot say it is without risk, perhaps even death. But if you choose to take the risk, I will gladly have you join me."

Kemal bows before me. "This is my home, haseki. For all that it is. Perhaps one day I can rise to Chief Eunuch. This is the fate I have been given. There is nothing else in the world for me now, as you know."

His smile breaks my heart. "Go with God, Kemal."

"And you, haseki."

I watch as he slips away into the darkness.

I hurry to my chamber. In the satchel, along with the eunuch's clothes, I hide the jewels Pasha has given me—gold and diamonds and emeralds that may buy me a new life. I tuck my Giaour's rose in with the embroidered scarf he brought me from the Indian merchant. I wrap a sash tightly around my waist and fasten the yataghan into it, concealing it under my midnight-blue entari with golden stars at its hem.

KHAYYAM

March 10, 1845

Cher Ami,

I hope this letter finds you well.

Because you are a man of letters, I will not insult your
intelligence or my own with a verbosity of feigned feelings. I have
enjoyed our time together these past months. But the devotion you
seek from me I cannot give. Though your attentions are flattering
and your compliments pleasing, I must beg you to turn your
thoughts elsewhere, even more for your sake than for mine.

For a woman in my position, at my age, a decade your senior,
alone though I may be, and necessarily so, for my fate commands
it, some may counsel me to accept the warmth of your feelings. To
pass my days and nights in the embrace of one whose ardor for me is
true. But I dare not allow us to continue as we have, knowing your
true heart, for such a game would endanger both of us. I think too
highly of you to do such a thing.

And, to say it plainly, my heart belongs to another. Forever.
Until I meet him again in jannah, where at last our star-crossed

love may find peace, liberated from the shackles this earth cast upon us. To him I am betrothed until my dying day. I can love no other. And to that oath I have been true these three decades. Indeed, when I saw him bleed upon the sands of my old home—so distant from me now in miles, but still so close—I knew that a part of me would remain there. That is the part of my soul that you seek. The part I cannot give.

Consider evenings spent with me as time lost. Time that might be best spent in pursuit of a real love—constant and true, not this shadow. Not what we have shared, a flameless passion—yet one that has still brought me a kind of happiness. A smile to my face that I thought had been erased by time.

Yours in friendship,

Leila

"We found her," I whisper. I give Alexandre a half smile.

We're nestled on the couch in my apartment. Alone. Thankfully. My parents left a note saying they'd gone out to meet some friends. While I'm relieved I didn't need to come up with an excuse for why we're breathless and dusty and dripping with cobwebs, it finally strikes me how terrifyingly close I was to getting busted by the police and my parents. My heart races, wild from nearly getting caught and our new discoveries. I move my fingers across the page delicately, like if I'm not gentle, I could bruise Leila.

"We did find her," Alexandre whispers back. "But there are even more questions now."

"I know. Who was she? And where did she come from and who died? And—"

"What's jannah? It's not a French word."

I look at him, surprised, though I don't know why I'm shocked. It's not as if everyone would know that word. "It means heaven in Arabic. Even Muslims who aren't Arab know that jannah is what paradise is called in the Quran. Leila was Muslim."

"In Paris. In the 1840s. A Muslim woman. Wow. An immigrant or refugee, maybe? Maybe that's why she says she was alone."

"And her one true love died—" My voice catches in my throat.

Alexandre puts his hand on my arm. "Are you okay?"

"I don't know," I say, my words catching in my throat. "This . . . this feels like eavesdropping on a private conversation. We're trespassing on other people's lives."

"But I thought you wanted to find her."

"I did. I do. Dumas became famous, and she's not even a footnote in history. I want to find out more. There has to be more there." I don't add that I need more for my essay, too.

Alexandre shifts closer to me on the couch. "We can go back, but maybe not tonight?"

He wraps his arm around my shoulders. I gingerly fold up the letter and place it on the coffee table. It might be the only piece of Leila that still exists—it is precious. Then I collapse into Alexandre's arms. He kisses the top of my head. Something squeezes my heart. I should be floating from this discovery, exhilarated and adrenaline crashing from our near miss with the cop. I am, but I also feel, I don't know, conflicted? A pinch of melancholy, even. Maybe because the raven-haired lady is real now. Fantasy can be quixotic and swashbuckling. But the real Leila didn't live in a starry-eyed romance; she was a woman, utterly alone, who fought to survive.

"You're right," Alexandre says. "This can't be it. This is only one note from her. If there's more, we have to be the ones to find it. Besides, this is one hell of a breakup letter. I'm dying to see what else she's written. I can't wait to tell Uncle Gérard about this. He won't believe it."

I look into his hopeful eyes. "Am I ever going to meet this uncle you keep talking about? I feel like he's the virtual third musketeer on our quest."

"Oh. I . . . well, he's a bit antisocial . . . and boring," Alexandre stammers.

I know I can be slightly paranoid at times, but it's weird to me that every time I suggest maybe meeting his uncle, Alexandre veers away from the topic. I'm about to press him, but I freeze at the sounds of keys jangling and footsteps in the hall. I jump up and run into my room to hide the letter, then race back and take a seat at the opposite end of the sofa from Alexandre.

He chuckles. I give him a raised eyebrow in response. Yeah, I'm a prudish American. Deal with it. I don't want to get busted by my parents while making out with a random French dude they've never met. Or any guy, for that matter. Zaid knew that instinctively. Kissing in front of parents would've been too disrespectful, too lacking in tameez.

My parents burst into the apartment laughing.

They stop abruptly when they see us.

This is it.

The moment my parents meet Alexandre and when the parts of my life I'd kept separate start to cross and tangle.

Yes, they know about Alexandre. They know about Dumas and my search for the raven-haired lady because I told them.

Alexandre knows that I bombed on that Art Institute essay. But each knows things the other doesn't. And I want to keep it that way. I'm one hundred percent not ready to tell Alexandre about Zaid. And there's no way I'm telling my parents what Alexandre and I *actually* did tonight. I need time to stop. I need this meeting to happen when I'm ready. Which is not now. Too many variables and too many ways for this to blow up in my face. At least I'm the only one who knows the real reason I'm posting to Instagram. But that's not even the worst of it. What if my parents say something about how lucky I was to meet Alexandre for the sake of my research? What if he thinks that's the *only* reason I'm hanging out with him? What if my parents blurt out something about Zaid? I've been utterly careless. Twice in one night.

I jump up, thinking I can avert the disaster that is about to play out in my living room. Instead, I hit my shin against the table. I right myself before falling. But this is going to bruise. I shake my head. *Typical.* I try to prevent a painful situation, but instead, I induce it.

Alexandre pops up from the couch, and my parents step over, converging on me as I rub my shin.

"Are you okay, beta?" Mom asks. She nods at Alexandre with a smile. My dad grins. Ugh. Too many knowing looks.

"Uh, yeah. That table is a hazard," I say with an uneasy chuckle. "But um, anyway: Mom, Papa, this is Alexandre."

He steps forward to kiss my mom on both cheeks and shakes my dad's hand. My parents have these wide, goofy grins on their faces, and it's mortifying.

"Um, Alexandre was actually heading out," I say, taking him by the elbow.

"Beta, where are your manners?" my mom scolds. "Alexandre, would you like to join us for some tea?"

"He can't. He has to get home," I say.

My mom raises an eyebrow at me. "I believe he also speaks."

Alexandre chuckles. "That is kind of you, but Khayyam is right, I must be on my way."

I'll have to thank him later for following my lead. I could imagine Zaid in this same situation being utterly amused, and lingering. He loves lingering at the most embarrassing times. From the twinkle in his eye, I think Alexandre is finding this moment pretty funny, too.

But my parents don't step aside and bid him adieu. Of course they don't.

"Alexandre," my dad begins in French, "Khayyam tells us you are a descendant of Alexandre Dumas. Fascinating."

My mom jumps in, also switching to French. "And Khayyam tells us you are in pursuit of a raven-haired woman mentioned in a letter—"

"Yes. We are searching for a lady with raven tresses who Delacroix and Dumas mention in correspondence about the *Club de Hashischins*."

"And perhaps more? It would certainly be an incredible find. I'm sure you'll be sharing credit for any noteworthy discoveries with our daughter. Planning on authoring any papers?" Yup, my mom went there, because it's never too early to warn your daughter's date about intellectual property theft.

This can't end soon enough.

Alexandre seems taken aback. "Absolutely. I hadn't considered . . . Of course I will. We will. Khayyam is as much a part of this as I am."

"Good," my mom says with a smile. "I'm sure she's told you we're professors."

God. This is the Hyde Park academic version of meeting a gentleman caller on the porch with a shotgun. I position myself behind Alexandre, shooting daggers with my eyes at my parents. "He knows," I mutter, then yawn dramatically. "It's getting late, and I'm tired. Like I said, Alexandre was about to leave." I give him a little nudge.

"Yes, a pleasure to meet you. I hope we meet again. Au revoir."

ALEXANDRE AND I step out into the hallway, and I sigh as I shut the door. "I'm sorry. My parents are, you know, over-protective. And also real nerds."

"In other words, they are parents. I understand. And you know I meant what I said," he adds. "You're part of this."

I nod. As Alexandre and I walk down the stairs, I feel a pinch of guilt. Finding this mystery woman and possibly even a missing painting—that is the objective. And spending time with Alexandre and making Zaid a bit jealous—that's the icing on the cake, but it's all leaving a bad taste in my mouth.

"Want to meet tomorrow? Try to discover more about Leila? Perhaps a little more sneaking around in dark places with dark corners?" I turn and step closer to him so our bodies touch.

He rubs his hands up and down my arms, distracted. "I have a couple things to do for my family tomorrow. My uncle is coming up again in the morning . . . Then I have plans in the evening." He drags his words and glances away for a second. "But the next day? I'm all yours."

I manage a half-hearted smile, but Alexandre doesn't notice. He quickly kisses me on the cheeks before slipping out the door.

As I close it behind him, the magic of the evening fades away. I'm left with the same lingering questions every time we part. He mentioned staying in Paris for work this summer, but what's his job? And what's up with the eccentric, enigmatic uncle? Maybe it's all boring crap he doesn't want to get into. I need to focus on the *real* mystery at hand.

Still, there's this irksome voice in the back of my head reminding me that I've also only been honest with Alexandre *to a point*. In that case, maybe I'm not the only one hiding things.

I pause. I don't want to go upstairs yet, so I linger in our building's cobblestone courtyard. In medieval Paris, the courtyards housed a shared pump or were a place to dump garbage. Later, all the fancy hôtel particuliers wanted them for inner gardens and privacy and stables. Our courtyard has the garbage and recycling bins hidden off in a corner, surrounded by a wooden picket fence and potted pines. The rest of the courtyard has large containers of red-and-yellow lantana that blooms in colorful clusters the size of large buttons, overhanging the terracotta pots. Around the perimeter are weatherworn metallic troughs of lavender that scent the entire little square. It's amazing because you can't even smell the garbage on the hottest days of August.

The apartments facing the courtyard are mostly dark. I look up and see stars. The sky is clear and crisp, making the stars seem brighter. On nights like this, when I was little, I would come out here and make one wish for every star I could spot until I ran out of stars or things to wish for.

I want to wish for something now, something besides proving that I'm smarter than Celenia Mondego and that I deserve to be in her stupid program.

But I don't know what.

To find Leila? To discover more about her? To know how Zaid truly feels about me? To understand what Alexandre thinks? Too many questions unanswered. Unasked. Unfortunately, they're both good kissers. And that fact mucks up my thinking. But I need clarity and focus. I need to decide the best thing for me and my future. Zaid and Alexandre should be beside the point. *Are* beside the point.

That's what my mom would say if she knew all the details. Julie, too, probably. Zaid was never Julie's favorite. I wonder if Alexandre would be? No. Her favorite in this whole saga would be Leila—the one who really deserves my undivided attention. Leila might have a sad story, but she seems like she was a force, and, according to her letter to Dumas, she knew how to make a decision. And stick to it. Lesson learned.

Leila

 ❧❧❦❧❧

I step lightly and quickly toward the Hall of Guests.

 A cold fear grips me, tendrils wrapping around my ankles, pulling me back. But this is no time for my courage to fail. I have chosen my path.

 When I reach the poet's quarters, he races to meet me and grabs me by the arm. "We must leave now," he says. "Your Giaour has been discovered."

 The blood leaves my face, my entire body.

 I imagine Pasha's cruel laugh. His fury.

 The poet takes my satchel, the vestiges of my entire world, and hands it to his valet, who hastens their departure.

 "I cannot . . . I cannot leave without him. There is no life without him." I speak, but I am already a ghost.

 "You have no choice. Your Pasha will kill you, too, if—"

 I break free from the poet and run out into the courtyard. Torches light up the arches between columns.

 Pasha's janissaries surround me.

KHAYYAM

It takes a sleepless night for me to come to terms with the realization that my restless uncertainty isn't about what I want—well, some of it is—it's really about *Alexandre* and what he wants. About who he is. And what we are together. There are moments when he's warm and present and others when he's aloof. Why does he hedge when I ask about his uncle? Why is he busy on so many evenings and kind of cagey about it?

I guess he has the right to be busy. Technically we haven't defined what we are. Par for the course, given my relationship with Zaid. But how does Alexandre see us? Nerdy researchers who make out? An unusual, amusing summer fling? Transatlantic friends with PG-rated benefits? What he does in his free time is not my business. Maybe Alexandre doesn't owe me any explanations, but I still want the whole story.

Facts are reliable. People aren't.

I learned that from Zaid, who first ghosted me and now is bombarding me with texts. I want to believe this speaks volumes about his feelings for me, but in reality, it means nothing. The messages aren't a hand to hold. They're not a romantic picnic in a pocket park. Even so, there was another one waiting for me this morning.

I'm planning a surprise.

Zaid's surprises are usually last-minute, like, Picnic at the Point—I got tacos and Mexican Cokes. Or, Meet me at 57th Street Books, the new issue of Ironheart is in! Besides our first date at the Music Box, I don't think he ever really planned a single outing for us. Did he take our relationship for granted? Julie only mentioned that, oh, a thousand times, and I always made excuses for him. Maybe Zaid regrets how he's treated me. This time apart, the pictures of Alexandre and me, maybe it all made him realize he was wrong.

Gah. I don't like surprises. I don't do well with ambiguity, either. I only count on what I know for certain.

Neither Zaid nor Alexandre should be a factor in terms of my future, much less part of the absurd conversation inside my brain. Where the through line is doubt. What if I try again with the contest and still bomb? What if I *am* a failure? Are these dumb romantic distractions enough of an excuse to crash and burn *again*?

SOMETHING IS NOT right. When I walk out of my room, my parents are already dressed. They're not lazily reading in the sun at the table on our balcony, their usual morning routine.

"Where are you guys going?" I ask, rubbing the sleep from my eyes.

"We're taking the train to Jouy-en-Josas to see an old friend of my mother," my dad says.

"Who?"

"It's a woman who went to school with Maman. I haven't seen her since the funeral. She doesn't haven't any kids or much family left . . ." My dad clears his throat.

"We thought we'd pay a visit," my mom adds. "Your papa heard that she isn't in the greatest of health right now. It's not far—close to Versailles. We'll probably have a late lunch at the hotel near the palace grounds and then head back in the late afternoon or early evening."

I nod. "Sorry about Grand-mère's friend, Papa. That sucks."

My dad sighs. "C'est la vie." My mom reaches for his hand and threads her fingers through his own, which seems to give him the strength to smile at me. "We did enjoy meeting Alexandre last night."

"Sure. It was perfect and not awkward at all." I have never been able to hide my sarcasm, and I've never wanted to, either.

"Well, you did catch us by surprise." My dad raises an eyebrow at me.

I tense. "It's not like we were doing anything."

My mom steps forward. "We know, beta. We do hope we get to see him again. He was certainly charmant." My mom giggles a little. *Giggles*. Then she turns to Papa, then back to me, and snaps her fingers. "Oh. I almost forgot to ask! The woman with raven tresses you mentioned? Did you ever find out anything else?"

I shake my head. "Not much. Only that the letters were around the 1840s." I wonder if I've given away my criminal activity, but there is no way my mom could know where we were last night—or what we found.

"That makes total sense," my mom says.

"It does?"

My mom wags a finger, her favorite way to make an academic point. "I thought it was funny when you mentioned Delacroix and Dumas using the English phrase 'raven-tressed' to describe the woman's hair."

"Because that's not proper French. The word for raven is corbeau," my dad finishes. "Anyway in French, the construction would be—"

"'The lady with tresses raven,'" I finish for him. "The noun before the adjective. But they constructed it the English way—the adjective before the noun. So?" I shrug and stare between the two of them, at a loss.

My parents exchange a look. "Byron," they say at the same time.

I frown. "It's from a Byron poem? It's definitely not *The Giaour.*"

"No," my mother replies gently. "I know how well you know that one. It's from 'She Walks in Beauty.' Not sure what year he wrote it—maybe 1814? 1815? There's a woman that he describes as having waves in every 'raven tress.' The French literati—even three decades later—would surely have been familiar with that poem, as they were with many English Romantics. Maybe that Byron connection to Delacroix and Dumas runs deeper than you think."

Delacroix's words to Dumas come rushing back to me: *"And see the words of the poet come to life."*

Holy crap.

How did I not even consider this possible connection? Celenia Mondego, head judge, pops into my brain with the answer: *slipshod research—a catastrophic inability to grasp obvious facts.*

Ugh. Screw you, Celenia. I'm not going to repeat the same mistakes. The puzzle pieces are in front of me, and I swear to

God, this time I'm going to make sure they click into place. My heart, my stomach, every cell in my body flutters and buzzes and whatever other words can describe being struck by lightning. I take a breath.

Be calm, Khayyam. Think.

As my parents leave, only one thought occupies my brain: Forget Zaid and Alexandre. I have a date with Lord Byron.

I GOOGLED THE Byron poem the minute my parents left. But I want to hold the book in my hands, too. Papa always says I am my mother's daughter, and maybe he's right, because poetry feels more alive to me when I can touch the page. Besides, it gives me an excuse to visit my favorite bookstore in Paris, and probably the most famous: Shakespeare & Company.

It's a mostly English-language bookshop on the Left Bank on a small, one-block street that dead-ends on a pretty square a stone's throw from the Seine. I've spent hours here with my mom, and I adore the charm of its uneven floors and the friendly cat that winds its way through your legs or makes its way onto your lap as you've sat down to read a book. It's a crooked, rickety old indie that's been around since the 1950s. It was built in homage to the original store that opened in 1919 on a different street that was shut down by Nazis when they occupied France. When you meander through its rooms, the history of this place feels alive, tangible—you're literally walking in the footsteps of famous writers and artists—expats in search of a community who found a home.

My favorite part of the store is the second floor. The short, narrow, twisting stair-bookcase (yes, a diagonal shelf of books runs along the outer rails of the stairs) spells out a message on each step: *I wish I could show you when you are lonely or in darkness the astounding light of your own being.* A quote from Hafiz, my mom told me on one of our annual visits. A fourteenth-century Persian poet. A Muslim. "See," she whispered to me at the time, "we're everywhere."

Up those well-worn, possibly not structurally sound red stairs are the old books. And the nook I adore the most— a cozy typewriter alcove with a single chair and tiny desk that can fit exactly one person, its three walls lined with scraps of paper people have typed on. I love ducking into that niche and reading people's anonymous notes. They're all wishes and dreams and words to lovers, and it feels like you're reading someone's diary, except that you're also helping them bring those words to life. I wonder what the store does with the old notes. I hope they burn them in a bonfire so that all those hopes can travel to the stars on a trail of smoke. Those anonymous dreams deserve a happily ever after.

I know I told Alexandre I'm a realist and not a dreamer, and that's true, but I'm not completely oblivious to the poetry of life. That's the too easily wounded part of me I keep hidden from everyone.

BUT TODAY, I don't let myself linger over other people's secrets. Today I'm leading with my head, not my heart. I walk right past the typewriter to the poetry section.

I have a mission. Find that Byron poem.

I run my finger across the spines until I come across a simple black paperback: *George Gordon Lord Byron: Selected Works.* I pull it from the shelves; flecks of dust catch the light. Byron might have been the most famous and flamboyant of the Romantics, but apparently even his books can sit on shelves untouched for ages. Still, at least we know his name.

I search the table of contents and find the title of the poem my mom mentioned right away:

She Walks in Beauty

She walks in beauty, like the night
Of cloudless climes and starry skies;
And all that's best of dark and bright
Meet in her aspect and her eyes;
Thus mellowed to that tender light
Which heaven to gaudy day denies.

One shade the more, one ray the less,
Had half impaired the nameless grace
Which waves in every raven tress,
Or softly lightens o'er her face;
Where thoughts serenely sweet express,
How pure, how dear their dwelling-place.

And on that cheek, and o'er that brow,
So soft, so calm, yet eloquent,
The smiles that win, the tints that glow,
But tell of days in goodness spent,
A mind at peace with all below,
A heart whose love is innocent!

There she is on the page—the woman with the raven tresses. I whisper across time, "Leila, could this be . . . is it you?" I run my fingers over the words on the page like they are something sacrosanct, a relic to be prized and guarded. I read the poem again, slowly this time, my index finger under-lining each word. *Leila, if this is you, if you are Dumas's raven-tressed lady and Byron's, could you be the Giaour's Leila? The one the Pasha killed? But how?* I pause. These questions are too simple. Leila isn't defined by the men whom she inspired. She is the inspiration. Some men tried to shape her into their fictional fantasies; others tried to muffle her voice. But she had her own story.

I feel that melancholy again—what I felt when reading Lei-la's letter to Dumas. When you're living, when you're alive, especially when you're young and feel immortal, you don't always think about what comes after you're gone. I don't mean heaven or hell. But what comes after *on earth*, when you're dead and buried and the memory of you fades from the living.

I flip absentmindedly through the pages of the book. My thoughts fly from Leila to my grand-mère and her old, sick friend who my parents went to see this morning. What hap-pens when a person dies and there's no one left to remember them? I see my grand-mère's apple-cheeked smiling face. She always had a bloom about her, a youthful roundness even as she got older. At least that's how I remember her. Maybe I need to write that down sometime, make her a character in a story. Maybe that's the best thing we can hope for after we're gone— that someone tells our story and makes it true. Or true enough.

My eyes stop on the poem I have to read again: *The Giaour*. God. This poem is twenty pages long. But this is where Leila's story, inexplicably, improbably, first crossed my path. And I didn't even know it. I can't wait to blow Alexandre's mind with this.

I'M A BIT lost in a research daze and with the dizzying

realization that maybe, perhaps, my Leila theory might actually be right. I step out of the dimly lit store, shielding my eyes while they adjust to the brilliant daylight. I blink a few times. A couple of pale-skinned, red-headed kids—brother and sister?—splash each other by a Wallace Fountain, one of the iconic green cast-iron fountains that dot the city landscape. It was a gift from an Englishman in the 1800s so the Parisian poor could have access to free, clean drinking water when the city was riddled with disease. They're the prettiest drinking fountains ever. And there it is again, the history of Paris still alive, still working in the present day.

I jump back a step when a few droplets land in my direction. The parents scold the kids in English—tourists, as I suspected, because in France, redheads are "exotic." I laugh and tell them it's no problem. They seem surprised I speak English, also happy. It never fails when you're in a foreign country: you're probably friendlier to folks from back home than you'd be otherwise. Maybe it's like Alexandre said when I was snippy with the American couple that asked me to take their photo. They're only trying to enjoy their vacation and maybe everyone wants a little feeling of home when they're far away. The kids wave at me as they set off.

I turn right and take a few steps to the café.

As I take in the tourists sitting outside, enjoying their coffee in the sun, I spot a Parisian. *My* Parisian. Alexandre huddled close over a table with a waify blonde girl.

I FEEL LIKE I've been punched in the stomach.

I stare at them. The detritus of afternoon coffee—empty sugar packets and milk froth–stained spoons are spread casually across their tiny, intimate table. They're laughing, and she leans into him and whispers something in his ear. His arm is causally draped across the back of her seat.

No. No. No.

Time decelerates enough to painfully draw out every excruciating detail of this . . . stranger. Perfectly painted red lips. Flawless fair skin. Diaphanous blue silk scarf knotted on the side of her neck—an exact match for her eyes. Audrey Hepburn sunglasses positioned like a headband. As the breeze rustles her hair across her face, she tucks a few silken blonde wisps back behind her elfin ears.

Dammit.

Standing here, frozen, I'm totally aware of how opposite she and I are. Physically, obviously—I mean she's pale enough to get sunburn on a cloudy day in winter. But it's much more than that. I'm the girl in a *Notorious RBG* T-shirt, dark skinny jeans, and All-Stars the color of a robin's egg. She's wearing a gray linen sheath that drapes over her body perfectly. On me it would look like a potato sack; on her it's Parisian chic. I'm too American with a slightly off French accent. She's fluent. I'm a visitor. She's the native. The one with home-court advantage.

A guy bumps into me; the world screeches back to full speed. He also steps on the back of my shoe, giving me a flat tire. He was walking backward, trying to get a shot of the bookstore.

His phone clatters to the cobblestones.

I lurch forward to help and end up dropping my book. All of a sudden, I'm trying not to fall, but too late, because now we're a tangle of legs and bags and apologies in Dutch, then French, then English. The Dutch speak so many languages. Why are Americans so bad at learning other languages?

Crap. Get up, Khayyam. Stop bemoaning our piss-poor

linguistic skills. I jump up and grab my book and bag, hoping Alexandre doesn't notice.

Could it get any worse?

The danger about asking yourself that question, about even letting it flit through your brain, is that the answer is always yes.

Of course he sees me.

Everyone at the café is staring at the embarrassing tourist jumble. My face is aflame. My entire body burns in humiliation. I head in the opposite direction and leave the Dutch tourist with a quick wave of the hand, only then noticing the little scratches and cement burn on my palm and the inside of my left wrist, which has started to throb—

"Khayyam?"

Alexandre's voice.

It *can* get worse. So. Much. Worse. I'm already walking away, ignoring him. *Please don't,* I beg him telepathically. But I hear the scrape of a chair against the pavement. Then footsteps. Dammit. I rush down the sidewalk and hop down onto the narrow street, run past two restaurants, and take a right to dash across the snarl of traffic on Quai de la Tournelle. A throng of scooters passes, and when I see two slow lumbering buses, I know it's my only chance. He's still calling my name as I sprint into traffic and make it across in a flurry of honking horns and two ambling bicyclists who have to swerve not to hit me.

"Désolée!" I call out to them.

Only then, the traffic safely between us, do I turn.

Across the street, Alexandre puts a hand up and motions for me to wait. I shake my head. My body trembles. I'm near sobbing. He steps out as a taxi crosses inches in front of him, the driver honking and swearing out of his window. I take the moment to turn away. Alexandre yells out my name again, then some other words I can't make out because I'm already crossing the bridge to Île de la Cité, lost in the mass of people heading toward Notre-Dame.

The great thing about being surrounded by hundreds of eager tourists and pilgrims heading to one of the world's great holy sites to pay homage, even if from a distance, to her resilience?

No one notices a girl with tears streaming down her face.

Leila

There is no time to protest or even scream. My hands and feet are bound and my mouth gagged. The janissary aga carries me over his shoulder and drops me to the ground at the Gate of Salutation.

I raise my head to see Pasha standing before me, dressed in full battle uniform, his kilij unsheathed in his hand. He pulls me to standing. "You have allowed yourself to be sullied. Thanks to the sharp eye of the Valide, you and your Giaour shall both meet the fate you deserve."

I try to scream, but I choke on the cloth in my mouth. Pasha steps in front of me; I feel his breath on my face and see the daggers in his eyes. He lowers my gag and kisses me hard on the lips. When he steps back, I spit on the stones at his feet.

He laughs. "Spirited until the end. Midnight eyes and raven hair and luscious lips. I showed you favor and mercy despite the rumors of your devotion to the courtyard jinn. I was willing to overlook some of your peculiarities, but now you have shamed me. And now you will know my wrath."

"If any has sullied me, it is you." I spew my words like a

curse. "*May you never leave an heir. May history forget your name. May your suffering follow you from this world into the next.*"

He slaps me across the face. Then he pulls the gag back over my mouth and motions to his janissaries, who step forward with a large burlap bag. I scream into the gag, swallowing my own blood, and flail against the aga, who lifts me up and places me into my burial sack.

"I'll dispose of her myself," Pasha says.

Hands lift me up and place me sideways over the saddle of Pasha's horse. He mounts, and we ride toward the sea.

KHAYYAM

"Khayyam, I'm so sorry. I guess you're ignoring my texts. Not that I'm blaming you. I should've told you the truth about Haydée from the beginning. It's over with her. Absolutely over. Finalement. I just . . . it wasn't a clean break. I wish . . . I'm sorry. Oh, this is Alexandre. In case . . . well"— long sigh—"obviously you know it's me. Sorry."

That is the voice mail I woke up to. *Voice mail*. After finally turning my phone off last night, after an entire afternoon of Alexandre's texting me apologies and explanations. After I poured my heart and spleen into an email to Julie, even though she's not going to get that email anytime soon. After all that, he actually called me and left a scratchy-voiced, sad message. That is desperation. A stitch of guilt sneaks up on me because I understand the pain of relationships that end without really coming to a close. Maybe Alexandre is desperate, but that doesn't mean he can't be sincere, too.

A KNOCK ON the door pulls me out of my guilty-angry brooding funk. "You need to come out and eat something." My mom knocks again. "It's almost eleven. Papa went to Pain de Sucre and brought that fraise crème gâteau you love."

"Fine, Mom. Give me a minute," I say with virtually zero enthusiasm, but the prospect of cake for breakfast . . . er . . . brunch propels me to the door. I twist my hair into a bun at the back of my head and run a pencil through it to keep it in place. The dirtier it is, the easier it is to keep knotted up. I take a quick glance in the full-length mirror propped up on the wall opposite the bed. I'm currently rocking the death-warmed-over look: blue-and-green plaid cotton boxer shorts and the same RBG tee I've been wearing for the last twenty-four hours.

My parents wait for me behind the bar in the small kitchen at one end of the large common space of our apartment.

I trudge over to a stool and slide on to it and face them. An espresso and the promised cake are waiting for me. "Merci, Papa," I say with a sheepish smile.

"De rien, chérie. You know it's not winter, no need to hibernate." My dad winks at me.

I raise the small pale-green espresso cup to him like I'm making a toast, then take a little swig, licking the crema off my upper lip. It's strong and smells chocolaty, but all I taste is the bitter. There's this verse by Omar Khayyam:

> *Whether the cup with sweet or bitter run*
> *The wine of life keeps oozing drop by drop*
> *The leaves of life keep falling one by one.*

Basically, c'est la vie. Sometimes life sucks. Get over it, because one day you'll be dead. How cheery! It's like I have my own personal scribe chastising me from the beyond.

If I have to have the bitter, might as well take the sweet,

too. I pick up the fork and devour the fresh strawberry slices, cream, and vanilla biscuit-y thing on the bottom of this pastry. Pain de Sucre is a matchbox of a pastry shop, but obviously ancient sorcerers run the kitchen. There is no other explanation for the alchemy occurring in my mouth right now. If I didn't know better, I'd say the pastry chef laced this cake with some kind of love potion, because it's so good I want to marry it. And with my luck, that is exactly how a love potion would work for me. At least it wouldn't cheat on me. Khayyam + Pastries: a love story in four bites.

I glance away from my pastry to notice my parents trading worried looks. "Hello. I see you. I'm literally in front of you. I'm fine. Just tired."

"What do you think about getting out of town for a bit?" my mom asks. "Do you remember that Papa and I are going to Brittany this afternoon for a couple days?" She points to their overnight bags by the front of the door. "A little trip to the sea would do you good. My ummi would always say the salt air cures whatever ails you. And sometimes turmeric. What do you say, beta?"

I scrunch up my nose and gently shake my head. It's basically a romantic getaway—for *them*. Brittany is code for my parents' favorite thalassotherapy hotel and spa where they emerge rejuvenated and feeling twenty years younger. But that would put me solidly into the pre-embryo stage, so I'm gonna pass on this rollicking, old-timey French fun and sulk with pastries in Paris and avoid Alexandre's entire arrondissement, which fortunately leaves me nineteen others to mope around in.

"Thanks," I say, trying to sound like I have even an iota of interest. "But I need to do some reading—trying to figure out if Dumas's raven-haired lady is the same woman in the Byron poem you guys mentioned. If I can link it to the Delacroix, maybe I can piece something together for another attempt at the prize. You know, find the lost story of this woman that might have been hiding in plain sight all along, like you said, Mom."

Seconds tick by, then more concerned looks pass between my parents. My mom rubs the back of her neck and, in an unusual move, presses me. "Beta, are you really okay?"

She thinks something is wrong. She always knows. When I was little, I used to call that sixth sense "mommy magic." I found it comforting back then. If I'm willing to admit it to myself, maybe I need that comfort now, too. But that parental balm feels harder to accept—like if I accept it, if I *need* it, I'm conceding some kind of personal failure, another one. I desperately want a win, even if it's insignificant.

"I would be more okay if you guys stopped grilling me. I'm fine. I promise. Besides you two can get some alone time, and without me, you'll be the youngest people at the spa!"

"Yes, chérie," my dad says. "The upside to child abandonment is a brief reclamation of our youth. Fantastique."

"Take it where you can get it, Papa." I chuckle and reach across the bar to squeeze his hand. "Anyway, I have to sulk around the city being contemplative, or it would be a total waste of a vacation in Paris."

My parents both laugh. My dad shakes his head, steps around the bar, and kisses me on the cheek, then nods at my mom before stepping into their bedroom.

My mom waits until he closes the door, then says, "Beta, you know you can talk to me about anything. Is that kerfuffle with Zaid still upsetting you?" My mom is that person who can use "kerfuffle" without irony, yet sounds charming and not like an old biddy. I love that about her.

"It's nothing," I reply. "I dunno, teen angst or something?" I suck in a deep breath, look at her reassuring smile, and decide to tell her the truth—part of it, at least. "Or . . . maybe it's Zaid . . . *and* . . . Alexandre. I like both of them, but they're problematic faves. Both of them have done stupid stuff, and I'm trying to figure out if I should give one or both of them a second chance. How do I choose between them when neither is perfect?" I shrug, then open the lid of the pastry box to grab another gâteau. This is definitely a two-cake conversation.

My mom takes a deep breath. "First, depending on the severity of what they've done wrong and how you feel about it and if you've been hurt, neither necessarily deserves a second chance. You should never feel belittled or taken for granted, and you should never, *ever* feel like you might be in even the remotest danger or that you're being forced to do something you don't want to do. Not even a whiff."

"Oh God. I know. It's not like that. Neither of them has made me feel unsafe. At all. But they've both kind of had their jerk moments. Dishonest moments."

I don't detail any of my own skirting of the truth, how maybe I'm guilty of the same thing I'm mad at Zaid and Alexandre for. I know my mom would be disappointed in me. And man, does her disappointment cut to the bone.

"Well, then, it's about how you feel," Mom says. "And what you're willing to forgive. None of us are perfect. We can hurt those closest to us. But love should make you feel good. Love should feel like home. A place built on trust and honesty. Not every moment is going to be perfect. But during the hardest times, you want that relationship to be your shelter from the storm."

"I don't know if either of them makes me feel that way. Or if they can. Or if anyone can or will." I gaze into my mom's kind eyes and blink back a tear. "It always seems easy and natural with you and Papa."

"Oh, jaan, if that's what you want, I hope you find it. But trust me; your papa and I, we work at it. Love requires work. But it's good work. Rilke called it *the work for which all other work is but preparation.*"

I manage a wan smile. "Honestly, I'm not sure if either of them inspire that kind of work. And I'm definitely not sure if I'm in love with either of them. Like, yes. But love?"

My mom smiles with obvious relief. "Maybe you have your answer, then. Maybe you don't have to worry too much about love or finding the right one. You're young; enjoy the journey. Love yourself. Forge the path you want. You know, your namesake had two rules for living: better to starve than to eat whatever; better to be alone than to love whomever."

"And that is why I avoid blue cheese."

My mom laughs. "Avoid moldy rot is an excellent metaphor."

"Who's being metaphorical?"

My mom leans over and kisses me on the cheek. "Perhaps what you seek is seeking you."

"Khayyam didn't write that, did he?"

"It's Rumi."

Persian Sufi poets are getting a lot of play in this morning's life talk.

My mom bites her lip, then continues, "Listen, I wasn't going to say anything because Zaid asked me not to . . ."

I straighten up in my seat. What. The. Hell. "Zaid has been talking to *you*? Why? What did he say and why didn't you tell me before?"

My mom puts her hand on my arm. "I'm sorry, beta. He said he wanted to send you a surprise. I thought it would be okay. It should be here tomorrow or the next day, I think."

"So I need to be here anyway to get it." My brain floods with questions. Zaid has never been the big romantic gesture type, but he actually took the time to reach out to my mom? To plan something? I'm keeping my expectations low, but it doesn't stop me from smiling because maybe something actually has changed. "Do you know what it is?" I ask, almost breathless.

"No. But he didn't indicate it was anything perishable like flowers."

"Ha. Right. Flowers? Julie had to remind him to get me a corsage for prom, so, no, probably not flowers. Could be garbage cookies from Medici."

That would be perfect. Like those T-shirts we exchanged? This would be our type of romantic gesture. He knows of my deep affection for garbage cookies, because they are filled with every good thing—chocolate chips, M&Ms, nuts, butter, sugar, oatmeal. Once, we found a week-old one in a paper bag in Zaid's backpack. We split it—he even let me have the bigger half. And it was still delicious, because unlike blue cheese, garbage cookies never get moldy and start to stink. Their shelf life is eternity.

"Well, if garbage cookies put a smile on your face like that, I hope that's what he's sending," my mom says softly. "Don't tell Papa, though. I don't think he'll approve of having pastries sent *to* Paris *from* Chicago."

"They're not pastries. They're cookies. They can coexist."

My mom seems satisfied with my smiles.

Garbage cookies are home and comfort and laughter.

If that's what he sends, Zaid won't be off my shit list, not exactly, but he'll definitely move down a notch. Though, I guess, Alexandre already took over the number one spot. With a bullet.

Still, I get what my mom says about love and work and forgiveness. I get that it's not always perfect. And I understand what she means about me making my own choices for *myself*. That's where my head needs to be right now.

If only my heart weren't going rogue.

Leila

❦

The wind roars in my ears as it rushes past us.

Pasha speaks as we gallop. We both know his are the last words I will ever hear. "In a way, I am sorry it had to end like this. You have brought me much satisfaction. But you should never have been disloyal. Valide always despised your strong-willed temperament, yet that never bothered me. It made you less of a bore than the others. But to give yourself, willingly, to the Giaour? You were never worthy of being haseki. It turns out you are a common concubine after all."

The horse comes to an abrupt stop, nearly throwing me to the ground. I smell the salt air and hear the siren call of the ocean's deepest waves. I know what awaits me. I squeeze my eyes shut and say a silent prayer: Lighten my journey, O God. Make this distance an easy one. In you, I seek refuge.

Pasha dismounts and throws me over his shoulder.

He speaks to a fisherman whose reverence makes clear he knows that it is Pasha who commands him and that he must obey. He rows us out in his little craft. Pasha keeps me on his shoulder, even as the fisherman draws us out into the inky black sea and small waves rock the boat. The fisherman stops. I hear Pasha mutter words under his breath, a prayer for mercy.

I do not know for whom he prays.

KHAYYAM

After bidding my parents bon voyage, I didn't want to stay in the apartment alone. Instead, I'm spending the afternoon getting jostled by tourists in the courtyard of the Palais Royal, weaving around the Colonnes de Buren. It's unlikely that I'll run into Alexandre here. I kind of hope I do, though. Part of me wants to yell at him for the sucker-punch shock of seeing him with his ex, and part of me wants to come clean about Zaid because obviously I get it. Also, I still need to get all the information his family has about Leila. Maybe I can finally focus only on finding her. It shouldn't be such a challenge to do the right thing for myself, but with my heart and mind in constant battle, there's no clear winner.

Alexandre appeared, a potential real-life deus ex machina—the key to my revenge on Celenia Mondego and to turning around my failure. Then he became a gorgeous distraction from Zaid. An Instagram jealousy magnet. And then more. But what, exactly?

My phone buzzes. It's Alexandre again: Mes yeux ne brillent que pour toi. My eyes only shine for you. Ugh. The beauty of the French language makes it hard to stay mad sometimes. I get a messy breakup, but seeing him with her, right there in front of my eyes . . . flowery words can't erase that image or take the hurt away. I slip my phone back in my pocket without responding.

For now, my best option is to eat my weight in macarons, but I can't even do that, because my brain is elsewhere, and I've forgotten my wallet at home.

BY THE TIME I get back to our building, I'm desperate for macarons. But somehow, as I trudge up the winding stairs, my resolve not to text Alexandre softens, like I've stomped out my anger and want to give him a second chance. Don't we all deserve one? After all, I haven't been totally honest, either. As far as he knows, my life in Chicago begins and ends with a failed essay, and if I'm mad at him for what he hid, I guess I need to tell him the truth, or else I'm a hypocrite. As I approach our landing, I reach into my bag to grab my phone—I stop short. I let out a little gasp.

What the—

Zaid is sitting cross-legged in front of our door. He's so engrossed in his phone he doesn't even notice me. His army-green backpack leans against the wall. Those caramel bangs conceal his face as he looks down at his screen. I panic, half-thinking I should run back down the stairs before he sees me—but too late. He glances up, and a huge smile takes over his face. He yanks out his earbuds and stands, holding out a crumpled, oil-spotted brown paper bag.

He smirks. "I got Ice Capades." Then he shifts his weight awkwardly from one foot to the other and adds, "Actually, they're garbage cookies. Your favorite, right?"

I freeze. Glued in place. Staring at him staring at me. Each of us in anticipation that one of us will say something else. All my words are lost. I take the last couple steps so we're both on the landing, face-to-face. I remind myself to breathe. In and out. He lowers the bag of cookies to his side and takes a step forward, closing the distance between us. He kisses me on the cheek. I don't move. I can't move.

For a second it feels like he might lean in to kiss me on the lips. I have to admit, I almost lean in, too. It feels natural to kiss him, like it's muscle memory. An echo of home. But I don't let myself fall into that old habit.

Zaid steps back, and we smile sheepishly at each other, like seventh graders at a dance when a slow song comes on, and they're not sure if the person they like likes them back.

I shove my phone in my bag and fish out my keys. "How . . . how did you get here?" I sputter, breaking the silence.

He grins. "On a plane."

"*Here*, on my doorstep." I'm a little terse because I'm not in the mood for dad jokes. "How did you get in?"

"I buzzed the building concierge. I told her I brought you les cookies d'amour from America. I think she found me charming."

I have to laugh at that. "Madame de Villefort. She's ancient and probably thought you were an actual delivery guy."

I ignore that Zaid has now used the word *love* for the second time since I've been in Paris—a word that never crossed his lips in Chicago, at least in regard to me.

"Can I come in? Or should we do this whole thing out here?"

I'm not sure what *thing* he's talking about exactly, but I unlock the door and step into the apartment, sweeping an arm toward the main room. "Voilà."

Zaid drops his bag in our small foyer, steps into the sunlit living room, takes a look around, and then collapses onto the couch. "It's nice; I like it." He's already totally at ease. Odd that I don't feel the same way right now, even though this is *my* actual French home.

I step into the kitchen to grab us some water. I fill two glasses, letting my mind drift to Alexandre. I was going to text him, tell him my whole truth. And then part of that truth appeared on my doorstep. What the hell do I do now?

I walk out of the kitchen. Zaid makes room for me on the couch. I hand him his glass and take a seat at the other end with mine. "Besides charming my concierge, how did you get to Paris? And aren't you leaving for Reed in a couple weeks?"

"My grandparents paid for it. They hadn't gotten me a gift for graduation yet, so I asked for this."

Must be nice. I honestly can't imagine asking anyone to pay for a little jaunt to Paris. Zaid clearly gets the message from my raised eyebrows and quickly adds, "I think they got it with miles . . ."

"Well, then, you're clearly not their little prince if they only bought you a ticket with *miles*." I put down my glass and gently punch Zaid in the arm.

"You're the only one that calls me out on my privilege," he says as he takes my hand. "I like it. Sometimes I need it."

Zaid knows how his privilege is different than mine. I'm a kid of academics who inherited an apartment in Paris that they never could have afforded. But he has über privilege. Finance money privilege. The kind of money that may not be able to pay for a brand-new building at the school, but definitely a classroom or wing. To be fair, Zaid's parents are pretty good about not being showy, and their politics lean left—far left—and they donate to all the right causes. I mean, we live in Hyde Park—Obama's old neighborhood. (The dry cleaner he used to frequent still proudly displays a sign declaring: DRY CLEANING HOME OF THE 44TH PRESIDENT.) And if you're an ostentatious, conservative prick, people call you out on it. Zaid's family, they're gauche caviar, as my dad says. In the American vernacular, limousine liberals.

At first I pull my hand away. But his laughter and warm smiles tug at my heart, so I let him pull me closer. This banter, this space between us, it's easy and comforting. It's home. He puts an arm around my shoulders and draws me closer, closing the last inches between us. I lean into him.

Zaid kisses me on top of my head. "I'm sorry. I'm an idiot."

"I know," I say.

Leila

It's not what they say it's like. Death. There is no soft, beckoning light. Or feeling of peace. There is nothing but me screaming and every fiber of my body burning and ripping apart and a whooshing in my ears that is loud. So loud.

And the water, everywhere, all at once. It does not rise up slowly from my feet and ankles, but swallows me whole as I sink below the surface. I force my eyes open so I can meet Death with courage, but in front of me is only water and this burlap shroud that will hold my body until I'm devoured by sea creatures, until my bones are worn smooth and eventually become grains of sand that wash to the shore. In the end, I'm not brave. I'm nothing but writhing and failed attempts to wiggle out of the ropes that bind my hands and feet. You cannot fly with stones resting on your wings.

I pray, not for help, but forgiveness. Will my spirit ascend to jannah? Will Allah forgive me my trespasses? God knows there have been many.

My throat closes, and my organs press outward against my

body. *Every part of me struggles to escape these earthly bindings. This sack, these ropes, these waves, this body.*

This fate.

My mind—is it my mind?—shrieks, panics.

This cannot be my last moment.

In this life where I controlled nothing, where cruel circumstance fixed my fate, I will, at the last, take this moment for myself alone. I close my eyes and see my beloved's face, feel his cheek against mine. Then a single image rises like a benediction. A rose against my lips. His rose. A damask rose-scented night that descends into darkness.

KHAYYAM

My sense of ease with Zaid fades, too quickly overtaken by nerves, so I rush us outside. I'm not worried that I'll *do* something I shouldn't but rather that I'll *say* something I'll regret. I have so many questions, but I don't think I'm ready for the answers. Even now with everything that's happened, I know Zaid can talk his way out of anything, and I'm too easily swayed by his charm and my own sense of nostalgia and longing for any comfort that feels like home.

I steer clear of the Latin Quarter, the entire Left Bank, in fact. That's Alexandre's side of the city. I might have resolved to text him, see him even, but not like this. I steer Zaid toward the Right Bank. And for now, I'm going to ignore that I live on an island in the river between the two halves of the city. My brain will explode from the symbolism if I think about it too much.

Fresh air and sunshine are the best cures for Zaid's jet lag and for my fear of too much truth before I'm ready. For now, I show him my favorite places, like Rue Montorgueil— a narrow and cobblestoned street bursting with life at all hours. Shops and cafés and their customers spill out onto the sidewalk, pushing pedestrians to walk on the road, making it nearly impassable by car and all the more pleasant. We quickly fall into step with old routines—comfortable side by side without unnecessary words. Maybe outside wasn't an escape from awkward conversations about us. Because wherever we go, there we are.

Zaid grabs my hand and pulls me toward a tiny floral shop, a riot of colorful blooms bursting out its doorway and into buckets on the sidewalk. He chooses a small bouquet of deep red flowers that look almost like roses. He hands the florist ten euro. She smiles and tucks the money into her pocketed green apron. "Renoncules," she says, pointing to the flowers.

Zaid looks up at me through his long bangs, flipping them to the side with one hand and handing me the ranunculus with the other. His deep brown eyes look tired, but still shine through the jet lag. I sink my nose into the flowers. They don't have a particularly sweet scent, but they are quite stunning, and I'm quite stunned. I need a moment to recover from this swoon-worthy moment. This is basically epic-level romance for Zaid—the boy who had to be reminded to get me flowers for prom and then forgot them in his car.

I turn back toward the street and the crowd of people, but Zaid draws me toward him, wrapping an arm around my waist. I forget the flowers and the people around us. At first, my mind hesitates, but my body pulls me into a kiss. This kiss tastes like home—and I surrender to the nostalgia, the memory of what Zaid and I once were to each other. I'm drawn to him like a moth to the flame in one of my mom's beloved Urdu ghazals.

A LOUD, LONG whistle yanks me away from Zaid.

I turn my head and catch a glimpse of a scruffy guy with

messy dirty-blond hair who slows down his scooter to yell, "Elle est bonne, ta meuf!" Zaid laughs and gives the guy a thumbs-up as he roars away. I smack down his arm.

"Ow!" Zaid winces. "What did you do that for? That guy said you were pretty, right?"

"Um, no. He said, 'Your girlfriend is good.' But *that* good means . . . well, it has implications."

Zaid looks down at the cobblestones, half-embarrassed, half-smirk.

"Don't be so pleased with yourself," I say.

"What? He's basically saying I have good taste. Which, obviously, I do."

"Oh my God, Zaid. Have you ever considered that maybe everything isn't actually about you?" As the words tumble out of my mouth, I realize this is something I've known all along. It's so simple, so obvious, but maybe because I'm in a different country, because of the distance between us, I finally have some perspective.

It's Zaid's world, and he wants the rest of us to live in it. The truth is, he's never even lied about that—never pretended to be someone he's not. He is who he is. He's not going to change. More importantly, he doesn't want to. And that kiss we shared? The one that took me back to that moment under the rumble of the Brown Line 'L'? The feeling of home in his arms . . . well, maybe we're both guilty of operating under the soft, filtered focus of nostalgia. But I can't let sentimentality cloud my judgment. I'm not going to let myself be a paragraph buried in Zaid's story—even if it is epic.

I walk absentmindedly down the street. Zaid rushes to catch up and takes me by the elbow. "Hey, what happened? Was it that guy? I'm sor—"

"I'm fine. My mind wandered for a minute," I say.

"I've heard my kisses can have that effect," Zaid says, a twinkle in his eye.

"Please. Get over yourself." I shake my head. This is Zaid. This is the goofy, solipsistic guy I fell for, eyes wide open. "You do know it's possible for the world to revolve around someone other than you?" I nudge him with my elbow. "I was actually thinking about the Delacroix. I discovered a new—"

"You mean the painting from your Art Institute essay? Is that still bothering you? Here we are on this beautiful day in Paris, together, and you're obsessing on a little academic mess-up? It's not like it was for a grade."

I squeeze the stems of the flowers in my hand. "There was nothing *little* about it. Okay?" I can feel my anger rising, and I take a breath before I explode. "You of all people should know how important that contest was to me. How hard I worked. And I'm not wallowing in my failure, by the way. I'm fixing my own problems. I've discovered a new angle. It's about this mysterious woman who might be a connection between Dumas and Delacroix. And I probably should've—"

Zaid cuts me off. "Shoulda, coulda, woulda. I get it, Khayyam. You know I'm still pissed for missing out on being valedictorian. But I try not to live my life with regrets. Maybe you should do the same. Leave the past in the past. Don't dwell on it. Live for the now. Carpe diem, baby." He gives me a warm smile and puts his arms around my shoulders, like I'm the perfect prop for the Zaid show.

I'm too stunned to speak. Zaid has a lot of skills. Recognizing irony isn't one of them. We continue walking down the street, a beautiful bouquet in my hand, people passing us by probably thinking we're what we look like, a young couple on a romantic stroll. But the face of things isn't always what they are. Because right now, Zaid and I might be walking with hands clasped, but there's a chasm a universe wide between us, and it's filled with my rage. For myself. For Leila. For every woman who's been told to stop acting crazy, to calm down. For every woman who had to step back from center stage because she was told the spotlight wasn't for her.

"You should check into your hotel," I say. "Please don't tell me your grandparents got you a room at Le Meurice." We haven't talked about his sleeping arrangements, but even if my parents are out of town, he knows he could never stay at our place. I'd never offer anyway, especially not now.

A shadow of disappointment passes over Zaid's eyes before he answers.

"That's cool. I can grab a nap before we get dinner. And for your information, I'm not staying at a fancy five-star hotel. I wanted to be close to you, so I got a room at a little hotel in the Marais—the Beauchamp. It's a few blocks over that bridge . . . Pont Marie, I think." He tucks his hands into his pockets. "I left my bag at your place, though."

WE HEAD HOME. My pace is brisk. I don't speak. I don't look at him. The air between us is heavy with confusion and all the words we're not saying. I've been gripping the flowers so tightly, the tissue paper wrapped around the stems is crinkled and damp with sweat.

After an excruciating silence, Zaid finally speaks, trying to fill the awkwardness with conversation, telling me what he wants to see and do in Paris in the next few days. He's acting like the last hour never happened. Like we've rewound time, like it's before our pseudo-goodbye and before him making cameos all over Instagram and before me trying to make him jealous with pictures of Alexandre. Before Alexandre, period.

We're halfway across Pont Marie when I stop in the middle

of the sidewalk. He smiles and tries to touch my cheek, but I turn my head away. "Aren't you going to say anything about the pictures?"

"What pictures?" Confusion passes over his face.

He can't be this oblivious, can he? "The pictures on Instagram of you with every other girl at Lab sitting on your lap."

Zaid's mouth hangs open for a second. "Are you serious? That was nothing. I mean, literally, nothing. Lucien had a party, and Rekha and I were hamming it up for stupid selfies."

"She wasn't the only one."

"C'mon, babe. I don't want to fight," he says and tries to take my free hand. I pull it away and ball it into a fist at my side. I can feel my temperature rise like I'm a cartoon thermometer and the red mercury is about to burst out of the glass.

I turn away and start running home. God, I'm such an idiot. Zaid runs after me, calling my name. He catches up with me across the street.

"Khayyam, listen, I'm sorry. Okay? I didn't know it would bother you. I mean, we weren't . . . together anymore. And anyway, you were posting pictures with the gangly French guy."

I grit my teeth and start walking away, even angrier than before. I know that what Zaid said earlier is true. Maybe I should leave the past in the past and live in the now. I'm always reacting and never leading. It's like all my choices have been taken away. In perpetuity.

Zaid jogs to catch up with me. "Hang on. I have to get my backpack."

Begrudgingly I pause, and we continue the short walk to my apartment. My heart thuds in my ears, and I slap my soles against the pavement like a four-year-old having a tantrum. My thoughts are a mess of crossed lines and wrong connections and regrets—a loading wheel that keeps spinning. I'm not a tech genius, but even I know when you need to pull the plug and reboot.

I let Zaid into my apartment and step into the kitchen to put the flowers in a tall glass of water. I have no desire to search for a proper vase right now. I plop down on the sofa. Zaid's standing in our little foyer, his backpack slung over his shoulder.

He turns toward me, but his gaze is on the floor. "Khayyam, look, I'm not sure what happened. I thought we were having a good time. I thought you were happy to see me."

"Were you not listening?" I yell, then lower my voice, thinking about the neighbors. "I am glad to see you. That doesn't mean I wasn't also hurt. Those pictures on Instagram with Rekha . . . you make it all seem like a little innocent flirting. But you forget that I know you. It had to have been more."

He rubs the back of his neck and sighs. "Fine. Okay. Yes. It was more than flirty pictures on Instagram, but you got on a plane to Paris, and I'm heading to Reed in a couple weeks. It felt like a goodbye, you know? Without all the unnecessary drama."

I thought an admission from him would be like a hammer to my heart. It's not. It's more like lemon juice on a paper cut. It smarts, and I can feel the tiny sting behind my eyes. But I don't cry. This moment is not fall-on-the-fainting-couch, weep-my-eyes-out, nineteenth-century-novel pain. It's more melancholy . . . regret, maybe. And anger. I take a breath. Then another. I soften the sharp edge in my voice. "Why did you come here?"

"I wanted to see you and—"

"And all those pictures of me and Alexandre made you jealous."

"That's his name? Alexandre?" He slips the bag off his shoulder and joins me on the couch.

I nod.

"All this time you've been pissed about Rekha sitting in my lap, but you've been . . . what . . . making out with a French dude all over Paris?"

"No. That's not how it was. I didn't even meet Alexandre until after you'd ignored all my texts and were getting handsy with half of Hyde Park."

"That's not true or fair. Besides, you used that guy as some kind of revenge or something? That's warped."

Zaid calling out my hypocrisy in this situation infuriates me, and it's hard to parse out who I'm most angry at—him or me.

"No . . . I . . . uh . . . I thought maybe the pictures would get your attention. And obviously, it worked because you flew to a different continent to . . . I don't know . . . assuage your guilt!" I lower my voice almost to a whisper. "And you wore the CTA tee in that shot with Rekha."

Zaid frowns down at the Brown Line 'L' T-shirt he's also wearing right now, pulling at it between pinched fingers. Then raises his eyes and meets mine. "What does this stupid shirt have to do with it?"

"I got you that stupid shirt for our one-month anniversary. Because of our first date? *While You Were Sleeping*, remember? Kissing under the Brown Line 'L'? Or did you bury that memory and leave it in the past, too?"

Zaid's shoulders slump, and he runs his fingers through his hair. "Khayyam, I didn't realize . . . I'm sorry." He takes my limp hand in his. "You know I'm not good at remembering stuff like that. I would never hurt you on purpose. Don't you get it?"

"Get what?" I stare at him. This beautiful boy I was pining over who somehow still doesn't understand what is important to me, who doesn't understand that this moment isn't a vacuum—that the past isn't something you can simply ignore.

"You're important to me. That's why I flew over here. It's the big gesture. Those pictures of you and the French guy *did* make me jealous. Like, I was going out of my mind thinking of you kissing him. And it made me realize that I didn't want to lose you. Those other girls don't challenge me like you do. We belong together."

My body relaxes for a moment. I look into Zaid's eyes. I understand that this is a big gesture for *him*. But the big gestures aren't important if the little ones don't exist. He flew across an ocean to proclaim that he finds me challenging? It's not finally declaring, *I love you*. It's not the *what's important to you is important to me* assurance. It's still about him. And I finally see the obvious—this is all he can give.

Zaid tucks a stray hair behind my ear and looks into my eyes. My anger has mostly melted into disappointment. I open my mouth to say something, but a knock on the door interrupts me. As I get up to answer it, I see Zaid smile—I think it's more at himself than for me. Of course it is. I shake my head and open the door.

Alexandre is standing in the hall, a giant bouquet of purple and pink flowers in front of him.

Leila

❧❧❧

Si'la says that humans cry salt tears because we emerged from the sea searching for a new world to conquer, but are bound to carry our first home with us forever. A blessing. A curse. A reminder of what we lost.

And it is to the ocean's waves I am destined to return.

Is it possible to cry when you are drowning? Can you distinguish between the salt of your tears and the salt of the sea? Does the ocean weep with you?

God, grant me safe journey from this darkness.

The sea swallows my prayer as water fills my mouth.

KHAYYAM

Since I was a kid, people have given me quotes from Omar Khayyam as gifts—embossed on journals or lovely framed prints. There's one postcard my mom sent me when she was away at some conference that I keep tacked to the bulletin board above my desk: *Be Happy for This Moment; This Moment Is Your Life*. My mind flashes to that saying as I stare at Alexandre and the beautiful bouquet in his hands, because if this moment is my life, my life is a rotten-blue-cheese-level-stinky mess.

"Khayyam, I'm really sorry. I hope you—" Alexandre's gaze darts past me into the living room; he purses his lips when he sees Zaid.

Oh God. This is happening. And there's nothing I can do to stop it.

I stumble over myself while stepping out of the way to let Alexandre in. Zaid rises from the couch.

"Alexandre," I say, "um, this is, um, Zaid. A . . . friend from Chicago."

They give each other the guy-sizing-up-the-other-guy head nod. Alexandre absentmindedly hands me the flowers; I drop them on the kitchen bar as I watch him step fully into the living room. He's taller than Zaid, but Zaid is bulkier. And I can feel them trying to figure out this situation. Though I guess it's self-evident.

Zaid finally walks forward and extends a hand. "Boyfriend. I'm her boyfriend from Chicago."

My jaw drops. Not only has he never called himself that; he's never even said he loved me, and now suddenly he's acting possessive?

Alexandre turns to look at me. "Khayyam," he begins, then shakes his head. He doesn't even need to say anything else. I can imagine what he's thinking: *You have a boyfriend? You're angry because you saw me with an ex, but you've had a boyfriend this whole time?*

"Alexandre. Désolée." My brain whirs, but the right words are slow to come.

"What are you apologizing to this guy for, babe?" Zaid asks. This time his use of the diminutive enrages me.

"So *now* you're my boyfriend? *Now?* According to you we already had our goodbye in Chicago. We went our separate ways, remember?"

Now Zaid is the one with his jaw on the floor. "I thought—"

Zaid is talking, but I can't take my eyes off Alexandre, because even if he's guilty of being clueless and a jerk, he's the only one who was totally in the dark in this situation. I see a shadow of hurt pass over his face.

Zaid notices me looking at Alexandre. "Un-friggin'-believable. I flew all the way over here . . . for you . . . to tell you . . ." There's a scratch in Zaid's voice as he speaks. It's not merely anger; it's resignation.

"To tell me what?" I ask. "You can't even say it. You came here because you were jealous of something happening between me and Alexandre—"

My eyes keep flitting from Alexandre, who stares off in the distance, to Zaid, who has this look on his face like a small animal that's half in pain and half raging. All my synapses are on rapid fire, and I can almost feel my brain melting a little. I breathe. I think about homework. When I have a ton of homework, I usually start with my least favorite thing. The thing I know will be the worst so I can get it out of the way.

My gaze falls on Zaid.

"You don't want to be with me, Zaid," I say, the softness in my voice catching me by surprise. "You want me now because you can't have me. You want the chase and not the quarry."

"What the hell does that even mean?" Zaid shoots lasers at me with his eyes. "You know what? Save it. Seriously. Screw this, I'm out of here. I can't believe you, Khayyam." He's usually a long-fuse, big-bang kind of person, and while I'm stuck in some kind of suspended animation in this moment, it seems like his fuse has burned down and a time bomb is about to explode in my tiny apartment.

Before I can de-stupefy myself and respond, Alexandre jumps in. "Don't talk to her that way." His voice is measured, but seething.

"Don't tell me how to talk to her. I've known her for years. I'm part of her story. You're a footnote," Zaid spits.

"Shut up, both of you. Stop talking about me like I'm not here and can't speak up for myself. And Zaid, what the hell? You don't get to act all noble when you've been running around making out with half of Chicago. It's out of sight, out of mind until someone else's interest in me makes me the shiny new object again that gets your attention."

Zaid clenches his jaw and strides toward the door—shoving past Alexandre with an unnecessarily hard body check. Alexandre staggers, catches himself, and shoves Zaid in the back. Zaid stumbles, rights himself, grabs his backpack, then spins around like he's about to take a swing at Alexandre.

"Stop it!" I yell, stepping between them.

Zaid curbs the arc of his backpack, but not before it smacks into the small side table in the foyer, sending a blue-and-white porcelain teapot to the floor, where it shatters.

"That was my grandmother's, asshole! Get out!" I yell at Zaid, who shuffles backward, twisting his hands around the strap of his backpack, a stunned expression on his face.

I sink to the floor and start crying—maybe more than a broken teapot warrants. Surveying the broken shards of everything. There are so many pieces. Too many. I force myself to take a few deep breaths, trying to slow my racing heart, calm my mind. I blink away my tears and look into Zaid's wide eyes, my voice shaky but deliberate. "Maybe sometimes history *is* more important to me than the now. Maybe that's my problem. But you were right about one thing—some things do need to be left in the past. And one of those things is us."

Zaid opens his mouth, then clamps it shut and stomps out, slamming the door behind him.

"IS IT TRUE, what he said? You were using me to make him jealous?" Alexandre asks.

The apartment still echoes with Zaid's departure as I study the mess. I look up at Alexandre. I stand up, stepping carefully over the broken pieces of my grand-mère's teapot. I walk into the kitchen to get a dustpan and broom, but I stop and lean against the bar to steady myself. My head hurts, and my eyes burn. I take a deep breath and turn to face Alexandre. He's made his way to the sofa. But I hover in the kitchen, keeping a little distance.

"Is it true? What you did? Deceiving me about still being

involved with . . . with—" Maybe it's childish to mimic his words back to him, but I don't care.

"With Haydée." Alexandre clears his throat and nods.

"Yeah, her. So what right do you have to be mad at me?" I ask, crossing my arms in front of me.

"I never faked my feelings for you. I didn't use you to hurt someone else," he responds. His words slam into my chest.

"No. You hurt me directly, all by yourself." My voice cracks as I speak.

Alexandre's shoulders sag. "I always liked you, Khayyam, from the moment we met. I ended things with Haydée before— was trying to end them, anyway. It's complicated. At least I wasn't posting pictures of us in the garden and my library and kissing you on the cheek to make her jealous, I—"

I'm about to apologize, but I pause. "Wait. How do you know what I've been posting? Are you stalking me on Instagram? I made my account private *before* my family came to Paris. Before you and I even met. I haven't approved any new followers since. So how?"

Alexandre stands up. Then sits back down. "I-I followed you before then."

"What the hell? No way. No. Not possible. I would've recognized someone named Alexandre Dumas on my follower list."

"My handle is Georges Munier."

"Who the hell is Georges Munier?"

"That story I mentioned, that Dumas wrote before Monte Cristo? Georges is the main character—not a slave but a descendant of slaves. Not completely white, but absolutely passing as white."

I step toward him. This is too much. I can't process it. My head throbs. I clench my fists. "That is friggin' twisted, Alexandre. Oh my God." My breathing is shallow, my pulse pounding in my ears. I feel light-headed. I try to slow my breathing, suck in some oxygen, so I can speak. "You knew I was going to the Petit Palais. I posted that. Did you—what the—you have been stalking me." I cross my arms in front of my chest.

"No. I haven't. I'm not a stalker. I would never . . ." Alexandre stands up and takes a step toward me, but I put my hands up and he stops. "Merde," he says, scratching his head. "I'm sorry. It was my uncle. He—"

"What does your uncle have to do with this?" I'm half rage and half utter exhaustion.

"I know how this looks, but it's not like that. I would never hurt you. My uncle and I, well, we're the only ones left who seem to care about Dumas's legacy. And well, Uncle Gérard has all these web alerts set for any news on Dumas, and you use the #AlexandreDumas hashtag all the time. There was an article about the Art Institute Young Scholar Prize that mentioned your essay and how you tried to link Dumas and Delacroix. He suggested I follow you and . . ."

I cannot believe this is actually real life. My life. There was one tiny article in a stupid online art blog that I didn't think anyone read. My worthless, catastrophic essay is biting me in the ass again.

I'm still too stunned to speak. My brain cannot process all of this at once.

Alexandre continues. "When I saw you were coming to Paris, my uncle suggested that I try to find a way to meet you, because . . . because we think that you were onto something. You were the one who made us believe there could be a missing Delacroix that belonged to our family. That rumor you uncovered about the possibility—that gave us hope."

"Cherchez la femme, trouvez le trésor," I whisper. "Oh my God. You planned this whole thing so I could help you find the treasure? You are a stalker. And a liar." Tears splash down my cheeks. "You wanted to use me for . . . for what? My research?"

"Khayyam, please. I'm sorry. I saw you post about going to the Petit Palais that morning, and I went to introduce myself to you and to ask you about your project. But when I got there, everything happened so fast. There you were, cleaning merde off your shoe, and—"

"Dog crap. You're blaming dog crap for your lies? For this whole charade?"

Alexandre shakes his head. "No. No. I'm not explaining it right. I went there, all business. Then when we met, it was so . . . spontaneous, and I was charmed by you. And it felt, I don't know, like we were always supposed to meet. And I wanted to see where things would go naturally."

"Naturally? What is wrong with you? You deceived me. You used me."

"I swear, I wasn't trying to hurt you. I was trying to save my family." There's a pleading quality to Alexandre's voice, but I honestly don't care about his feelings right now. Or his family. It's not lost on me that this is the second time this afternoon that a guy I like—who I thought I knew and trusted—has told me that he would never intentionally hurt me, so how come it keeps happening?

I twist away from Alexandre and move toward the balcony. There should be dark clouds. There should be storms. But I step outside into a clear, bright afternoon. I hear him turn on his heel and shuffle away. He closes the door softly behind him. I don't turn back to look.

THERE SHOULD BE a universal law that when you need your best friend the most, she can just magically appear and not be on some retro technology-free family sabbatical. Julie would probably tell me to go for a run by the river. But currently, I'm getting my wallow on. How long is too long for romantic wallowing? Is there a prescribed length when it moves from therapeutic to pathetic? I think there should be a chart. Obviously for serious breakups, like divorce, or finding out that your spouse has a whole second family or something, then I think days—if not weeks or months—of lamentation are definitely in order. What about for two doors slammed in my face by two different boys who both hid things from me? Who lied to me? What about then? When it's not clear because I hid things, too? When it's a mess of porcelain shards waiting to cut you? A few hours? It seems like a few hours is fair.

A few hours to contemplate what was almost surely a goodbye with Zaid. It would've been nice if we'd had a softer ending—one that was kinder to both of us. He may not have been perfect, but neither was I. And there were things between us that were good, a space that was warm and felt like home once. A hand that was so often there for me when I needed it, without me even having to ask. There was laughter, too.

Then there's this other nagging thought in my head. Well, there are a million. But one sticks out. What did Alexandre mean when he said he was trying to save his family? Like save them from what? And how could I possibly help? I know he's worried about the Dumas legacy and all, but saying he's trying to save them seems a little melodramatic.

I force myself off the couch and grab my laptop and do what I should've done when I first "coincidentally" met Alexandre. How could I ever have believed it was an actual coincidence? What I should have realized, what I know, is that the probability of us meeting without outside intervention was actually infinitesimal. It's math! Yet I bought it without question, without even bothering to check out Alexandre's story. Celenia

Mondego's criticism about my "slipshod research" passes through my brain yet again. Point taken. I'm not the one on an Internet-free holiday. But I was too focused on the dead Dumas in history books to even bother Google-stalking the living Dumas I was making out with amongst the archives.

I barely have to lean into my cross-referencing skills; *Dumas. Family. Legacy. Estate. Save.* And I unearth a treasure trove. Thank you, google.fr.

There are newspaper articles, blog posts, photos of the old Dumas château, interviews with Alexandre's mysterious, horrible uncle. Sure, I've been burned by fake Dumas news once already, but how could I not have even looked up the uncle? The one who probably has a Google Alert on me. The headlines jump out at me:

Q All   📧 News   🖼 Images   🗺 Maps   🏷 Shopping   ⋮ More

About 9140 results (.25 seconds)

Dumas estate in deep debt

Dumas foundation attempts to raise a million euro to pay back taxes

Billionaire American developer plans to turn Château into luxury resort

Legacy of France's beloved Dumas in hands of billionaire American?

Dumas family and foundation appeal for more time before foreclosure

All for one and one for a Dumas luxury resort?

And there she is again, Celenia Mondego, whispering in my ear: *a catastrophic inability to grasp obvious facts*. Fine, okay. I should've googled.

I open up an article to check out an interview with Gérard Dumas, Alexandre's uncle:

> *Unfortunately, Alexandre Dumas died penniless, and his beautiful estate fell into disrepair after passing through many hands, eventually coming under the guardianship of the Foundation de Monte Cristo. Together we are working to preserve the legacy of one of France's greatest artists. We believe the Dumas estate holds many treasures and must remain, forever, a French national institution.*

Treasures, he said. The estate holds many treasures. *Cherchez la femme, trouvez le trésor.*

Damn. It's like I have all the pieces of the puzzle, but I can't fit them together. Leila. Byron. Delacroix. The treasure in Dumas's note. But the Leila in *The Giaour* died in a sack death, killed by the Pasha, which is why the Giaour avenged her. That's the whole inspiration for the Delacroix painting. How could she have survived being bound in a sack and drowned? What's fiction, and what's the truth?

I run into my room to grab the book of Byron poems I bought right before my whole world became the Upside Down. I flip to the chronology of Byron's life and run my finger down the years. There it is. 1810–1811: Byron's Grand Tour—basically a gap year for wealthy nineteenth-century British dudes. A deeper Internet dive leads me to a map of his Tour that looks like it took him around the

Mediterranean and to the Bosporus. *The Giaour* was published in 1813. So was "She Walks in Beauty." I can feel my brain trying to fill in the blanks, but I can't see the big picture.

Maybe Alexandre and I left things . . . well, unspoken, and I will probably be eternally pissed at him for what he did, but I also need his help to put together all these pieces. I pick up my phone. Take a deep breath. And text him.

> Me: I'm still mad. But I need your help. I still want to find Leila.
> Alexandre: Do you hate me?
> Me: Like 40%
> Alexandre: So that still counts as a passing grade?
> Me: Not for Asians.
> Alexandre: I'll take it. And of course, I'm going to help. I want to find her, too.

I weigh whether or not I should say something to Alexandre about finding out about his family—about the bankruptcy of the Dumas estate. About understanding why he wants to save it—even if what he did was awful. But it doesn't feel right to say it in a text. Too many words. Not enough space.

> Me: I have a theory—Byron and Leila are connected. She's the Leila in THE GIAOUR and another poem, too. She's real. Somehow.
> Alexandre: Didn't you read the note???
> Me: What note?
> Alexandre: I slid a note under your door about half an hour after I left. I spoke to the Dumas archive collector in New Zealand and asked him to search his files. I got an email early this morning. It's a note from Leila.

I hurry to the door. In my wallowing, I must've dozed off or been totally out of it. There's a white envelope with my name on it.

Me: Found it.
Alexandre: Read it. You have more than a theory.
Alexandre: In case you need to hear it again, I'm sorry for everything.

I put my phone down. I'm too distracted to judge the sincerity of Alexandre's remorse. My hands tremble as I pull out a copy of the letter:

November

Cher Ami,

 Say not that your heart is broken. With all that I have seen and felt and known, I hold, even still, that the heart is the singular miracle God gave to each of us—an organ that heals itself. A wizened old hekime in the harem once told me that the human heart is the size of a fist. Yet the heart is much bigger on the inside, not bound by its physical form.

 And so, may I humbly advise you to do the thing I have tried to do all these long years since the night in the desert when I watched as my beloved was struck down by Pasha's sword. Let this love you profess for me be enclosed in a small chamber in your heart. Seal it. Open the door to it no more. And there let it live, evergreen, but not consuming. Perhaps one day, it will fade from your memory entire when rosier cheeks and lips occupy your imagination and enter into your embrace.

When the poet and I alighted on English shores, I knew I could not remain with him. Indeed, the very sight of him served as a cruel reminder of the last night I spent in the warmth of my land's sun and the clear, devastating beauty of her starry nights. Though he offered himself to me, proposed a life where neither of us were bound to the other, and a comfortable life it might have been while he lived, I refused to accept it. I did not escape one gilded cage at so high a price to simply enter another.

Begging his leave, I secured companionship with a kindly, older French woman of diminished noble birth, but wealthy enough to be a patron of the arts, a lover of the Orient. And thus I came to France all those years ago, not merely to forget, but to try and live without regret in my heart—to build a life on my own terms.

In this, you have helped me, perhaps unknowingly. Your friendship, your encouragement, your amiable nature brought me a sense of comfort and returned a part of my own self to me. And for that I shall remain eternally grateful.

Yet now I must ask that we sever our connection permanently for your own good. For I know myself. What you seek from me, I cannot give. I know what I ask of you. I do not ask it lightly.

Forever yours in friendship,

Leila

I let the letter fall to the table. In Byron's poem, the Giaour kills the Pasha to avenge Leila's sack death. That's the story the Delacroix paintings tell, too.

But if this is real, it's all turned upside down. Leila survived. She had to watch helplessly while the Pasha killed her lover. Then she fled to England with Lord Byron. And then here to Paris to try and make a life for herself. Byron wrote a fantasy, an opium-induced fable because he thought his fiction was the better story.

He was wrong.

Leila

❧❧❧

Before I slip past this world, I am seized and tossed in a whirling tempest of water and air that leaves me gasping for breath as the ocean enters my lungs one moment and is wrenched out of me the next.

It ends with a thud. Pain surges through my body.

I am on land—the sack in tattered shreds around me, and my hands unbound, bleeding. I sit up, trembling, coughing, spitting out water. I unsheathe my yataghan, miraculously still at my waist, and cut through the ropes at my feet. I untie the gag from around my mouth. My lungs and nostrils burn. I turn back to a sea that is illuminated from below by a cerulean light. Si'la leans into the waves and whispers and drops an opal into the churning water that calms at her command. The blue light fades.

I turn to look for Si'la, my mouth open to scream, but no sound comes out. A horse gallops toward me. I squint into the darkness. I rise and hold my yataghan aloft. The rider stops short; his horse snorts and brays.

The poet dismounts and reaches out his hand. "You need to come with me now."

"How did you find me?"

The poet's eyes are wild. "A blue light rose from the sea. And voices, whispers, led me this way. I . . . I can't . . ." He takes a deep breath. "My valet and the other men have traveled forward and await us on the *Salsette*. We must hurry. There is no time. The janissaries have granted us safe leave, but I believe that promise would be rescinded if they see you alive. Which is—"

"A story for another day. Do you have my satchel?" The poet hands me the bag that holds my entire life. "Please turn." He doesn't move. "Please. I can't accompany you wet to the bone in these clothes." He turns, and I quickly undress, slipping into the eunuch's garments, tucking my hair into a simple turban.

"I am ready," I say and climb into the saddle, yataghan in hand.

The poet looks me up and down and grins. "And I was under the mistaken assumption that it was I who was mad, bad, and dangerous to know."

"I'm only dangerous to those who cross me."

He nods and mounts his horse. We dash toward the dock.

I have no intention of boarding the ship.

KHAYYAM

Yesterday after reading the letter, I spent more time googling Byron. Turns out what I need to look at is a book in an actual library—my mom would be thrilled. I texted Alexandre late last night and asked him to meet me. And here he is, waiting outside the front door of the American Library in Paris, body inclined against the pale yellow-gray stone. Like always, he looks lean and relaxed, but as I approach, his nervous smile betrays him.

He pushes his sunglasses to the top of his head, and that's when I see his bloodshot eyes. "Salut," he says as he bends to kiss my cheeks, but then stops himself.

"Salut," I respond, my shoulders stiffening.

Clearly, neither of us has slept, and we have no idea what to say. This sucks.

I shift my weight from one foot to the other. I spent most of last night waffling between rage and resignation, between hating Alexandre and seeing a piece of myself in what he's dealing with. I don't want to bring up his family's financial situation, but it's one of, like, five elephants in the room, and it's so crowded I can barely breathe. "Alexandre, why didn't you tell me?" I mutter.

Alexandre looks stricken but also confused. There are so many things we hid from each other, why would he automatically know what I'm talking about?

"I mean, about your family," I say. "The back taxes and the Dumas estate being near foreclosure. That's what you meant when you said you wanted to save your family, right?"

Alexandre nods almost imperceptibly. "But how did you—"

"You're not the only one with cyberstalking skills," I say. It's petty, but it's also true. And I feel at least a little entitled to this moment.

Alexandre's shoulders sag. "Khayyam, I'm sorry. I was an idiot for listening to my uncle. I should've been honest with you from the beginning. About everything." A wave of anguish passes over his face.

My body tenses. Yes, I feel sorry for him. But I still feel like a giant gaping wound of a person, and my sympathies are limited. I nod. "We both should have been." A moment of silence passes so weighted with regret and longing and things unsaid that I practically have to yank my words out of my belly with a hook. "Look, we both want to find Leila. You want to find the treasure so your family can pay off the estate debts and save Dumas's legacy, right?"

"Yes. If it is a Delacroix that was gifted to Dumas, it would be worth much more than just the back taxes. We could preserve the estate. Rebuild it. Restore his name—our name." Alexandre is matter-of-fact. Focused.

I nod. "Well, maybe there's a treasure I want to find, too."

"Yes, your paper. The prize—"

"No. It's not just that . . ." I wave my hand. It's not. There's more to it. More to me. I want to find Leila because she deserves to be found. "We both basically want the same thing, right?" If Alexandre can be businesslike, I can, too.

"Here's the deal. We put things behind us and pretend we're normal people trying to solve a centuries-old literary mystery, okay?"

I need to leave the near past in the past, so we can spend today searching for the long-ago past. Compartmentalize. Save my messy feelings for another day. It doesn't feel logical, but somehow it makes sense to me.

Alexandre grins, and the smile reaches his tired eyes. "Yes. D'accord. We are one-hundred-percent normal people. Okay, tell me why we're here again?"

I let out a breath. This is okay. This is going to work. I have to imagine that my ex-boyfriend isn't wandering around Paris right now after what might have been our last goodbye. I have to pretend that the cryptic puzzle I'm trying to solve to find a missing nineteenth-century woman isn't leading me on a treasure hunt with a descendant of Alexandre Dumas who Insta-stalked me and who I like making out with. Sure. No problem. People undersell the importance of denial as a coping mechanism.

"Byron sailed from Lisbon to Constantinople on his Grand Tour—basically a gap year for rich British men in the nineteenth century," I explain. "That's when he could've met Leila. Byron was also a letter-writing fiend, and I'm betting he wrote to Leila. If she inspired two of his poems, she must have been important to him. Harvard published some volumes of his letters—he wrote over three thousand. They're not digitized, but there's a set of the books here." I point to the doors.

THE AMERICAN LIBRARY in Paris is exactly like any library in the States—except that it's two blocks from the Eiffel Tower and a boulangerie with heavenly pain au chocolat.

Everything is in English, and the furniture is utilitarian library chic. Even the air-conditioning is set at the normal American level of near-frigid—I feel like I've stepped through a portal and am suddenly back home, and that sensation is oddly comforting.

I copied the call number from the website last night, so I head straight to the lower level. Alexandre follows.

"It looks like you know your way around this place. You've been here before?" Alexandre asks as I search for the right shelf.

"It's a truth universally acknowledged that an American in Paris in possession of mediocre French reading skills must be in want of English books to read on vacation."

Alexandre wrinkles his forehead.

"Oh, sorry. It's a reference to Jane Austen. *Pride and Prejudice*?"

"Ahh, oui. A wildly popular book about repressed feelings. How British."

I laugh out loud, and it warrants a couple turned heads from studious library patrons. Maybe this denial thing can work. Sadly, it's all too familiar. We slip between the stacks, and I run my finger across the spines, looking for *Lord Byron: Selected Letters and Journals, 1788–1824.* I'm focused, but not so determined that I don't feel the nearness of Alexandre as he follows closely behind me. I can't completely deny his existence. Or my attraction to him.

Found it. I pull a worn blue book from the shelf. Its cover is encased in plastic, and it has that faint stale library smell. Judging from the creaseless spine, barely anyone has cracked it open.

We find an empty table tucked into a corner in the back of the room. I open the book and flip to the index. All the letters are listed by name of recipient. I run my finger down each column—twenty pages, two columns on each page. No mention of a Leila. "Dammit. I thought there would be something." I slam the cover shut. Dead end. Without a connection between Leila and Byron—a real, provable one, I have nothing but another hollow theory.

"Let's not give up yet. Weren't you the one wearing a *Nevertheless, She Persisted* T-shirt the other day? Maybe we can still find a glimpse of Leila in some other letter," Alexandre says as he gently takes the book from my hands.

He's right. I can't give up yet. Maybe I'm down, way down, but I'm not out. Besides, Leila is counting on me.

Alexandre reopens the book to the title page. "1788 to 1824. He didn't live long, did he?" he asks before turning to the index.

I nod. "It's sad. Imagine all the other things he could have done. But at least he's not forgotten."

It's kind of morbid to consider the upside of someone dying when they're thirty-six. But it's also true. Byron had the incredible good fortune of being born a titled British white man. Leila and countless others are forgotten or are only known because they happened to cross paths with famous men. That thought gives me pause.

"Hey." I nudge Alexandre. "Like your illustrious ancestor, Byron had a lot of lovers. Let's look at some of the other women he wrote to."

A roguish grin sneaks across Alexandre's face. I inadvertently lean my shoulder into his, and he pushes back ever so slightly. I reach for the book, and our hands meet. Alexandre turns to me and holds my gaze. "I meant what I told you before. Mes yeux ne brillent que pour toi."

"Stop it," I whisper. "That's not part of the deal." My face flushes. I take the book without looking at him. I study the index, pretending I don't feel the nearness of him.

"Here's a letter to a countess." I point it out to Alexandre, who leans closer to me and reads over my shoulder, whispering Byron's words in my ear:

August 25, 1819

My dearest Teresa,

. . . [Y]ou will recognize the handwriting of him who passionately loves you, and you will divine that, over a book which was yours, he could only think of love. In that word, beautiful in all languages, but most so in yours—Amor mio—is comprised my existence here and hereafter. I feel I exist here, and I fear that I shall exist hereafter, —as to what purpose you will decide; my destiny rests with you, and you are a woman, seventeen years of age, and two out of a convent. I wish that you had stayed there, with all my heart, —or, at least, that I had never met you in your married state.

But all this is too late. I love you, and you love me, —at least, you say so, and act as if you did so, which last is a great consolation in all events. But I more than love you, and cannot cease to love you.

Think of me, sometimes, when the Alps and the ocean divide us, —but they never will, unless you wish it.

Byron

I gulp. I'm not sure a love letter was the right choice at this moment.

Alexandre chuckles. "He was quite the romantic, wasn't he?"

"He's writing this to a married woman," I say. "He's a total narcissistic jerk who had no control over his passions or his ego. That's why one of his lovers called him mad, bad, and dangerous to know—his entire life was about himself and his excesses and his incredible ability to seduce women and men."

"He obviously couldn't help himself when surrounded by temptation," Alexandre says.

I roll my eyes and elbow him. He starts laughing.

"Let's pack it in," I say. I don't think I can handle any more flirting in the stacks.

Alexandre and I stand up to place the book in a "to be reshelved" cart. "I'm sorry we didn't find anything about our lady with the raven tresses," he says.

I stop short. "Oh my God," I nearly yell. "That's it. It's so obvious."

"What? What did I say?" Alexandre asks.

I don't reply. I'm too nervous. *Please let me be right*. I cradle the book in one hand and flip back through the index, quickly running my eye down the columns. All the letter recipients are listed alphabetically by last name. But what if Byron didn't use a name but an endearment? My hands get clammy as I search for her. Maybe it's luck. Maybe it's destiny. But it doesn't matter, because there she is: *Lady, Raven Tresses, of the* . . . page 312. Alexandre squeezes my elbow.

"Holy crap," I whisper.

January 12, 1815

My Dearest Lady of the Raven Tresses,

Though fate, and, in truth, your own will, have distanced us since our return, know my love is a fix'd mark. Neither time nor place can alter its course. I am ready, upon your word, to arrive with all haste to Paris. Indeed, if you bid me fly to the moon, I would give up all pleasures of this earthly realm and build a ladder to the heavens to live with you amongst the stars. I can think of no more rightful place, for your beauty is celestial; more so, your heart.

You have made your own feelings clear. And of mine, you can be in no doubt. God knows I wish you only happiness and a peace, which I hope comes through time, dripping slowly through the days and hours. I know your heart longs for another. Mourns for he who was cut down so cruelly in front of your tender eyes. Would that I could return him to you, had I but that power.

I write in no true hope to sway your course. Merely to declare, once more, that I am, as ever, in your service. This is no time for mere words. Yet I offer you these verses enclosed here. Though I have kept your identity hidden, I write these words that you and the world may ever know that I was and am yours, freely.

Ever Yrs,

I close the book and look at Alexandre. I want to throw my arms around his neck and squeeze, but I muster all my self-restraint and suppress my feelings. But then a smile sweeps across my face as I library-whisper, "Boom."

ALEXANDRE INVITED ME to his place to look at a couple other old books that could yield clues. But I said no—not wanting to tempt fate or be tempted. And part of me wonders if it wasn't an excuse to spend time with me in his library where we shared our first kiss.

I walk home, my mind whirring with things lost and found. It's overcast, and there's a slight breeze—a welcome break from the heat that's been pretty unrelenting all month. Tourists pass by, oblivious to me and the cautionary tale that is my life, in a rush to get to a monument or museum that's been waiting for them for centuries, to pose for a photo that probably will never exist on paper. Is a JPG even a memory? Or as the French say, a *souvenir*? I have literally thousands of pictures on my phone, but I barely look at them and definitely don't remember them all. Byron wrote thousands of letters during his life, and he died when he was thirty-six. And here I am, hundreds of years later, reading them. *That* is a souvenir.

I sigh. I always grow into Paris when we're here. Despite the chaos in my life this summer, as I watch windswept tourists pulling along little kids with ice cream melting down their arms, I feel content in my own French skin. Like I belong here. Like it's okay to have more than one home. That home is a place I can carry with me.

I notice a missed call and a text from my parents, who apparently are having such fun taking the waters in Brittany, they're staying on a couple more days. I haven't told them a thing about Zaid, except to say that his big surprise was garbage cookies like I suspected, which is, in part, true. I didn't tell my mom about the ugly scene in our apartment. I didn't tell her about how I wished I could've given Zaid and me a better ending. Looking back, maybe we were always a bit of a mess together, but sometimes it was a beautiful mess.

Anyway, if I told my mom everything, my parents would be on the next train back. I know she's been worried about me, more than usual, but there's nothing she can do about Zaid or Alexandre or my confusion. I wished them a happy second honeymoon and told them I was fine. And honestly, I am okay. There is so much unrequited love and straight-up trag-edy in these notes and letters we've found that it makes my troubles seem small.

Leila watched while the love of her life was killed. In a way, a part of her died that day, too. Dumas was doing his best to woo her, and even after they were apparently sleeping together, he didn't have her heart. And Byron, damn, was he pining away—though he probably deserved it. Talk about an ugly, tangled heap of emotions. Decades of heartbreak and death make Instagram scandals seem small. Byron sent that letter from England to Paris by ship. I was going bonkers when Zaid didn't text me for four days. I cannot imagine the nail-biting anxiety of having to wait months or to never even know if the letter of your heart ever reached the intended. I'm suddenly overwhelmed by gratitude that fate landed me in this era. I mean, when my parents reminisce about the 1980s and '90s and mix tapes and talking on a landline and watch-ing TV with commercials, it feels like the Dark Ages. It's snail mail. It's a poem being hand carried over land and sea.

My phone dings. I stop on the street in front of my build-ing. A text from Alexandre. A photo of another Gautier essay he found in the *Revue* he wanted us to look at. Okay, maybe inviting me over wasn't an excuse to relive our romantic moments. Seems this Gautier article may never have been published, though, because Alexandre says he found it in an appendix. I unlock the door and read as I walk up the steps to my apartment.

SEPTEMBER 1849

... Ceremonially dressed in Arab costume, as my compatriots, I notice a somber mood has befallen our usual jolly gathering. Few partake tonight in what Baudelaire has termed his "playground of the seraphim." Dumas broods in the corner, and his dark humor fills the room. I dare not ask what troubles him. Even Delacroix, his confidant, cannot convince him to indulge in the green sweetmeat that may open the door to celestial voices. "I do not seek a muse," he utters under his breath. "There is no solace for me here. Only pain." It is only when the concealed panel opens and Leila—for we have come to know the tarot reader by this name—emerges from her hidden chamber that his mood lightens and an expression reminiscent of a smile dares appear on his face. But it is merely a ghost of what once was, I fear. The tarot reader finds her seat at the small wooden table in the corner. She takes care to cover it with a crimson scarf, placing her deck in the center, then folds her hands in her lap, waiting for the evening's first customer. She observes the room from her advantageous positioning, smiling at each of us in our turn. When her face falls upon Dumas, her eyes warm to him, and she gives him a discreet nod that only I, attuned to minute observation, comprehend.

Dumas rises and places himself at the mercy of the

cards. The lady with the raven tresses gestures to the deck with an open palm—bidding Dumas to separate it into three small piles. He whispers his question to her, then reaches out, but rather than the cards, takes her hand in his. Swiftly, she removes it to her lap, her smile faltering only briefly. But her eyes soften, and an unspoken understanding seems to pass between them. Dumas looks down. Since I first entered these doors, I cannot recall a moment where Dumas seemed so overcome by melancholia. He chooses three cards: past, present, future. L'Amoureux, La Roue de Fortune, La Mort. Even the tarot reader, insouciant though she often seems, gasps and pushes back from her chair. She utters her apologies and retreats to the hidden chamber that none but she is allowed to enter.

Those are the tarot cards we found—well, two anyway— the Wheel of Fortune and Death. A lump wells in my throat as I unlock the door and step into my empty apartment that suddenly feels full of ghosts. I'm not sure why I feel sad for people who are ancient history. Their story just feels so real. So of this moment. I text Alexandre:

Me: We need to go back to the Hôtel.

Alexandre: The secret chamber?

Me: Obviously. Tonight.

Alexandre: Okay. Then pack your bags, because tomorrow we go to the Château de Monte-Cristo.

Me: I'm not staying overnight there with you. My parents would freak.

I don't add that I am freaking out *right now*.

Alexandre: Sorry. I was trying to use that American idiom. The Château is only 1 hour by train.

Me: 😅😅😅

Alexandre: . . .

Alexandre: . . .

Great. My assumption was so ridiculous he can't figure out how to respond.

Alexandre: I will come by your place at 9 P.M. I will bring no bags.

Leila

⌖

The wind in my mouth, I fight back tears. If my Giaour is alive, I will go find him. If Pasha has already struck him down, then it will be Pasha's last night on earth.

At the dock, a skiff awaits us, ready to carry us the short distance to freedom. The poet takes my hand, but I resist.

From the east, a charge of hooves. The poet pulls me down onto the sloping, sandy bank, his arm around my shoulders and his breath on my neck. My Giaour bursts through the night, his white horse a beacon in the darkness. Pasha rides on his heels, his black steed snarling fire. I scramble from the bank, screaming my Giaour's name. He pulls back on the reins, and his horse's neighs echo out across the water. He turns to me. I stand and remove my turban. Pasha blanches and slows his horse when he sees me.

My Giaour raises his hand to his lips, brings it to his heart, and then gestures toward me. With his other hand, he unsheathes his kilij.

He turns and charges at Pasha. Their blades clash and send sparks into the sky. I try to run toward them, but the poet holds me back. I kick against him, but he grips me tighter.

Pasha and Giaour circle each other in an arabesque of death, an elegy of swirling white robes and blades and bodies. Their horses fight, loyal to their masters, baring teeth, their muscles tense beneath their hides. Pasha pushes his steed into the side of my Giaour's mount and then skims the edge of his kilij just beyond the white steed's saddle. The horse cries out and rears and bucks, my Giaour clinging to the reins, trying desperately not to be thrown.

The Pasha arcs his kilij through the air—a single motion that slows time, makes the earth stand still—and brings it down against my beloved's throat. For the briefest of moments our eyes connect, and then he falls, a river of crimson at his neck.

KHAYYAM

"You're quiet this evening. Everything okay?" Alexandre asks as we round the corner of my block to Quai d'Anjou, steps away from the Hôtel de Lauzun.

It's true. I'm quieter than usual, but I don't think I can explain to Alexandre that I've been at home alone, waiting for my phone to ring or hoping that maybe Zaid would show up at my door so we could resolve things better, find some semblance of closure. The story of us wasn't all bad, and we deserved better than slammed doors and angry words. But I can't control all my endings—or beginnings, apparently. And now I'm all exposed nerves and bruised ego. The sadness of, well, everything growing on me. Not growing, exactly, more like burrowing a hole where all my memories live.

I stop walking about twenty feet from 17 Quai d'Anjou and look up at Alexandre. "Sometimes saying goodbye is difficult. Even if you think you're ready. Even if it's right," I say. If I were talking to Julie instead of Alexandre, I might've added that part of me is wondering how I'll say goodbye to him, to Alexandre. It's not going to be today, but it's coming, and I'm not sure how I feel about that.

Alexandre simply nods, then tilts his head in the direction of the Hôtel.

As we approach, a man with light-brown skin and salt-and-pepper hair steps out of the street door that leads to the courtyard of the Hôtel, talking loudly on his cell phone. Alexandre grabs my hand and pulls me closer. I feel the warmth of his body next to mine and the familiar scent of his home—old books and oranges—as he hurries us toward the entrance. All smiles, he says, "Monsieur, s'il vous plaît." The man turns to look at us and then catches the door; he pulls the phone away from his mouth and says, "Bonne soireé!" Then he wiggles his eyebrows. Alexandre nods at him and grins as we slip through the door. I pull my hand away as soon as we are safely inside the courtyard and give him a look.

He shrugs. "The men in Paris, we have an understand-ing—"

"You mean a bro code?" I roll my eyes. "Let's get on with the breaking and entering," I say, perhaps a little too loudly.

"Sssshhh." Alexandre gently places a finger on my lips. I thought I'd already conveyed my deep irritation at being shushed the first couple times he did it, but apparently not sufficiently. Also, I might be imagining it, but I swear he lets his finger linger against my lips a second longer than necessary before I twist away and scowl at him.

There's no one in the inner courtyard. We can slip right in the door of the Hôtel—it's not like someone fixed the lock in the last few days. It's probably been busted for years. We head straight to the winding stairs to the landing with the worn velvet tapestry and yellow border that Gautier mentioned in the first article we found. I can't get over that it's still here. Though there are probably tapestries and paintings older than this one hanging all over apartments in Paris, like that Delacroix etching in Alexandre's foyer. Age increases the value of some objects and diminishes others. It's a bit of a crapshoot, assigning an object—or a person—worth, isn't it? It's luck, and it also kind of sucks because for most of history, the people who got to assign that value were men who didn't look like me.

But I suppose love assigns value, too. Like the portraits I do every year in school that line our staircase back home in Chicago. Those mean as much to my parents as that Delacroix does to Alexandre's family—maybe more—but they're not hoping to sell them and save the family estate because, well, my skills aren't exactly Delacroix-etching level, and our house is not exactly an estate.

"I don't remember seeing another door last time," Alexandre says as we enter the dusty old parlor that is exactly as we left it. As I step into the room again, my heart races. I keep glancing at the windows, hearing a siren, but it's only in my mind. I grimace, remembering the crack I made in the buffet table drawer. The red silk scarf we found last time rests where we tossed it before making our quick escape after seeing that cop outside.

"Well, it was dark, and we had to hide and—"

"You were distracted by all the kissing," he says.

"You wish," I scoff, trying hard not to smile. "*You* were distracted by all the kissing."

"Without a doubt."

Don't flirt, Khayyam. You're sending mixed messages. To yourself.

Why is it so hard to do the thing that's best for you when you know it's best for you? Sometimes I wonder how human beings have survived from the Paleolithic to now. We always seem to operate against our own better judgment. I'm guessing

Byron might say that's what makes life worth living—Dumas might say the same, too.

But I push their voices out of my head. It's Leila's voice I'm here to find.

ALEXANDRE HEADS TO the opposite wall and begins tapping it like Velma in *Scooby-Doo* trying to find a secret passage. If only there were a giant fireplace with a sconce that was actually a lever revealing a hidden room. Before I join him, I want to look in the cabinets in the buffet we didn't get a chance to investigate the first time we were here. One is empty, but when I open the other one, I see several ripped pieces of paper scattered on the shelf inside. I gather them up to take a look—it's bits of a torn-up tarot card. I piece the dusty fragments together. I beckon Alexandre over to show him.

"It's the last of the three cards Gautier mentioned. The Lovers."

"L'Amoureux, La Roue de Fortune, La Mort. Past, present, and future for Dumas."

"He must've been pretty upset, but ripping up a tarot card isn't exactly logical."

"You know what they say: le cœur a ses raisons que le raison ne connaît point."

"The heart has its reasons that reason cannot know?" I smirk. It hits a little too close to home. Like, why do I still want to kiss Alexandre even when I'm mad at him? And why can't I stop wanting to text Zaid when I think I've already shut that door?

"The heart is a mystery." It's too dark to see Alexandre's expression clearly, but I hear the softness in his voice.

"Don't you think there's a funny contradiction in French

culture? It's all about reason and logic except when it comes to love."

"There is no logic to love. So I don't see the contradiction," Alexandre responds flatly, and it's hard to tell if he's serious or joking. Could legit be either one.

Now seems like an excellent time to change the subject. "Gautier said there was a hidden panel, right? Or door?" I circle the room with light from my phone, trying to keep it away from the windows. It's a risk using the lights, and my shaky hands remind me not to press our luck, but we need to get a closer look. The walls are all panels—rows of intricately painted flowers and elegant carvings of cherubs and garlands of ivy and rosettes along the edges where the wall meets the ceiling. It's faded glory—the frescoes cracked and broken, paint peeling, the gilt borders tarnished, and bits of glass missing from dusty, ornate chandeliers.

"The only door in this room besides the entrance is to that tiny closet we hid in."

Alexandre chuckles. "Oh, I remember that very well."

He's not helping make the situation less awkward. What's more, he clearly doesn't want to.

I ignore his leading comment. "Maybe one of these panels is *the* panel. We need to see if any of them have doorknobs or keyholes."

We start at the far end of the room. I move in to get a closer look, crouching to examine the length of each panel while Alexandre guides his light over the surface. There are no keyholes anywhere. Gautier didn't give any more specifics about the hidden door Leila emerged from. But maybe . . . I straighten up. Like so many things in this mystery, sometimes the meaning behind a thing isn't what it seems at first.

"Hey, what exact word did Gautier use again? To describe the door Leila went into?"

Alexandre scrolls through his phone, a few seconds that feel like forever. "Cachaient. Meaning something is concealing the door."

Two floor-to-ceiling tapestries hang against the wide wall at the back of the room. "Something like one of those, maybe?"

We grin at each other. I have a sudden urge to pull the tapestries down, but I don't want to destroy any other French antiques. I step closer to one, examining the worn threadwork and fading forest scene, trying to figure out a way to handle it with care, like all lost things deserve. I decide to slip behind it, giving rise to plumes of dust that make me cough. The thick fabric feels heavy against my back. I run my fingers along the wall, feeling for a door.

I hear Alexandre walking on the other side of the tapestry, then a gasp, and a metallic squeak. The tapestry slides off my back along the wall. I whip around, and Alexandre points to the ceiling—the tapestry is attached to a heavy rod with metal rings like a drape. An easy way to hide a door. I step back. There's no keyhole anywhere. No doorknob. We begin running our hands over the entire wall, pushing the panels, but nothing gives.

Then my finger catches on the edge of one of the panels. Alexandre shines his light on it. A narrow pocket door. I catch my breath, fit the pads of my fingers in a tiny grooved indentation along the side, and pull.

The panel groans and creaks and slides into the wall—a low, slim door, big enough for one person to squeeze through.

THE ROOM BEHIND the pocket door is tiny and spare, furnished only with a narrow bed and thin bare mattress, a nondescript side table, and a small slanted, wooden writing desk tucked up under the only window in the room. It's almost painfully austere. I can't say for sure this was Leila's, but I want it to be so much that I'm willing to believe it is based on one line in an article and my gut feeling. It's not exactly sound science.

"It's like a nun's room," I whisper.

Alexandre shakes his head. "No. It's a prisoner's room. It's like the room in *The Man in the Iron Mask*."

"Who's that?"

"Dumas wrote about him in the last Musketeers novel— the king's twin, imprisoned for his whole life, so he wouldn't challenge him for the throne. He was forced to wear a mask to hide his true identity. When we first meet him in Dumas's story, the prisoner is in a sparse room in the Bastille, and there's a wooden desk tucked up under the only window." Alexandre points to the desk under the small, dirty window.

"Oh my God," I whisper. "When was it written?"

"1847? 1850? It was a serial based on a true story from the 1600s, except that, even now, we don't know the true identity of the man in the iron mask." He runs his hand through his wavy hair.

"I know," I say, my pulse starting to pound in my ears. "The timing. He would've been writing it when he knew Leila. He could have seen this place. This could be her room."

I walk the length of this tiny cell of a room in about ten paces. There's not a lot to look at: bare floor, bare window, bare walls. I'm caught by a stitch of sadness. If this was Leila's room—and I want to believe that—it's almost painful to imagine her living like this. How did she survive? Money from tarot readings and séances? That could hardly have been enough. There are too many dots that we can't connect and maybe never will.

I sigh loudly.

"What's wrong?" Alexandre asks. "Aren't you happy we found this place? It matches Gautier's description."

"I'm thrilled. Amazed." I take a second to collect my thoughts. "But it's infuriating that no matter what we find out about her, we'll never know the whole story, or even half of it."

"It's the cruel irony of being human." Alexandre inches closer to me, so we're almost touching. "We spend so much of our life trying to be known, only to be forgotten."

Alexandre's assessment may be bleak, but it's also true. One thing he's forgetting, though? It's not just the human condition because the histories that do remain, the people we remember? They're almost all men. I watch as he crosses the room to the narrow bed and takes a seat, sending more dust into the air.

I move to the window and trace the grooves in what could be Leila's desk. Maybe she was a writer; maybe these marks are from the metal nibs of her fountain pens that bore the weight of her loneliness and rage and passion. *You must've had stories to tell, Leila. I wish I could've heard them.*

I hear a soft thud behind me. When I turn, I see Alexandre on his knees reaching under the bed. "I kicked something with the back of my heel," he says, then pulls out what looks like an extra-large cigar box—thin, rectangular, wooden. I sit down next to him, resting my hand on his shoulder. The box opens with a little creak of its hinges.

The first thing I see is a dagger.

Alexandre delicately pulls it out from its sheath. The metal shines, luminescent, almost like moonlight under the beams from our phones. It has a sharp point and a sort of curved edge that backs into the handle that looks like it's made of bone. Ivory, perhaps? There's a word carved into the handle that I can't decipher, written in what looks like Arabic or Persian or maybe even Urdu script.

Beneath the dagger are papers. I leaf through a few—receipts, tickets of some sort. Some of them were probably written in pencil because they're not even legible. I hand Alexandre half the pile. He gasps. "It's an invitation to a housewarming party—the opening of the Château de Monte-Cristo."

As I look at the invitation over Alexandre's shoulder, I stop short. Out of the corner of my eye, I spy a letter written in black ink at the bottom of the box.

My gaze falls on the signature line: *Ever yours, L.*

Leila

The poet tries to hold me back, but a mere mortal cannot stop me. I tear through the air, ready to plunge the tip of my yataghan into Pasha's heart, to cut it out and cast it into the sea.

He dismounts. His mouth opens in a laugh so cruel seraphs weep.

The earth rumbles at my feet, dust swirls around me, and I'm pushed back by a gale force. Shadows rise from the dirt, their eyes glowing yellow as they set toward Pasha, shifting into hordes of screaming hyenas. The ghul claw at him, sharp teeth ripping soft skin, devouring him. Perhaps he screams. Perhaps he pleads. But I refuse to hear his cries. He stole my life and my love. He will not command another second of my time.

I fall to the ground, pounding my fists on the earth, remembering Si'la's warning: I fear you will not escape wholly as yourself.

My heart is cleaved and will never be rendered whole.

"Rise, Leila. Leave this place." Si'la's voice is soft, but direct.

"Strike me down; let my blood mingle in the earth with his," I beg.

"Your life has many tales yet to tell. I pray your Giaour is granted mercy as I pray for you." Si'la cups my chin. She touches my opal, and its warmth courses through my body.

I look up at Si'la. Leaving means losing her, too.

"Go now. You must hurry," she warns. "If you are found, the janissaries will be ruthless. You will carry his love in your heart always. And mine. May it be a balm for you in troubled times ahead. Peace be with you, little one."

"Goodbye, Si'la. I will never forget what you have done for me. Peace be with you on this day and all days." I have no other words. They all catch in my throat.

I stand and return to the poet. His eyes are filled with tears. I bend down and grasp my satchel, clutching it to my chest. The poet takes my hand, and we walk to the small skiff. We row in silence to the Salsette, where his men help us aboard.

KHAYYAM

I wake to the early morning light filtering through the windows in my living room. I sit up with a start, and then sink back into the sofa, rubbing my dry, scratchy eyes. My neck hurts, and I could barely sleep—too many feelings about what we found last night, too much catastrophizing about what could go wrong. I turn to the soft snoring next to me. Alexandre's body is half curled into a comma, long legs extended, eyes gently closed. He nodded off a few hours ago. Somehow, despite everything, he looks peaceful, unbothered.

I honestly can't imagine the position he's in—the weight of history and family burdens he's carrying. I've tried, but I can't stay angry with him. He lied to me and made stupid choices to save his family. But what keeps coming around to kick me in the ass is that I lied, too—to save myself. I'm too tired to be mad. It's too exhausting to stay angry. It feels too hypocritical. I might not be ready to forgive him completely, but maybe Alexandre deserves a second chance. Maybe I do, too.

We haven't kissed since before the drama outside Shakespeare & Company, but I can't ignore the times we've almost kissed since then or how the space between us crackles with

possibility. We're in orbit around each other, and it's taking
a lot of energy to make sure we don't collide and burn up. I
can't deny it would be nice to nestle into his arms and close
my eyes and let the world drift away for a few silent hours.
But I'm not ready to let my guard down again.

My eyes fall on the ornate blade in its sheath atop the
papers we found last night. Only one of the notes was legible,
but that was enough for me to connect some of the dots. The
dark fairy tale come to life—death and blood and an enslaved
harem girl, fighting to live the life she wanted. It's the Giaour
and the Pasha and Leila, at her most exposed and heartbreak-
ing. It's Leila speaking for herself.

July 10, 1845

My Eternal Love,

   *Think me not unfaithful, though I undertook to write to you
yearly on the anniversary when we were parted. In this endeavor
I have failed, yet in my vow to remain true—to live and live only
for you—I have not wavered. More than three decades have passed
since Pasha's kilij struck you down and cleaved my heart in one
fell swoop. Every day I have prayed for you, that God grant you a
place in jannah.*

   *Time has been kind to me, though I fear you would no longer
recognize me should you, through some miracle, walk through this
door. My hair is grayer, and wrinkles meet my eyes when I smile;
my smiles are but a shadow of the joy I shared with you. Though
it came at too high a price, your youth is eternal in my mind's
eye. The soft waves of your black hair bear no hint of age, and*

the flecks of gold in your eyes, those warm eyes, dance as they did thousands of nights ago in our courtyard of hollowed trees. Hallowed trees. I have promised myself not to mourn you all my days, yet to hold you fondly in remembrance, but my love, I must confess, it is difficult, and with each passing day, you grow more distant from me.

There is little luxury of the harem here. But I do not long for it. A cage, though gilded, is still a cage. And here I am free. The old woman who took me under her wing passed some years hence but left me a small living. And while I long ago sold the jewels that accompanied me on this voyage, living frugally has allowed me to reap, even still, some benefit from those gifts. How it pleases me to know that my easy disposal of those jewels would anger Pasha.

But I have built this life from almost nothing and without regret. I have scraped together a material living using my wiles, learning to navigate this world of men even as I did the world of men back home. It is a simple life, but it is mine.

The poet, too, died some time ago. Though we were little in touch, I felt his passing most deeply—the last unwitting connection to home. He was a petulant child and selfish and also beautiful and daring. And ever one who lived freely. As of late, I have fallen into favor with a group of French writers and artists. Using skills and arts I learned in the harem and in my travels, I read their fortunes, and, when on occasions they take hashish in their coffee and wish to commune with spirits and find their muses, I am at their service. I can only imagine how you and I could have laughed at their folly together. For this amusement, I am given a modest room in a once-opulent hôtel particulier that has seen better days. As have we all.

There is one in particular, a novelist, with whom I have been passing the time, and he quite pleases me. He has a round face and wild, unkempt hair and a mirthful mouth. And his stories amuse and fascinate me. Alexandre woos me with words and long letters professing his love. But he knows my heart. When I told him our tale, so different from the fiction the poet created in your name, Alexandre bade me—nay, challenged me—to put pen to paper and tell my own story, that the truth would be known. Perhaps I will, so that when my memory fails me, as it will almost certainly, I may gaze upon those words, and within them, you and I will live once more as we were. Star cross'd yet also young and beautiful and alive and in love. With an emotion so rapturous and pure, jinn and angel alike surely wept when we were parted.

It is late, my love, and the candle is nearly at its end. Tonight, I burn sandalwood incense in your memory. I pray its perfume wafts me to sleep that I may dream of you. And now as I do each evening, I whisper my goodbye to you: My love, may our separation be brief. May our paths join again at water's edge. May God keep you always in his care.

Ever yours,

Leila

Alexandre and I read it over and over last night, but rereading it this morning, there's still a lump in my throat. I'm sad, but it's more than that. I barged right into someone's most sacred, intimate moment and didn't even bother to ask permission. Leila's note was private—a wish, a prayer, a confession to a lover long gone. There is obviously an amazing essay in here that I'm sure would blow away the Art Institute judges, but there's a quiet whisper in my mind telling me that we haven't only been trespassing at the hôtel; we've been trespassing on someone's life, too. Is Leila's life my story to tell?

Alexandre shifts in his sleep.

I think about his family and how afraid they must be of what they might lose. How the possibility of finding a missing Delacroix carries a kind of burden for him that it doesn't for me. He's trying to save his legacy; I'm trying to build my future. And the fact of the matter is, I have more options than him, more chances. It wasn't coincidence that brought us together; it was his uncle. But somehow when he reached for the past while I grasped for the future, our hands linked and formed a circle.

I get up and stretch, then pad into the kitchen to start some coffee. The smoky, nutty smell swirls through the room, and slants of bright light fill the apartment, rousing Alexandre from his sleep.

He twitches, yawns, and pulls himself up from the sofa. "How long was I asleep? You could've woken me," he says in a gravelly morning voice and runs his fingers through his messy hair.

"A few hours. And it's okay; one of us deserved some beauty sleep."

He smiles, reaching for his phone. "I'm the only one in this room that needs it." Then he crosses the room, excusing himself to freshen up.

I realize I haven't looked in the mirror, so I quickly splash some water on my face from the kitchen sink and finger-comb my hair. I'm relying on this coffee to take away my morning breath, so I add an extra cube of sugar and whirl it around with milk and take a big gulp before Alexandre comes out.

When he reemerges, he walks to the kitchen and drapes himself across the bar. I'm distracted by his tousled bedhead that somehow makes him more attractive. But I snap out of it when he sets down his phone in front of me. "Check out this email. It's the reason I wanted to go to the Château de Monte-Cristo. My uncle Gérard—" He catches himself and pales.

I wince when he mentions his uncle—the one who hatched the whole Insta-stalker plan. I may have softened slightly toward Alexandre, but Gérard Dumas is still high on my shit list. I nod at Alexandre, giving him the silent okay to continue.

He takes a swig of his coffee. "Apparently, there's a legend that a mysterious Middle Eastern woman might've inspired the sack death in *The Count of Monte Cristo*."

"The *Giaour* sack death? Leila being thrown into the sea by the Pasha? But Byron made that up; I mean, she's alive. *Was*. The poem was a fiction. You saw her letter."

"That's exactly it." Alexandre runs his hand over his face. "Dumas would obviously have known about the Byron poem but also the truth of Leila's story. My uncle says there are stories of cryptic journal entries Dumas left when writing *Monte Cristo*—maybe about the sack death—but he's never seen the originals. Could be rumors."

I chuckle. "Oh, so I guess it's up to us meddling kids to do the grunt work to find them, right?"

Alexandre gives me this blank look. Apparently *Scooby* references don't translate, and I don't take the time to explain. "It feels like Dumas's ghost has masterminded this whole mystery, because we have the makings of a classic

Dumas novel—intrigue, family secrets, hidden treasure, duels—"

"Don't forget hope and romance." Alexandre looks at me with expectant eyes.

"Don't forget jealousy, deception, and revenge," I counter.

Alexandre sucks in his breath. "I could never forget. But Dumas also wrote about the strength of friendship and finding a way to carry on after everything feels lost."

I put a hand on his arm, directing our attentions back to his phone. "What exactly am I looking at?"

"My uncle has a letter to the lady of the raven tresses. A copy, anyway."

"What!" I yell. "And he's been sitting on it? I thought he was the one who orchestrated this whole thing." I wave my hand in the space between us. "Unpaid labor to find the missing treasure that's going to benefit your family that he couldn't find himself. Now you tell me he's been holding out?"

"Uncle Gérard didn't even remember it until I told him about the letters we found and how Baudelaire's name came up in one of the *Revue* articles."

"And?" I cross my arms and raise my eyebrows.

"Dumas died at his son's house in 1870. Supposedly, there was a copy of Baudelaire's poems, *Paris Spleen*, by his deathbed. It was packed away with his things, and decades later, some archivist found a letter tucked between the pages. The letter is at the Bibliothèque Nationale. The book is at the Château."

"Unbelievable. It's literally filed away in the archives here in Paris? And he never gave the letter a second thought. No one was curious about the woman? Until now, I guess, when she could be worth money." I shake my head. This is how stories are lost.

"You have to understand that there are literally thousands of letters and journal entries and unfinished stories and essays, unpublished novels. I guess he disregarded it because Dumas had dozens of known affairs—"

"Oh. Of course. How could he possibly have thought it was important—it was just a note to some insignificant woman, right? Another notch in Dumas's belt."

"I'm sorry. The men in my family, well, I guess we haven't exactly been chivalrous or easy to forgive." Alexandre bites his lip. "Maybe we don't deserve it."

"What's in the letter?" I demand.

June 15, 1870

Chère Madame aux cheveux raven,

By now, perhaps, you are long gone, reunited at last, I hope, with the one love that lay claim to your heart when you were young.

I am old now and near my own end. Time and fate, as is their wont, have proven recalcitrant. I am resigned; there is always an end to every story, and so, soon, there shall be one to mine. And it is thus, in the reminiscences of an old man, that I find my mind returning to you again and again. To the time you were known to me. To those brief years you graced my life. To the stories you told and entrusted me with.

Fear not, fickle and inconstant though I may have been, too easily swayed by the fairer sex, it is certain, but as to my word to you, I have remained true. I have sheltered your secrets and the treasures of your heart. How I longed to share your words with the world to rectify what your poet misrepresented, but neither he nor the world were ready for your truth, nor did I have your permission, and so I curbed my temptation that it would heel to your desire—that your story and your secret be concealed. Though I believed your fantastical tale should find its place amongst the great love stories of our time, of all time, I tried desperately to understand that in a life with little privacy and little freedom, you longed for this to be yours. Did the writing of it grant you some peace at last? Were the words on the page a balm for your heart? If, as your letter, now surely turned to ash, was to be believed, and neither I nor the world have reason to consider your word to be less than truthful, then I am content that, having writ the words on the page, you at last knew the freedom—the agency—you longed for, dare I say, lived for. But who amongst us knows what the future may hold? Whose lives and tales will be remembered and whose lost?

These are questions that trouble the mind of this old man, long past his vigor but still keen in spirit. These thirty years have I wondered what happened to you. I have been tormented that in some final desperation you may have died by your own hand. At first, I feared this, leaving me as you did, abruptly without proper goodbye, and yet, guardian of these last vestiges of your beloved. Were we not friends, at least, in the end? Did I not deserve a final glance at your beauty? Was our ardor not worth a kiss at the close? I searched for you and searched in vain. Had our friend Delacroix not stayed my hand, I might be searching for you still, would my health allow it. Our dear, loyal friend produced a likeness of you for me. I confess, I needed it not—though my memory fades, your raven hair, your piercing eyes, your lips the color of damask rose are preserved in the amber of my mind. Have I myself not written that the body's sight can sometimes forget, but the soul remembers forever?

All my treasures now have I laid to rest, hidden from the world's eyes, perhaps never to be found, where my love is ever-green and Paradise blooms eternally for you, my beautiful spirit. That should please you, does it not?

How my own words, now connected forever to you, come back to me again and again, as I have thought of you and what you searched for and the gift you left me: happiness is like the enchanted palaces we read of in our childhood, where fierce, fiery dragons defend the entrance and approach.

It was Delacroix, too, who reminded me of what I am as I sat brooding at the loss of you—neither the mirth nor the ego—but rather, simply, that I am a storyteller. So, my dear, I choose to imagine you in a life content and quiet. Far from the remind-ers of the past at long last, breathing deeply. How often did you speak of a life by the sea—closer to your own beloved—where you saw him fall, so would you now go that he may rise and rise with you. I see you there, on water's edge, the soft sound of the waves upon the shore, as the poet captured so perfectly, "a heart whose love is innocent."

Imagining you in this place, your monsters at last slain, I must confess, pleases me. For what in the end are we but stories?

Ever yours,

Alexandre looks up from his phone and whispers, "Khayyam. What's wrong? You look like you've seen a ghost." He reaches across the bar toward me, but I pull away.

I rub my tired eyes. "I don't . . . It's . . . private and sad. No one gets a happily ever after in this story, do they? It's what Dumas said, it's all turned to ash."

"But it hasn't." Alexandre shakes his head. "Don't you see? Here we are, talking about them, reading their words. Breathing life into their stories. They live through us."

I understand what Alexandre is saying, feel it, even, because the proof that the past lives through us is standing right in front of me.

He continues, the strength of his convictions rising. "If we can find the painting and save Dumas's home and legacy, we can help the story live forever. That's why we have to go to the Château de Monte-Cristo. My uncle thinks if the treasure—the painting—still exists, it could be hidden there."

"We can't," I say, almost catching myself by surprise.

Alexandre furrows his brow. "What do you mean? Don't you see? You were right all along. There *is* a missing Delacroix."

I step farther into the kitchen, away from Alexandre, and shake my head. Anger courses through me—I'm ready to explode and I can't figure out why. I choose my next words carefully, cautiously. "We can't go to the Château—"

"We have to go," Alexandre insists. I can tell he's trying not to yell. "It's not even a question. Do you have any idea what this could mean? For both of us? Finding that painting—"

I lash out with words that mean to cut him: "It means you'll use Leila like everyone else did. If there is a Delacroix, your family will sell it for millions more than what you owe in back taxes and get rich off it. Off *her*."

Alexandre scowls. "And what about you? It's not like you decided to pursue this purely because of your love for art history. You want to use this story—*my* family's story—to win some stupid contest, hoping it will gain you entrance to your dream university."

Ugh. Gut punch. I realize that by not taking Leila's story public, I might destroy my only chance for academic redemption. Maybe that's why Alexandre's words hurt so much—because they're the truth.

I take a deep breath. Then another. And struggle to calm my voice. "Don't you see? It's not about the essay for me. Not anymore. Somewhere along this wild journey, a part of me changed because of Leila. The treasure is her story. And maybe it needs to stay buried. Maybe that's what Leila wanted for herself."

"What are you talking about?" Alexandre seems totally confused. And I admit, I'm a little confused myself. I can't decipher what I truly want. Or what's right.

I sigh and rub my face. "I'm saying you're right. We're both invested in this treasure hunt. We both have things to lose. But please take a step back and think about it. Say the treasure is the painting, and that's part of your family's story. I know why you need to tell it. But you don't get to own Leila's story, too. To me, that's the real treasure. And she didn't want it told. Dumas says as much in that letter. Whatever story she might have given Dumas, whatever he might have hidden, it's *personal*. It's none of our business. Even Dumas wouldn't break her trust. Do you think it's right for us to dredge up the past they both kept silent about?"

"This is absurd. The stories are connected. Delacroix. Dumas. Leila. Byron. Us." Alexandre turns his back to me. I guess my attempt at reasoning with him isn't working. "Have you forgotten the note Dumas left for his son? 'Look for the woman, find the treasure'?" He spins back around to face me, his shoulders tense. "Dumas wanted his son to find it. He knew it was important to our family. It's not just a story. It's our legacy." He throws his hands up and shouts, "It could be a missing Delacroix!"

I don't yell back at Alexandre. Strangely, as his anger rises, I feel calmer, more assured. "Maybe you have the right to the Delacroix. But your family has no claim on Leila's story. Everything was taken from her. Don't you get that? She can't just be a means to an end."

Alexandre steps closer to me, his eyes softening. "I understand what it means to lose something important. I know how much Leila's story means to you. That's even more reason why we have to be the ones who find it—then you can control Leila's story."

I let out an ironic laugh. If I've learned anything this summer, it's that if you believe you can control the story, you're only fooling yourself.

"What's funny?" Alexandre asks.

I shake my head. "Not a single thing. There is no one left to defend Leila. No one except me. And I can't let her down. It would be a betrayal."

"And so what? My family should lose everything—our legacy, our future—because you don't want to share a story that doesn't belong to you? It never belonged to you. Your essay—that's *my* family's story you were writing about. You want to protect a dead woman. I'm trying to save my actual, living family."

I clench my fists. "And Leila was nothing? Is that it? A forgotten footnote in the history of the mighty Dumas family?" I seethe. "You're as bad as your uncle. Worse."

Alexandre blanches. He opens his mouth, then snaps it shut and stares at the ground. Finally he looks back up at me. "I'm taking the next train to the Château." He doesn't yell. He speaks matter-of-factly, his voice dry as sawdust. "Come with me or not. If there is a clue to finding the Delacroix—maybe even the painting itself—I am going to find it. I'm going to discover the end of this story. The world has to know." He pauses. "*I* have to know."

"And it won't hurt if you get rich off the painting, if you find it," I spit.

"I only want to save the Château and Dumas's legacy. I'm not expecting to get rich off it. Of course, being an American, you think everything comes down to money."

"And I guess being a man, you think you can steal a woman's story and make it your own." The words roll off my tongue, filling up the empty, shocked space between us. If I'd had any inkling that stepping in a pile of dog crap was going to lead to this shit show, I would've stayed in the apartment this entire trip.

Alexandre grabs his book and tosses it into his backpack, anger and confusion in his eyes. He stops halfway to the door, and his shoulders relax. It seems like he's going to turn to me and say something. But he doesn't. He walks out without looking back.

Leila

⊶⊷

There is a great scurrying about on the ship, but the action moves around me in muffled silence. My rose in hand, I stand at the rail watching my homeland slip away, my eyes focused far in the distance at the blood-soaked earth where my Giaour fell. The dark sky above his body gives way to a halo of light that softens the gritty air.

"What is that?" The poet walks up behind me. His voice incredulous, eyes filled with wonder and despair on my behalf.

I raise the rose to my lips and breathe it in. "It is the last promise of love."

"Perhaps you are the poet."

"I am no poet. I am nothing but an orphan and a concubine."

The poet clasps my arms and turns me to him. "You are all that is beautiful of this night sky—the brightness of the stars, the deep stillness of the dark. And all that's best of those meet in your aspect and your eyes.

"My God, what your eyes have seen. What they have shown me. I hope you may find it in your heart to explain to me what I witnessed, though I fear it lies beyond words."

I smile at him, but there is no promise in it. For what could he understand of this? Of what I have witnessed? As all men, he sees truth as his own creation, a clay figure he can bend to his will.

"I'll leave you to your remembrance." He takes two steps away from me but turns back, touching my shoulder. "Though your heart may be broken, yet brokenly can you live on. And the privilege of being a poet is the ability to make beautiful that which the world has distorted."

I don't turn when he walks away. I don't mock his lyrical, naïve words. What he does not see, what he cannot see, is that the only privilege, the only freedom in my life, was the secret I kept in my heart. The secret that lies bleeding on the sands of my home as I drift away to another world.

KHAYYAM

Lying in my bed, I watch the bright stars fade into the liquid rose gold of dawn. I spent the night staring at my cracked ceiling, pondering the million tiny white veins and arteries in the centuries-old plaster that no one has bothered to cover up. A crisscrossed tangle of paths that lead nowhere. The birds are singing, but after hours of no sleep, their joy feels like an affront. Their symphony, a cacophony. But the truth is, they don't know I exist. They only sing for themselves.

I grab my phone off the nightstand. Julie hasn't responded to my earlier email; she's still cloistered with no Internet. No texts from Alexandre, either. No surprise there, but my hope deflates. Maybe I should apologize for some things I said yesterday, but so should he. I'm exhausted—tired of doing the wrong thing, stumbling over obstacles I've laid in my own way, believing in people who take me for granted. Lather. Rinse. Repeat. My path is a circle with no way forward, and every well-worn step is a little soul crushing.

That line Leila wrote keeps haunting me: *The heart is the singular miracle God gave to each of us—an organ that heals itself.* I wonder what *she* would say about my predicament—two guys I can't seem to communicate with, two countries that don't always feel like home, and an uncertain future I can't seem to control. I chuckle out loud at the irony. She actually might have good advice. A Muslim woman alone finding her way in the Paris of the 1840s. Brokenhearted, but not broken. Knowing that fate dealt her a crappy hand, but not ready to fold, fighting every day to survive.

Leila wrote the Giaour a letter knowing he would never receive it. She wrote a letter to find her truth. To find some answers for herself.

Without thinking too much about it, I open a blank email.

To: Leila @ ???

_____

From: Khayyam Maquet

_____

Subject: What would you do?

_____

Dear Leila,

I don't believe much in fate, but I've been feeling all along like I was the one meant to find you. That maybe your words were meant for me to unearth over 150 years after you wrote them.

You couldn't have known that your story would reach through time to speak to me. And maybe I'm not the only one they're supposed to speak to? Did you want your story untold because while you were alive it was too much to bear—the loss, the scrutiny it would bring, the notoriety? Were you afraid? My first instinct was to find you, then defend you, to fight for what you wanted—for your secret to be kept.

I could be wrong. Perhaps after all these years, the world needs your story. You couldn't—wouldn't—share it in your time, but maybe I'm meant to share your words in mine. Isn't that how history works? Isn't that how we learn? This is one thing women can do for one another—amplify the voices of our sisters that were silenced because the world told them their stories didn't matter. Maybe it's my job to make some space on the shelves for your story, Leila, because you deserve to be the protagonist in your own life. Every girl deserves to be. If you'd lived in a different time, you could have made a different choice because you would have had more fates to choose from, because you would have had a choice at all.

Maybe you never imagined that your life could change the world, but it's already changed mine. Thank you for the gift of your story.

Love,
Khayyam

I stare at my screen and save the letter in my drafts. Men tried to make Leila's story their own for her entire life. I won't let them own her legacy, too. Dammit. I have to go to the Château.

IT WAS ALMOST too easy to get here. It should've been an epic journey—a quest where I battled beasts or villains to find a treasure. But it was a train ride. A swipe of an RER ticket. Maybe I didn't need to fight monsters to get here, I only needed to fight myself to come face-to-face with the tall, wrought-iron gates of the Château de Monte-Cristo.

They're locked.

A sign reads: FERMÉ LUNDI. Closed Mondays.

This isn't dramatic as much as totally absentminded on my part—a lot of French museums are closed on Mondays. Should've googled it.

Sigh.

I take out my phone and text Alexandre: I'm outside the gates. He'll understand. Of course he will. Since he's a member of the *there are no rules, only suggestions* school of life, I'm sure he figured out some way to charm or parkour his way into the museum.

A moment later, he's ambling down the wide gravel path, a white hoodie pulled up over his head, slightly obscuring his expression.

"Did you break in here, too?" I ask, trying to cut the tension with the kind of small talk perfected by dads the world over. Wow. I'm only one step removed from the classic Chicago conversation starters: *How 'bout them Cubs (or, Sox, depending on the neighborhood)?* Or, *can you believe this weather?*

"No." Alexandre tries to muster a smile as he approaches the iron bars. "My family can come and go as we please. It's in the charter agreement with the Foundation."

"Of course it is." I manage a small smile in return.

He steps closer, grasping one of the poles separating us. "I'm sorry for the horrible things I said yesterday. I was only thinking about my family—and this place," he says, gesturing to the grounds behind him. "I didn't consider your feelings. Didn't want to acknowledge that you were right to question what we're doing."

I step closer to the gate and wrap my hands on the bars right below his. I'm still on the outside, but I want him to let me in. "I get it. I do feel protective of Leila, but I guess I also feel protective of me. Honestly, I'm not sure how to trust you."

Alexandre recoils when I say this. I don't want to hurt him, but I can't hide the truth anymore, and I can't pretend his deception didn't matter. He casts his eyes downward.

I take a quick breath and continue. "It's hard to know what the right thing to do is. Leila didn't want her story to be told, but if we find the painting—if it is her—we can't keep her hidden. Her whole life was about being hurt and used and discarded. I don't want that to happen to her again."

Alexandre moves his fingers down so they almost touch mine. "We won't let that happen," he says softly. "I know asking you to trust me—to forgive me—might be too much. But I promise I'm not going to lie to you again. If there is a Delacroix that we can sell to save this place, I want to find it. But if the only treasure is Leila's story, like you say, then I want to find that, too. Her story is enough."

We stare at each other through the gate, exchanging small, stiff grins like strangers forced to share a small space that each of them wants for themselves. But it's a start. A modification. A do-over.

I clear my throat and step back. "Are you going to let me in? Or do I have to pole-vault over the gate?"

Alexandre shakes his head. "Sorry. One minute." He disappears behind the high stone wall that borders the property and reemerges on the street, walking toward me. *This way,* he gestures. I walk up to him, and we give each other the required, slightly detached bise. We're silent. Waiting. Anticipating the other. Trying to figure out if there is anything else to say.

We hurry to an olive-green, splintered wooden door carved into the stone wall. Boughs from the small grove inside the wall partially obscure the door from the street; I probably wouldn't have noticed it if I'd casually passed by. Alexandre pushes it open, and we emerge in a green wood, the fresh smell of moss and dirt infusing the air. We take a narrow path, Alexandre in the lead. I imagine Dumas walking through here. Perhaps with Leila? It's quiet in Dumas's park—lush and romantic—and if I wrote love stories, this is exactly where I would want to write them.

Alexandre breaks the silence, the back of his hand brushing against mine. I'm not sure if it's an accident or on purpose. "Dumas had this built by a pretty famous architect in 1846. It was supposed to be his dream home. He called it the Château de Monte-Cristo, because the money he made from that book paid for this place. He also had a separate smaller place built, beyond the main home. The Château d'If—named for the island fortress Dantès was imprisoned in. It's actually a real place on a small island off Marseille."

I know all this information, but I don't tell him because his voice lifts as he's talking—as he's sharing a part of his family's story.

Instead, I chuckle. "He named his writing studio after a prison? Ouch. That's a rough metaphor."

Alexandre turns to me and smiles. I almost reach out to squeeze his hand but stop myself.

From the woods, we arrive onto a verdant, gently sloping lawn. Gobsmacked is the only word that comes to mind. I walk ahead, passing Alexandre until I reach the gravel path finally facing Dumas's Château de Monte-Cristo. It's not massive, basically a three-story house with two round-domed turrets. But it is stunning. The honey-colored stone façade is detailed with intricate carvings—flowers, angels, musical instruments, mythical beasts, a crest.

Alexandre appears at my elbow. "Is that Dumas?" I ask, pointing to a large medallion above the door. "Would he have his own face sculpted on his home?" Then I notice the windows in the domes. "And the grill over the windows, those are his initials?"

Alexandre nods. "He also had his personal motto engraved up there by the family crest: *I love those who love me*. And yes, that's him in stone in that medallion. But he also has Shakespeare, Dante, Homer, Virgil . . ." He points to each carved face as he says their names.

"Got it. Basically, he loved attention and had no modesty about his talents. And, apparently, you have a family crest?" I side-eye Alexandre. He grins and shrugs. The tension between us slowly starts to drain away. It might be because of our familiarity with each other, but also because we're both here, searching, hoping to save something or someone, maybe ourselves.

"He was supposed to have had a huge ego, but more power to him," he says. "He was a biracial man who faced terrible racism but still became one of France's greatest writers."

"Seeing this place, I understand why it's important to you and your family." I take a hesitant step closer to Alexandre. "Obviously it was pretty significant to Dumas—he literally stamped his identity all over it."

Alexandre nods and squeezes my elbow. "Everybody thinks of him as wildly successful, but Dumas grew up poor and had to fight for what he had. He faced a ton of discrimination. I think that's why he built this place and put his name everywhere. It wasn't ego. It was a way to look his detractors in the eye and say, 'I did this.'"

"Good for him." I allow myself a smile; I'm all for giving judges the metaphorical middle finger. "I'm glad you're here to help keep this place in your family and keep his story alive."

"That's why Leila's story deserves to be told, too. Not because of who she was to Dumas, but because of who she was. Period. I learned that from you," Alexandre says.

"Glad you were paying attention." I nudge him in the ribs. My heart lifts at hearing his words, but I'm still nervous about uncovering a secret that has been hidden all those years. A secret that doesn't belong to me.

Alexandre takes hold of my elbow. "Let's try to find this cache of Leila's treasures that my beloved great-grand-père supposedly hid here. I promise if we find anything, we will decide our next steps together."

I smile. "In that case, let's find out what your great-grand-père was hiding."

ALEXANDRE WALKS AROUND turning on the lights and opening drapes as if he's entered his family's summer home for the season. I take a minute to admire the craftsmanship of the Château as the crystal in the chandeliers twinkles in the sunlight that streams into the front parlor. It's a museum now, but I imagine how alive it must have once been, and as I float from one room to the next, I can hear the echoes of the past whispering to me.

While I'm leaning over a glass case examining some letters and first editions, I see it: Baudelaire's *Paris Spleen*, the one Alexandre's Uncle Gérard said was at Dumas's bedside when he died, where the note to Leila was found. The book is open to a passage: *"There are women who inspire you with the desire to conquer them and to take your pleasure with them; but this one fills you only with the desire to die slowly beneath her gaze."* The last phrase is circled multiple times.

It's hard to see Baudelaire's writing as anything but sexist and possessive and he was probably not thinking about Leila when he wrote that. But Dumas must've imagined Leila when he circled those words; maybe that's why he slipped that letter to her between these pages. The spirits of the past are all around us. I might not believe in actual ghosts, but sometimes the present feels like a palimpsest, and we're all just here trying to decipher words we can't quite make out.

ALEXANDRE GRABS THE top hat off the head of a mannequin suited in period costume and bows before me, sweeping his arm across his body and doffing the hat.

"Put that back," I whisper, though there is no one in here but us. "We've damaged enough French antiques."

"It's a replica," he says. "A lot of this stuff is. The Foundation managed to save the building—it was in total disrepair when they bought it—but most of the antiques and our family heirlooms were already long gone."

"Sorry," I say as my mind wanders back to the porcelain teapot that Zaid accidently broke. It had no real value except that every time I looked at it, I remembered Grand-mère serving me tea with madeleines or almond biscuits. I remembered her laugh, and in that way, the teapot was priceless.

Alexandre shrugs. "This place was almost razed to build apartment buildings a couple decades ago—that's why I'm desperate to save it now. It's survived all these years. I refuse to let some greedy American real estate developer turn a French national treasure into a resort."

"Too bad Dumas wasn't as good with money as he was with words."

Alexandre winces. "Story of my family. Dumas had to sell this estate for a fraction of its value only a few years after building it because he squandered all his money on his entourage and parties and building this property. Then he had to flee to Belgium to escape his debtors."

"That sucks." I shake my head.

Alexandre gives me a sad smile. "He eventually came back to France—his children and some friends saved him. Dumas was a genius, but not one who thought about the future. It kind of runs in the family." He shrinks back like saying the words hurts.

The irony is not lost on me. Alexandre doesn't talk a lot about his dad—another Alexandre Dumas—but it's clear that he hasn't exactly been smart about money or salvaging the family legacy. And here's history repeating itself again—another son of a Dumas stepping in, trying to save his family.

"Looks like Dumas had more hangers-on than actual friends," I say. "All those people passing through his life, but Leila was the one on his mind when he was dying even though he hadn't seen her in decades . . ." There are so many empty promises and unhappy endings in this story. I hope I can change that.

Alexandre gives me this wistful look and guides me into the hall. "Follow me. There's a room I want to show you."

WE TIPTOE INTO an intimate room with brightly colored stained glass. I look up at him, my mouth open in surprise.

"I know," he says. "They call this le salon mauresque."

"The Moorish salon? Uh, yeah, no kidding. It's an Orientalist's dream."

The ivory walls are decorated with stucco sculptures and arabesque designs—leaves and vines and geometric patterns—the kinds of motifs you might see in a mosque. The entire ceiling is sculpted in an intricate, intertwining design—rectangular shapes that somehow fan out into a flower. A brass lamp with panels of red, blue, yellow, purple, and green glass bathes the room in a soft glow. Divans covered with tufted ivory-and-red-brocade cushions are tucked into each corner. Even the now-boarded-up fireplace is decorated in gold, replicating the patterns on the walls and ceiling.

"All the work was done by Tunisian artists that Dumas commissioned on his travels and then shipped over. It's in much better shape than the rest of the château because the King of Morocco paid for the restoration of this room, like, forty years ago."

"Wow. No wonder this place bankrupted him." I take a look around the room. "Do you think he made it for her? For Leila?" I gesture to the corners. "Did you notice that each of the little divans has just enough space for two?"

"L'art de la seduction et de l'amour." Alexandre raises his eyebrows at me.

"Do you need that hushed tone and glint in your eye when you say that? Because those divans probably haven't seen any action in a hundred years, and that streak is not going to be broken tonight."

Alexandre laughs, and his shoulders shake a little. It echoes through this empty house, which once was probably full of laughter like his. I imagine the great artists and writers and theater people who must've danced through these rooms and what secrets were shared amidst the whispers and wine. I wonder if Leila was one of those guests at the grand housewarming party—we did find an invitation in her box of mementos. How did she feel walking into this room, one perhaps made for her? Did it feel too close to the gilded cage she had escaped? Did it remind her of her beloved dying before her eyes? I wonder if it made her heart ache for home. Too many questions without easy answers. And no real way to find them.

"What are you thinking about?" Alexandre's voice in my ear catches me by surprise. He's standing right next to me, and I can feel his breath against my neck. I shiver. "Are you cold?" he whispers.

I turn to face him, looking up into his warm eyes. He brushes a strand of hair away from my cheek. My skin warms at his touch. I suck in my breath. "Um . . . have they updated the plumbing since Dumas lived here?" Wow. Smooth. Who *doesn't* bring up indoor plumbing to avoid potentially romantic but anxiety-inducing moments?

Alexandre scrunches up his eyebrows. "Um, yeah. This place was actually a school for a while in the 1950s and '60s. There've been a number of renovations. Do you need to—"

"Oh no. I was checking because I wanted to be mentally prepared in case we were going to have to outhouse it." God, I'm a dork.

Alexandre laughs. "It is a museum now, and I think you'll find French plumbing standards have greatly improved since the 1800s."

My neck and face are so warm, I'm probably covered in red splotches right now. I walk toward a divan and pretend I'm intensely interested in the velvet cushions.

"I thought I would find the cache or some clues in here. It seemed an obvious place to start."

"But?" I ask.

"There's nothing. At least, not that I could find. There are no drawers or closets."

I scan the room. Alexandre's right. There aren't a lot of hiding places, but we're here, so might as well take another look. The carvings on the wall are attached, and I don't think we could look behind any of them without dismantling the place, which obviously we are not doing because, well . . . priceless heritage, cultural preservation, etc.

I gaze at Alexandre, who's standing with his elbow on the mantle of the small black marble fireplace. I tap my lips, then walk over and crouch down in front of the panel that seals the opening. Alexandre bends down next to me.

Running my hands around the top edge, I feel a draft. "It's not sealed. Do you think you can lift out this panel? It's not marble. Seems like wood painted to match the rest of the fireplace."

Alexandre knocks on it—there's clearly a hollow behind the wood—then he places his fingers next to mine at the top of the panel. The sides of our hands touch as he tucks his fingers under the edge.

He smiles. "Latches."

I take a closer look and see that two small metal hooks attach the wood frame to the lip under the opening of the fireplace. Alexandre inches closer to me, our bodies almost touching. My pulse quickens. "Help me," he says. Yeah, my thoughts exactly.

He carefully unhooks one latch, then the other. I place my hands on the wood panel so it doesn't fall forward. Alexandre feels around the edges and undoes two more latches. His hands meet mine in the center of the panel, and we ease it down, letting it tilt toward us. A cloud of black dust puffs out at us. We both cough. I close my eyes and wipe my face on my sleeve. When we finally ease the panel to the ground, our sooty faces look like pictures of coal miners from the early twentieth century. We seem to have taken the brunt of the dust, but there are still swirls of gray on the marble tiles around us.

Alexandre and I look at each other and burst out laughing. We look ridiculous. Soon, we're howling, my sides ache, and tears run down my dusty face. Alexandre reaches over and wipes my cheek with the cuffs of his once perfectly white hoodie. They come away streaked in even more dust, which makes me laugh harder. It's absurd, but I needed this moment. *We* needed it. Most importantly, we haven't broken any French antiques, but there is going to be some cleanup. Alexandre takes a tissue out of his pocket, wets it with his water bottle, and wipes the dust off my eyes, then my cheeks, then moves to my lips.

He leans in ever so slightly. I suck in my breath and pull away from him. I can't let myself get distracted again. Not now, when the truth feels so close. We look into each other's eyes, but neither of us says anything.

I brush off my clothes. "I should try and rinse off some of this dust."

Alexandre nods and leads me to a bathroom. Quiet the whole way.

Alexandre washes up first, then leaves me alone to go search for cleaning supplies. I rinse my face and hands. There's even soot inside my ears. I take off my clothes and do my best to shake out all the dust before putting them back on. I run my fingers through my hair and tie it up in a ponytail, then find a lip gloss at the bottom of my bag and swipe it across my lips. When I'm presentable again, I walk back to the salon, realizing that we've been utterly dumb. Alexandre has already replaced the panel and is cleaning up the dust with some hand towels and a small spray bottle. He looks up as I enter the room. He opens his mouth to speak, but I beat him to it.

"It makes no sense that we did this, does it?"

He shakes his head. "No. It's like I didn't even listen to

myself when I was telling you the King of Morocco recently refurbished this room. That's probably when they boarded up the fireplace."

"All this soot and excitement for nothing." I sigh.

Alexandre walks over to me, grinning, but he keeps a bit of distance between us. "Let's finish cleaning up and eat something. I brought some food with me. There's another place I'm dying for you to see. If my grand-père Dumas said he hid something, then I believe him, and I feel like he's trusting me to find it."

Leila

❧ ⚬ ❧

The rose-red thread of dawn appears on the horizon. Each wave carries me farther from my Giaour. This is to be our fate, then. One written for us without our consent. Our future, stolen.

Destiny is cruel. That it should so long favor Pasha, yet allow my love and me merely a fragile hope of freedom, only to rip it from us so violently . . . how will I ever know peace in this lifetime? I can only think that this world was not meant for us. For our story on this earth has ended.

Old lessons come to mind. And the painfully true words of the Persian poet: The moving finger writes, and having writ moves on.

I may curse fate, but fate neither hears me nor cares.

I whisper my final goodbye to my land and my heart: My love, may our separation be brief. May our paths join again at water's edge. May God keep you always in His care.

KHAYYAM

After a quick picnic lunch of baguette, cheese, and fruit in a lovely sunken garden right below the Château, where we sat on the edge of a defunct fountain, Alexandre and I walk through the property. The air is fresh and clean, and with these beautiful old trees and gently rolling hills, it's easy to see why Dumas chose this place as his escape.

Alexandre seems surprisingly nonchalant for someone who is about to dig up old family secrets and bring them into the light. It reminds me that even though I've spent all this time with him the last couple weeks, there's still a lot we don't know about each other. His manipulative uncle pushed us together, but we do share a common interest and more than that, too. We also have an idea of what we hope to find, but we have no idea what we actually *will* find and what the implications could be. I'm anxious, and I'm not even related to Dumas—I can't imagine how I would feel if the roles were reversed.

But then again, if there ever were any family treasures—at least on my mom's side in India—they were probably destroyed during Partition, when over a million people were killed and thousands of homes wrecked in the violent upheaval. Thanks to arbitrary borders devised by a cowardly British bureaucrat, entire family histories and personal identities went up in smoke. I can't imagine what it must have been like. Overnight, you're not Indian anymore; you're Pakistani. You're split apart from family and friends. Torn from your home, forced to leave a part of yourself behind with nothing to hold on to but fading memories.

My mind wanders from my nani to Leila. Maybe what saves them is us—the people who are alive to hear the stories and pass them on. To give them weight and power in the retelling. In the not forgetting. That's why we need to find Leila's story and tell the world, so that she can live again. She was probably never going to have a happily ever after, but maybe there's a way to give her a better ending than the one she got. Dumas was right to tell his son to find the treasure; we have to preserve our families' stories, because history is all we are.

"Just up the hill." Alexandre's voice pulls me out of my meditation. As we scamper up a small incline, my phone dings once, alerting me to a text. Then twice more. I yank the phone out of my pocket and see Zaid's number flash across my screen. I draw the phone to my chest. Alexandre scrunches up his eyebrows at me in a question. I raise a finger. He steps away and turns his back to me, pretending to be inordinately interested in the foliage on a nearby shrub.

I take a breath and turn to my phone.

Zaid: I'm sorry.
Zaid: You were right. We can't bury the past.
Zaid: I love you. I hope you find what you're looking for.

I walk over to a small stone bench set into an alcove of small bushes. Tears sting my eyes. I try to focus on my breaths, making them slow and deliberate. I've been waiting forever to hear those words from Zaid. To believe that I meant more to him than the awfulness of the past few weeks. That I had a place in his heart. And these texts break me a little. I know it's not him being jealous or his FOMO. It's the end. It's the goodbye. He's leaving me with a piece of himself that he could never give me when we were together.

I allow myself a moment. Consider whether I should text back. But I feel too raw to respond now. And truly, what else is there to say?

I stand up, slipping the phone into my back pocket. I leave a piece of my heart on that bench and take a step forward.

Alexandre meets me in the middle of the path. "You okay?"

I nod my head yes. Then shake it no.

Endings are hard. Even when you see them coming. Closed doors you sometimes have to seal forever with a small part of your heart inside. A part you can never give to anyone else. Love doesn't come with a warning label. Not like anyone would listen, anyway.

I guess human beings are mostly optimists, otherwise we'd always be alone.

I wish Zaid and I could have had a proper goodbye. Something more than a text. Something more tangible. But one thing Leila has taught me is that we don't always get the ending we want. Or deserve.

ALEXANDRE AND I walk in silence until we reach the crest of a small hill. I stop and gasp when I see the building in front of me. It's even more a jewel box confection than its mate.

"Voilà, le Château d'If," Alexandre announces.

A tiny pink neo-Gothic castle—it's like a child's palace brought to life. It has its own moat and is set into tall trees surrounded by shrubs. We walk across the narrow stone bridge to get to the door of Dumas's rose-pink stucco study. Facing the building, there's a single turret to the left and a small stone balcony on the second floor. Floral and geometric stone carvings cover the façade, and the eaves are decorated with brown wood cut in curves like the edges of lace. I hurry toward the steps but stop short. Nestled into the side of the stairs is a little alcove for a dog and his house. A sculpted dog keeps watch over the Château d'If. He's gnawing on a bone. This might be the most utterly delightful detail of this whole place.

"He's the guard dog." Alexandre chuckles, then points to the study. "Check out the façade. Dumas had the names of his novels and some of his favorite characters carved in stone."

I read out loud from the stone placards that surround the main door. "*The Count of Monte Cristo, The Corsican Brothers, The Castle Eppstein, Jacques Ortis . . .*" I start counting the titles. At eighty my gaze halts on a figure carved into the side. "Hold on. Is that—"

Alexandre nods. "Yup. Dantès. The character that inspired this whole place."

"Enchantée, Comte," I say, offering a tiny curtsy. I turn to face Alexandre. "Don't take this the wrong way, but I can see why that developer wants to make this estate into a resort—he'd make a killing."

Alexandre sighs. "For now, it's for your eyes only," he says, giving me a slight bow and then gesturing toward the door.

"What? Are you serious?"

"It's not open to the public because it needs renovation, but—"

"You have the Dumas all-access pass. But is it, like, structurally sound?"

"We'll find out if the roof caves in over our heads," Alexandre smirks. When I open my eyes wide at him, he adds, "It's fine, mostly superficial damage. I actually took an evening train yesterday and slept here last night."

Alexandre walks up to the door and opens it, ushering me in. I step through and am kind of . . . underwhelmed. Compared to the main Château, it's spare and feels sort of crooked, like it's leaning. Clearly all the expense was on the outside. Maybe it makes sense since this was his private study where he would retreat to write. It's a solitary place.

The main room is empty except for a nondescript wooden desk pushed up against the window. A dark brown, worn wooden chair with a curved back and arms sits askew to the desk, a hole in its wicker seat.

"Is that his real desk?" I ask, trying not to sound disappointed.

"No. They say it belonged to his son, Alexandre Dumas, fils. Dumas sold off a lot of his furniture when he went bankrupt." I think Alexandre senses my disillusionment. "It's kind of sad, I guess. But this place was his sanctuary from what I understand were the never-ending parties at the Château and his needy entourage. And isn't the light in this little room amazing?"

My cheeks flush with embarrassment. Like, who am I to judge the writing retreat of Alexandre Dumas? And when my Alexandre points to the soft light streaming into the room from the windows facing one another, I can picture the older, barrel-chested Dumas leaning over the desk scribbling, a ray of sun splashing across the page. If I were writing some of the

French language's greatest adventures, I guess this is how I'd like to write them, too. Surrounded by quiet, a fire roaring in the blue-tiled fireplace of my tiny castle, looking out into my garden and the woods beyond.

"Most of the house is empty—it's passed through so many hands, anything of value was stripped or shoved into storage and forgotten somewhere. When the property was a school, this building was faculty housing," Alexandre explains.

When Alexandre mentions teachers, my parents pop into my mind. I haven't been thinking about them much because it was easier not to, but they return tomorrow. How am I going to explain all of this to them? Apparently, without thinking, I've adopted Julie's life motto: *Ask forgiveness, not permission.* She's going to be mad she missed the live play-by-play. Who knows, my parents are nerdy academics, and they might even be sorry they weren't able to join me in these dusty old rooms. But they'll probably also be angry that I didn't tell them what I was doing. I know I'm going to have to tell the truth—share the secrets I've been hiding—at some point, but for now I nudge them out of my mind. No time to catastrophize about the future right now. I need to focus on where I am.

Alexandre steps into the kitchen and starts riffling through his backpack, while I take a few minutes to walk back through the main floor of the study, hoping that there's a hidden panel here, too. A vault, maybe. A loose floorboard. I tap along the walls and look behind some of the unremarkable paintings that decorate the entry. I step carefully on the wooden floors, listening for any telltale creaks, which is ridiculous, because every floorboard here groans under my weight.

I carefully tread up the lopsided staircase. On the second floor, I'm greeted by a few plain, sunlit rooms. One has a made-up mattress on the floor. This must be where Alexandre slept last night. There's a rectangular oil painting of a stone grotto on the wall. I recognize the spot from our walk on the property. It's not particularly remarkable, but it piques my curiosity.

"Who is this painting by?" I call down.

Alexandre doesn't answer, so I head back down, passing a few similar paintings—mostly scenes from the grounds.

I step into the functional kitchen that looks like it was haphazardly slapped together in the 1950s and hasn't been touched since. Alexandre is looking through some books and papers on the counter. "Who did all the paintings in the house?" I ask.

"I don't know. Honestly, I've barely given the paintings in here any thought. They're not exactly noteworthy."

"Guessing from the cheap wooden frames, maybe they were student work that got slapped up on the walls?" I suggest.

"I suppose?" Alexandre answers, but is clearly distracted. "Listen, I had this book I wanted to show you that has a passage about the housewarming party. But I can't find it. I think I might have left it at the main house. Do you mind if I run back to get it?"

THIS TRIP HAS been kind of a bust. I'm not sure why Alexandre's uncle sent us on this wild goose chase. I guess he's not concerned about wasting my time. Of course he isn't. I'm of no concern to him at all. This place is amazing, and I'm psyched I get the backstage tour, but it seems pretty picked over—if there ever was a missing Delacroix or anything of value, it's long gone. And if a painting by a master could be lost, whatever Leila might have given Dumas is probably food for worms.

While I wait for Alexandre, I turn on the tap to refill my water bottle, but the water comes out yellow, so I skip it, wanting to spare myself the lead poisoning. There's a dull whir coming from a retro mustard-yellow fridge; I open it and find four individual-sized bottles of Pellegrino, Mini Babybels, a pack of Le Petit Écolier biscuits, two clementines, and grapes. It's like Alexandre was expecting me. Like I said, people are eternal optimists. Maybe that's not always a bad thing.

I grab a bottle, shut the door, and lean against the fridge to take a swig. There's a matching mustard-yellow stove across from me, next to a small cupboard that looks like it was shoved into the space because it doesn't quite fit. And there's a crack parallel to the ceiling above it.

Wait. No. Not a crack. A seam.

I put my water down on the counter to my left and move closer to the cabinet. It's covering something up. The thin wooden door of the cabinet sticks, so I pull with a little more effort, forcing it open. A few chips of white paint fall to the floor. It's totally empty, except for the decades-old dust that touches everything in this place and what are maybe mouse droppings. Gross. I shut the door.

Since the cabinet doesn't sit flush with either the wall behind it or the counter next to it, I slip my hand in the open space along the side. It's narrow, but I can fit my arm through. I wrap my fingers around the back of the cabinet and try to inch it forward. It's empty, so it's not impossibly heavy, but it's cumbersome. I try fitting my hands around it, hugging the front, but my arms aren't long enough to reach the back of the cupboard.

It's probably another dead end, but no stones left unturned this time around. I'm in this till the end, and I'm here, so I might as well force the issue. Literally.

I open the door again and grab hold of the shelves to see if I can make any headway in moving the cabinet out of its space. I gain a few inches. There's a big enough gap between the cupboard and the wall now that it's clear there's a door behind it. I grab my phone to shine a light in the back. There's no doorknob, only a round hole where a knob should be. I lean over, stretching all the way from my toes, and can barely fit the tips of my fingers into the hole where the doorknob should go, but I can't get a grip.

I blow my hair out of my face and step back, trying to assess how to get sufficient leverage to pull this cupboard out. I twitch my nose partially from the dust, partially because I'm not sure what to do next. Then Zaid and his ridiculous physics jokes pop into my head. He would find this whole slapstick situation hilarious. He could probably make me laugh about this whole thing. And he would know what I need: *force equals mass times acceleration.*

Force. I need more force. And I'm the force.

I take a deep breath and grab the open cabinet door with one hand and the side of the cabinet with the other. I pull. Hard. The cabinet inches forward. I pull again; I feel a few drops of sweat beading above my lip. I can do this. A surprising buoyancy fills me. The cabinet gives some more and now is sort of twisted, the side of its open door angled toward the kitchen. This time, I grasp the door with both hands and pull hard with all my strength.

My right hand slips, and I fall right on my ass.

"Dammit," I say as I stand up, rubbing my backside and rolling my head to stretch my neck.

"What are you doing?" Alexandre stands in the doorway with a book in his hand. He puts it on the counter and walks over. "This breaking French antiques thing is getting to be a habit. I'm going to have to report you as a menace to the Minister of Culture."

"What?"

Alexandre points to the cabinet. The upper part of the door is off its hinge, and it's leaning forward at a precarious angle.

"Oh crap. Sorry. I was trying to get behind it."

Alexandre grins, amused, but also raises an eyebrow. "Why?"

"There's a door." I point behind the cupboard. "I hope this cupboard isn't on the historic register," I say, wincing.

"Don't worry, it's hardly a national treasure. But that door behind it—I've never seen that. Step back for a second."

I step aside, happy to give Alexandre the chance to pull out the cupboard or fall on his ass trying.

Alexandre wraps his long arms around the entire cabinet and first tries to lift it out, then resorts to dragging it forward, which works. I step up and help guide the cabinet far out enough into the kitchen so that we can slip behind it. The door is painted the same dull white as the rest of the kitchen and is much smaller than a standard door. It looks like someone painted right over the seams. I wiggle my fingers through the doorknob hole and pull. There's some cracking, but it doesn't budge.

"Hang on," Alexandre says, then grabs a dish towel from the counter and hands it to me. "Use this. That looks like a sure way to get splinters."

I lay the small towel along the bottom edge of the hole, place my hand on it, and try pulling again. "God, a million layers of paint are gluing this shut. Why would they do this?"

"A careless paint job? And then when whoever redid this kitchen saw it, they probably figured it was easier to stick the cabinet here."

"Grab a knife," I say. Alexandre hands me one, and I chisel through some of the paint on the side of the door. "Can you reach the top?"

Alexandre slips into the small space next to me. I hand him the knife, and he wedges it between the door seam and wall, working his way from left to right, inching closer to me. Dust and paint fall around us. If this were a movie, Alexandre being pressed up next to me as motes of dust waft down on us from above might be full of romantic tension, but in reality it's a little gross—a potent brew of adrenaline and endorphins and sweat and dust amidst the mouse droppings.

Alexandre draws his arms down and gently grips my shoulder. "Ready?"

I nod. I'm not ready, though. This little hobbit door could be another empty promise, but my heart races anyway. I may still be uncertain about sharing Leila's story with the world, but I can't deny how desperately I want to know all of it—know her.

We step out of this small space to give the door room to open. Alexandre fits his finger through the doorknob hole and tugs. The door creaks and groans and gives way. It scrapes against the floor, swollen from the heat and from being shuttered for decades.

The door stands ajar, and we peer into the space. It's a dusty, cobwebby old storage room.

We have to duck our heads to squeeze through. There are cardboard boxes stacked against the walls and an old wooden trunk with what looks like drapes piled on top. A wooden table with two chairs stacked on top is pushed up against the back wall. We step farther into the space, making sure we don't trip on anything, and shine our phone lights into the darkness.

I spy a set of wooden frames leaning against the wall beneath the windowsill and step over to take a look. The canvases are grimy, and some are damaged. They're mostly amateur portraits and scenes of the grounds in bloom. Some of the wooden frames are cracked and empty. As I flip through them, cobwebs stretch and break between the frames.

I turn to Alexandre. "I wonder how long this stuff has been in here?"

He's investigating the trunk, which appears to be filled with old textbooks. He shrugs, then sends a beam of light from his phone across the space. It catches on an object on the wall, hidden in a shadowy corner.

"Oh, merde alors," Alexandre whispers, almost reverently.

I reach toward a small rectangular painting inset in a simple but substantial wood frame.

I suck in my breath. It's her.

Leila

❧⁖❧

I write these words years hence, as time seems to fold in on itself. Where once the images of your red lips and dark curls and the feel of your rein-coarsened palms against mine faded into the creases of my mind, I find those images renewed, that touch reimagined. Time is funny in this way, a fickle master. But I can only believe it means that soon I will join you, my love, in the jannah of our dreams. Will I find you there? Did you wait for me? Does time pass achingly as it does on earth, or is there no time at all?

Each of these decades apart has felt like centuries, nay, an eternity of days, each one ending in the same way, as I looked for the last time upon the shores that were once home. On the land where our love blossomed. On the dusty earth where your blood fell. Each night when my eyes closed, there was the old heartache, made new again. Each night the wound, refreshed, in the stillness of my room.

I will away now to quieter shores, where I hope the lapping waves will carry you back to me as they once carried me away. I will admit I am afraid. For though I trust in the life after this one, I have moments of doubt that perhaps we shall not be reunited. Yet I try and keep my faith like the damask rose you once gave me, ever in bloom.

KHAYYAM

I am frozen in place, even as Alexandre inches ahead, awe-struck. It's too impossible to be real. Like a character has walked out of a book, out of my imagination, and into real life.

A wooden frame the size of a cookie sheet showcases a canvas with a dark-haired woman, her raven tresses falling in waves down her shoulder. She's standing to the side of a fountain, her face in profile. Even in this poor light, I can make out her dark scarlet lips and the olive-brown tones of her skin. We've never met, but I think I'd know her anywhere. "She's . . . she's . . ."

"Luminescent," Alexandre finishes my sentence. "It's the Delacroix mastery of color and light." His light follows the length and curve of Leila's figure. "See how even in profile, her features are really refined? And the embroidery on the robe?"

When we shine our light closer to the canvas, we see the midnight-blue of the robe or dress she is wearing is deep and rich. The silk cascades in folds along her body and onto the ground below, concealing her feet as she stands gazing into a fountain. The robe slips ever slightly from her shoulder and is bordered all along the hem with golden stars. Her left hand casually grasps a silver dagger at her side, its cream-colored handle showing between her fingers. It's the dagger that's sitting in my living room right now.

Alexandre gasps. "The dagger."

"I know," I whisper.

I honestly can't tell if this is real life or a dream—lately everything I hope for slips through my fingers, making hope feel too fragile, too dangerous, to believe in.

My heart races. I have to remind myself to breathe, because I think I stopped the minute a beam of light passed over Leila's face. She's young. Maybe nineteen or twenty in this portrait, though the Leila we glimpsed in the letters was older, middle-aged. This is the Leila of Byron's poem. She was beautiful and strong, and she deserved more than what life offered her. She was barely older than me. And alone.

"Leila's entire life, she was forced to hide," I mumble, my voice cracking. "Who the hell shoved her in this dark corner with a bunch of junk?" My voice grows louder with my anger. "Let's bring her into the light."

Alexandre squeezes my shoulder. "I couldn't agree more," he says, then gently lifts the small painting off the wall.

WE DUCK BACK through the door, Alexandre clearly taking care not to bump into anything. I wipe down the small kitchen table and then line it with paper towels, creating a semi-clean spot to rest the painting. We lean in closer. My breath is heavy, labored, like the weight of this moment is finally hitting me. Bending over the table, I search for the distinctive *Eug. Delacroix* signature but can't find it. It could be hidden beneath the frame, faded, or maybe he never signed it. But it has to be a Delacroix. I hope.

Alexandre steps away from the table and sinks to the floor. "I can't believe . . . finally. Finally, there's a chance. My family . . . we have to authenticate it first. X-rays. Multispectrum analysis. But the brushstrokes, the romantic nostalgia, the kind of dreaminess about the scene—it definitely feels like some of his later paintings."

I take a seat next to him and nudge him. He smiles. I smile back. Then giggle. He starts laughing, too. Nerves, I guess? I said there was a weight to this moment that made it hard to breathe. But weirdly, there's a lightness to it, too. A joy. A disbelief.

A thought occurs to me, something I remember from researching art provenance and authentication. "The back of a painting. We have to examine the back."

"Sorry?"

"Art historians learn as much from the back of the canvas as they do from the actual painting."

"Yes," says Alexandre. "Delacroix didn't sign all his paintings—"

"On the front," we say together and stand.

Alexandre steps over to the painting and lifts it up gently by the edges of the frame. I move closer. The back of the canvas is dark, a dirty beige. There's a yellowed piece of paper affixed to the top of the exposed wooden frame. It's small—maybe the size of a credit card. Faded black cursive on the back reads: Cherchez la femme, trouvez le trésor. There's no signature, no other words, no date. Celenia Mondego would probably say it hardly counts as evidence, but she's sitting behind a desk somewhere, and I'm here right now. For me, it is enough.

Alexandre's face erupts in a huge smile, every tooth showing. He carefully rests the painting on the table, then wraps his arms around me. Without even thinking about it, I return the hug but cast my gaze back to Leila and the fountain she's staring at. I'd missed it while I was busy staring only at her.

Oh my God.

"Alexandre, holy crap. The fountain." I pull myself out of the hug and bend over the painting again. "The last letter. The one from Dumas to Leila, from the Baudelaire book. Show it to me."

"Okaaaaay. But why?" He pulls out his phone from his back pocket and begins scrolling.

"Hurry up. Please."

He scrolls faster, clicks, and then hands the phone to me.

I read out loud from the last note Dumas wrote to Leila, "*Happiness is like the enchanted palaces we read of in our childhood, where fierce, fiery dragons defend the entrance and approach*. That's from *Monte Cristo*, right?"

Alexandre nods.

"The dragon . . . *defends* . . . the entrance," I say slowly. "He guards it from anyone who might try and trespass." I get goosebumps as I say the words; I finally see the pieces clicking into place. "Look closer." I point to the fountain. "That's the fountain from the garden. That little dragon is guarding Dumas's happiness. Or, I dunno, maybe Leila's. It doesn't matter, because that fountain must be where the Leila cache is hidden."

"*This* is the Leila cache. Cherchez la femme, trouvez le trésor. We looked for the woman and found the treasure: the painting."

"I swear, I know your great-grandfather better than you. For Dumas, the treasure wasn't the Delacroix; the treasure was Leila. Her story. Whatever it is she gave him." I walk toward the door and beckon Alexandre to follow.

"Where are we going?"

"The garden. To find the dragon that's guarding Dumas's happiness."

THE BASSIN DU Dragon juts out from the stone wall below the Château in a sunken garden. My heart thumps in my ears as we take the steps two at a time, skidding across the gravel to the basin.

Facing the fountain, actually looking at it this time, I see there are three rectangular sides. Two have carved medallions of lions' heads that once must have spewed water into the small basins directly underneath. But the center panel, the one I'm looking at, sports a sculpted faun's face. As with the lions, a small semicircular basin sits right below the faun, ready to catch any water. But what we're here for crouches below the faun, our little dragon on its own pedestal that would've emptied into the large basin at the foot of the fountain. Ferocious, with wings back, teeth bared, body at the ready, guarding this place from any who may try and trespass.

Alexandre steps right into the dry basin and bends down by the dragon, feeling around the stone. Unlike the two sides, this front piece is decorated with long, fernlike leaves carved behind the dragon and stalks that look like they could be . . .

"Birds of paradise." My mom's favorite flower. Alexandre is occupied with his task, so I say it louder. "Birds of paradise."

Alexandre shifts to look at me. "So . . ."

"This has to be the place that Dumas talks about in his deathbed letter to Leila—his paradise on earth. Where his love is evergreen and Paradise eternally in bloom. The birds of paradise flowers are sculpted, always in bloom."

There's this look of delightful disbelief in Alexandre's eyes, and the space between us feels full of possibilities. For a second, it seems like he might kiss me. But I tense, and my body sways back slightly.

"You're amazing," Alexandre says. "This is it. I can feel it. The dragon, the birds of paradise, even that." He points to the carved head above the medallion. "I think it's Pan. Dumas was a huge mythology buff—there are references to myths throughout *Monte Cristo*."

"Pan is the god of nature, right? The guy with the flute, surrounded by nymphs?"

"Exactly. Nymphs aren't goddesses. They're divine spirits on earth—young, beautiful maids who never aged."

"Leila," I whisper. "The beautiful spirit."

The strange juxtaposition of all these elements isn't lost on me. The dragon guarding the palace of happiness, the birds of paradise, and Pan. It's a hodgepodge, like a lot of Dumas's writing. Like Leila's story, like mine. Like all of ours.

"But this place was built before Leila disappeared from Dumas's life."

"The main house, yes. But not all the grounds. Dumas could have easily commissioned this fountain later; even if he was going bankrupt, he could've found a sponsor to pay for it or one more creditor. Also, this fountain hasn't worked in decades. Maybe Dumas made sure it never did because it's not a fountain. It's a hiding place. It would be very Dumas to build this in honor of her."

We set back to work feeling around the stone, checking for tiles or crevices that might give. The large basin's floor is pretty broken up. We can even pull up chunks of it to expose the hollow underneath. But there's nothing there but old, moss-covered pipes and bugs. Alexandre sticks his fingers into the mouth of the dragon and then moves to Pan. He also checks the god's pointy ears. I slide over to investigate the fish carved below the lions.

The fish on the left side turns out to be . . . a fish. The lion medallion above doesn't yield any secrets, either. I move to the right, stepping around Alexandre, who is now pulling at the dragon's teeth. I would like to believe I'm the Veronica Mars of art world sleuthing, but right now, I'd say we're a little more *Scooby-Doo*, believing that a dragon tooth is going to be the lever that reveals a secret chamber, and I'm getting hungry again, so a Scooby snack sounds good right about now.

I squat in front of the fish on the right—its tongue sticks out, mocking me, because upon close examination, like its mate, it proves to be a carved fish. This is starting to feel ridiculous. I sigh. Alexandre and I exchange a look that's a cross between a three-year-old who inadvertently popped their birthday balloon and a WTF-are-we-even-doing eye roll.

I stand up face-to-face with the lion on the right panel. That's when I notice *this* lion isn't carved into the stone like the other one. It's metal. Brass or . . . ? Looks like it was once painted over—a dull gray to match the stone—but the chipped, weathered paint reveals a brownish-green. Copper, maybe?

I run my fingers over the lion's face and mane, about the size of a dinner plate. It's not sculpted into the fountain like the rest of the figurines. "Alexandre," I say under my breath as I trace my fingers over the edges, hitting the groove of a nail—no, a small screw, then another. "Alexandre," I say louder, "we've got to get this lion's head off."

He joins me, and I point to the screws. We each begin madly working on one screw at a time. Twisting, pulling. Alexandre gives up and tries simply lifting off the entire lion's head.

"We need tools," I say. "We can't pull out screws and bolts with our fingers. There's all this rust and—"

Alexandre rushes off before I can finish. "There's a janitor's closet!" he yells as he runs up the stairs toward the Château.

I TAKE A seat on the edge of the stone basin, resting my chin in my hand. Evening is approaching, and it's been an exhausting and exhilarating day. I still need to text my parents, and regardless of whether we find anything in this fountain, the entire world is going to know at least part of Leila's story tomorrow. Secrets will be revealed. But not all of them.

Knowing how excited my parents get over even the tiniest of academic revelations, I can only imagine the uproar this will cause in the worlds of art and literature—in France, in England, with Ottoman scholars. And maybe even with the judges of the Art Institute's Young Scholar Prize.

The world can be turned upside down by a chance encounter. Or, in my case, one calculated by Alexandre's Uncle Gérard and carried out by Alexandre. Still. It makes my brain hurt to think about how little control we have over events in our life despite how hard we try to control everything. How hard *I* try to control everything.

Alexandre races toward me, carrying a screwdriver, pliers, and a small crowbar. The sheen of sweat on his face somehow doesn't diminish his cuteness. His wild-eyed determination heightens my own excitement amidst the bittersweet sentiments that course through me. It's weird how we can hold two—or more—emotions in our bodies at the same time. How do human beings just not explode from too many feelings?

"A crowbar? You're not planning on destroying this fountain, are you?"

"I'll do everything I can to avoid it." Alexandre is totally serious as he says this.

He passes me the screwdriver. My hands are clammy; I can't get a good grip on the rubber handle. I try to rub the sweat off on my jeans, but in a second my palms are sweaty again. The cycle of nervous anticipation. The screwdriver only succeeds in loosening the screws slightly—it's not the right size, which I suppose makes sense, seeing that the tool is from the twenty-first century and the screw is probably from the nineteenth. Alexandre steps forward with the pliers and begins gently pulling at one screw until it pops out. Then he gets the other, but the medallion stays in place.

We try to shift it. And it budges the tiniest bit. My mouth is like cotton, my pulse racing. I want so badly for this to be *something*.

Alexandre attempts to grip the medallion from around its edges and nudge it out of place. His faces strains from concentration; he grits his teeth. This time, tiny bits of stone fall from underneath the lion's head. It's getting looser. He wedges the screwdriver between the medallion and the stone column. I stand next to him, holding up the medallion by its slim edges so it doesn't fall forward on us. Alexandre shoves the screwdriver in the hollow we've made by shifting the medallion to the left and right. It gives. We both gasp and catch the face of the lion in our hands as it careens forward. We gently place the medallion behind us, then turn back to stare into the dark abyss of a hole in the side of the fountain.

There's nothing quippy on the tip of my tongue, but my brain brims—a synaptic tangle of thoughts and feelings and silent screams. My hand trembles as I reach into the darkness.

The hollow is cool, slightly damp. I stretch up on my tiptoes until my fingers skim the bottom. A shelf, maybe? My hand brushes against something. A jar. It slips from my fingers with a clink. My heart stops. Time stops. "There's a pot or something in here, but I can't quite grab it," I say as I remove my hand.

Alexandre reaches in. The searching look in his eyes transforms to wonder when he finds the jar. "Got it," he whispers and carefully pulls the pot out through the hole.

He cups it in both hands. It's a simple, milk-colored ceramic pot. A dirty one. I chip at the caked-on mud with my fingernail, and a leaf of dirt falls away, revealing a logo: CONFITURES FINES FELIX POTIN PARIS. It's a jam jar.

Alexandre stares at the jar. "I knew you'd find it."

"*We* found it. Let's hope it's not a-hundred-and-seventy-five-year-old rotten jam."

Alexandre puts a grimy hand on mine. I don't flinch. "Khayyam. Without you . . . I was wrong to deceive you, to let my uncle influence me and push me the way he did. You deserve so much better. I should've been honest from the beginning. You deserve the truth."

"Maybe that's what we're about to find," I say, my voice catching.

Leila

Though I will soon be forgotten, perhaps have been already, I leave this record now to tell my truth:

I lived.

I loved.

I had a voice.

And in this life, where I had so little to call my own, where my liberty and love were torn from me, I seize this power: the freedom to write my own story.

KHAYYAM

Stories are funny things. Even the mere idea of fiction. Facts exist. But I see now that facts are different than truth. Facts are supposed to be indisputable, unbending (at least until science tells us we were wrong about everything), but even the true stories of who we think ourselves to be are a kind of fiction we create. We build our worlds out of vestiges of history and the fairy tales adults tell us and scraps of poetry we hear: *Beauty is truth, truth beauty*.

A poem can be the truth. And a painting. And a novel. And this space right now, between Alexandre and me, in the fading light of early evening in a writer's haven in the French countryside where words gave life to an epic. And in these words, black ink fading into the weave of cream-colored paper, rests Leila's truth, revealed at last.

Alexandre and I stare at the wrinkled and creased sheaf of papers in front of us. The ceramic confiture pot is now back in the kitchen of Château d'If, where it must once have been long ago. Sealed away, it has done its duty, preserved the treasure of Leila's story, protected her words from rain and

predators and opportunists while waiting for us to find them.
That's what I want to believe.

We find a note folded on top of the story, and I read it out
loud, my voice breaking but my heart full.

Cher Ami,

*I find myself in your debt. For it is you who bade me write my
story that I could discover agency in this world, that in placing pen
to paper, I may at last rid myself of the specter of a life desperately
wanted but unlived. You were not the first who urged me so; Byron
encouraged me thus, but I was not yet ready. And finding me
indifferent, the poet fashioned his own tale, a dark fantasy, though
he had seen the truth with his own eyes. One our dear friend then
immortalized on his canvases. Perhaps I should have written sooner,
but I was younger, and I feared reliving those unspeakable final
days when my beloved was lost to me forever. I did not know then,
as I do now, that writing my story was the way for my Giaour to
come back to me, a way for me to come back to myself.*

*I leave these words with you now, my dear Alexandre, as I bid
you adieu. Take care of them. Guard them. They are my heart,
exposed.*

*In recent years, I felt my inquisitiveness shrivel, as one does,
I suppose, when age confronts you. I found that I had replaced
Pasha's gilded cage for one of my own making. But through our
talks and debates on our philosophies, indeed, in your sheer joy for
even the smallest things, I find my own curiosity for life renewed,
and thus I set out on one final adventure. Softer, perhaps, than
the grand voyage that brought me here, but a journey I wish to*

take, and take alone. Do not feel that I have rebuffed you in slipping quietly away. Though as a Muslim, we confess our sins and shortcomings only to God, I offer you this last confession in the hopes that it might ease your mind or your heart. Though you know my heart belongs to another, I have loved you in my own way, Alexandre. Perhaps not with the ardor you sought and conveyed, but in true admiration for your spirit and with a trust I have given no other since I fled my home.

My departure is bittersweet. Paris is the only home I have known beyond the harem, and yet neither of them was of my choosing.

I leave now, not as I once was, but something more and stronger. I leave now with my story, at long last my own.

Peace be with you, my friend, in this life and the next.

Ever yours,

Leila

I put the letter down as I repeat the words Leila quoted in her story: "*The moving finger writes, and having writ moves on.*" Words concealed in a jam pot all these years—a century and a half before I was born.

I shake my head, a lump welling in my throat. It's not possible.

"It's a beautiful line," Alexandre says.

"It's more than words," I whisper. "It's Omar Khayyam. That's the Persian poet she was talking about."

"Merde, alors." Alexandre covers his mouth with his hand. "I know you've said a million times you don't believe in destiny. But Leila's story was a part of your story all along."

I bury my face in my hands. I'm not sure what to believe anymore. I'm not even sure of the difference between fact and fiction. Maybe there is none. Maybe we're always becoming what we imagine ourselves to be.

Alexandre shakes his head. "What a life. This story—her story. A courtyard of hollowed trees, the yataghan the Giaour gifted her, the sack-death attempt, her rescue by jinns, her protector Si'la. It's too fantastical to be believed." He rubs the small of my back.

"For Muslims, jinns aren't simply fantastical, mythical creatures," I say, straightening. "I mean, yes, they entered into legend, but they are God's creations, beings made from smoke-less fire. Shape-shifters. Not singing blue creatures that pop out of magic lamps. Anyway, it doesn't matter what we believe, does it? It's Leila's story—it's her voice, telling us her truth."

"And now the world will know it. Know her," Alexandre says softly.

I sigh. I'm still not certain this is the right thing to do. Would Leila have wanted this story to be told? She wrote it for an audience of two. There's no way she could have imagined the audience that awaits her now. I see the academics and museum curators salivating already. And with Delacroix and Dumas and Byron intertwined in all of this, it's going to go viral in a massive way. My little ambitions to write a killer essay—to win a contest—seem so small right now.

Leila, forgive me if this isn't what you wanted in your time, but maybe your voice and your life have been erased long enough.

"You're still not sure, are you?" Alexandre asks.

"No. But I do think it's the only thing we can do, that

we should do. Leila isn't voiceless, but she was silenced. And honestly, if she inspired three different geniuses, maybe Leila's own brilliance and bravery should be uncovered for the world to see and to know. Besides, I'm sick of the old *behind every successful man is a great woman* BS. Time for this woman's story to be front and center—in the light of day and not in some man's shadow."

Alexandre nods. "Are you talking about you or Leila?"

I smile. "Both."

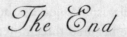

The End
THE BEGINNING

My parents warned me that it would be a media circus, and they were right. When I finally called them that night after we discovered Leila's story, they rented a car and drove straight from Brittany to the Château de Monte-Cristo. So many questions and talking and retracing our steps and explaining. And that was just for my parents.

The next morning, Alexandre contacted his parents and his uncle and the archivist of the estate, and then came preservationists and experts from the Louvre and the Bibliothèque Nationale de France and the Musée Delacroix and the Académie Française. And, wow, was there arguing. Alexandre's uncle—a skinny, wrinkled man with bushy gray hair who smokes too much—tried to shake my hand. Talk to me. Thank me. I turned my back and walked away. It was all too much. Maybe I've found a way to forgive Alexandre, but I haven't forgotten that his uncle was the puppet master. And I'm tired of people trying to pull my strings.

That was all before the various steamrolling adults and institutions finally agreed on terms for a press conference where Alexandre and I were presented as these two young sleuths who had performed this incredible service to France, having unearthed a part of her heritage that had been lost. Then they whisked us away without giving us a chance to talk—to tell the whole story, the real one. No surprise there.

But I had a little surprise in store for them, too. Using my best Sharpie skills and a plain white tee I liberated from Alexandre, I stood on that stage with #writeherstory emblazoned across the front of my shirt, making my loyalties and purpose clear. The press conference isn't the end of this story; it's the beginning.

My parents assured me that I would still get credit for the discovery—my name somewhere on an official piece of paper, on a plaque. That I could—and should—still write an essay about it for the Art Institute, but that now my essay could be published in art history journals, even mainstream media.

Me, I'm not sure what I want to do next. I only know that I want Leila's story to be heard and respected. I don't want her used and forgotten again. I'll do whatever I can to make sure she isn't.

Alexandre saved his family and Dumas's legacy. Sure, there's a bureaucratic nightmare of provenance and wills to unravel, but the letters prove that Delacroix painted Leila *for* Dumas. The family can sell the painting if they want and pay the back taxes on the Château. Of course, there will be a renewed interest in Dumas, and tourists will probably flock to this place. I heard Alexandre's uncle saying that the family would petition the French government to protect the entire estate as a national historical monument because of our discoveries. That means it would be safeguarded from slimy American real estate tycoons forever.

I'm happy for Alexandre. I guess in a way, I've come to

understand his motivations. His desire to help his family. Leila never had that kind of family. She was an orphan whose one true love was murdered before her eyes. Leila might not be related to me by blood, but she's my family now, and I'll make sure no one hurts her ever again.

TODAY IS THE goodbye. I'm not sure if I'm ready to face it, but it's coming whether I'm ready or not.

My phone rings as I step through the arches of Place des Vosges, past the *1764 Nicola* graffiti. It's Julie.

She skips the hello. "Are you okay? My parents send me to Internet jail for a month, and I come out to find this angry, weepy email from you and that your *#writeherstory* photo has gone viral. And there's some hot dude in a picture with you next to the missing masterpiece you found, and your face looks like you're going to cry when it should be beaming. What is happening?"

I laugh. It's great to hear her voice. "I've missed you, too. And, yeah, um, we have a lot to catch up on. A lot."

"I know! Give me details. Zaid. This French dude. Delacroix. Leila. Damn, girl, you've had a busy summer."

"I will. I want to. It's been amazing. And horrible. But right now, I'm about to meet that hot French dude and say goodbye."

"I'm sorry. That sucks. Especially after the BS Zaid pulled, which I am going to give him hell about, by the way."

I chuckle. "Nah, it's okay. Can't wait to see you."

"Text me your flight info. I'll be waiting for you on your porch."

"I know you will," I say before we hang up.

I'm usually excited to go home after our annual Paris holiday. And I can't wait to see Julie and tell her everything. It's weird, though. Chicago feels so far away right now. Like when I get there, a part of me will still be here in Paris.

"WHAT DO YOU want to do on your last afternoon here?" Alexandre asks as we sit on a blanket on the grass at Place des Vosges, his fingers busy finalizing the white clover crown he's been working on the last few minutes. He places it on my head and says, "You are the queen of your fate."

"You already used that line on me," I say, fingering the flowers atop my hair.

"Time is a flat circle," Alexandre says. "Time is infinite, but events are finite, so we are destined—or doomed in some cases—to repeat them. Nietzsche called it eternal return."

"Uhh, he totally stole that concept from Hinduism and Buddhism."

Alexandre grins. "He would probably say that proves his point. There is no new thing under the sun."

"Sounds like a sophisticated excuse for plagiarism," I say. We both laugh. "I guess I see it, though. Time is an endless circle, but it's a loop, so everything we experience or feel someone else has already experienced and felt before us. But what about the fact that the universe is always expanding? The universe isn't finite."

"Hmm, well, in the universe, space is time, right?"

I grin, then cover my face with my hands. Alexandre leans over and gently moves them away. Tears splash down my cheeks.

"Why are you crying?"

"I don't know. They're sort of happy tears, I guess? Time is weird and impossible. Doesn't it feel to you like we know Leila, like she's a living, breathing person right now? It's like words made her flesh, but now that the world has her story, she's receded back into history—a two-dimensional figure in a book to be studied. She was lost and then found, and now she's slipped away again."

Alexandre nods. "For a couple weeks, we were the only ones on earth who knew who she was, even though all we had was an inkling, a small idea of her. I think it's normal to feel protective of her. We were her guardians for a short time, after all."

"I still am. Always." I give him a soft smile and look off toward Victor Hugo's house.

In France, much more so than in America, the past and present live side by side. I guess it's inevitable then that sometimes those worlds collide. Parallel universes suddenly cognizant of each other's existence.

Alexandre touches my elbow. "I got you a little something to say bon voyage." He hands me a square brown paper package tied in a red satin ribbon. I turn it over to unwrap it and pull out a small wooden frame. Underneath the glass is a sketch of Leila we saw in the archive of the Musée Delacroix. It was a scrap in a file, forgotten, ink on paper, a close-up of Leila's face in profile looking off in the distance.

"Oh my God, Alexandre. Did you steal this?"

A smile spreads across his face. "No one knows that exists besides me and you. And I'm sure Delacroix would want you to have it. And so would Dumas."

"And you're basing this on . . . ?"

"Delacroix was a family friend and made that sketch for my great-grand-père. As far as I'm concerned, it is a personal heirloom. I'm completely within my rights to give it to you."

"I'll revel in your entitlement since it benefits me. Si tu n'as pas le droit, prend le gauche, non?" If you don't have the right, take the left.

Alexandre laughs. "How very French of you. Now you will have a Delacroix in your home like I do, a secret only you and I will know. A private souvenir."

A lump wells in my throat. "Thank you, Alexandre," I whisper. Another tear falls down my cheek. We haven't talked about what happens tomorrow when I leave for home. He lives here; I live in Chicago. And there are a whole lot of jagged truths between us.

Still.

I lean over and kiss him. It's a goodbye. It's a gesture that holds no promise. It's closure. It's not perfect, but it's how our story ends, at least for now, and that's okay.

I wonder what things would've been like if we'd really met accidentally or if he'd emailed me and asked me to coffee. I think about our first kiss in his library and how it tasted like books and Orangina. And how things were good and then chaos. And how lies and truths commingle in all our lives. I think about the flat circle and how at some point in that never-ending loop, our paths crossed, maybe in a different way, and we found Leila and we found each other and we found the truth.

If eternal return is real, and the universe keeps expanding and events keep recurring, then eventually this moment will happen again. And then once more, for an infinity of lifetimes. Maybe one of those times we'll get it exactly right.

Somewhere along that circle, the tale will be told and retold. There, Leila and Dumas and Delacroix and Byron and Alexandre and Khayyam will travel down a long, winding road that will eventually bring us together, unlikely companions finding one another through space and time to tell a truth.

In the end, we all become stories.

AUTHOR'S NOTE

This story is fiction.

But it also tells the truth.

All stories start with a seed and for me that seed was planted years ago when I first crossed paths with Lord Byron's epic poem, *The Giaour*, along with his deeply ingrained Orientalism and sexism. In college, I took a class that centered around Mary Shelley's *Frankenstein*, a novel that I found threaded with the Orientalist stereotypes of the time. Yes, even our favorite iconoclastic feminists held entrenched prejudices—mostly toward women of color (See: *Vindication of the Rights of Woman* by Shelley's mom, Mary Wollstonecraft, where she imagines Muslim women as servile and soulless, unthinking sexual curiosities). My seemingly fated meeting with the Romantics led me to my bachelor's thesis, which examined Napoleon's influence on British Orientalism—a corporate and literary institution that allowed the West to create, restructure, and appropriate the East in accordance with its colonial endeavors. Through my research I realized that the Orientalism of eighteenth- and nineteenth-century conquest was still very much present and flourishing in our world today. Control the narrative, control the people. Sound familiar?

I wanted to write a story that would bring those connections to light. I wanted to create a character, a girl like all the other girls finding their voices, a young woman who could reach back into the past to seize a stolen narrative and reclaim it—as a woman, as a Muslim, as a human being fighting for a space of her own. That character is Khayyam and the voice she freed is Leila's. Two young women connected through time both giving utterance to a powerful idea: they are the heroes of their own stories.

The Giaour, published in 1813, is a fragmentary poem of 1300 lines with three different narrators and points of view telling the story of a young woman, Leila—of her life in a Pasha's harem and her affair with the Giaour, an alleged infidel, her drowning in a sack death when her betrayal was discovered, and a fight to the death between the Pasha and the Giaour. It is a story about a woman, in which the woman has no voice. It is the story of the East told completely through the lens of the colonizer. It is the story of a Muslim, written by an Orientalist who fetishized the harem and who was convinced Muslim women had neither the power nor desire to speak for themselves.

While the Leila in Byron's *The Giaour* is fiction, some scholars suggest she was "inspired" by a sixteen-year-old girl who Napoleon took into his own colonial harem during his ill-fated attempted conquest of Egypt. When he abandoned her (along with his entire army) as he escaped back to France, she was killed by local authorities for her alleged collaboration with Napoleon—bound in a sack and drowned. The tragedy of this sack death that Byron seized upon for his poem eventually led to a series of paintings and sketches by

Eugène Delacroix informed by Byron's work. One of those paintings, *The Combat of the Giaour and Hassan*, was once believed to have been owned by Alexandre Dumas, père. An entire history of a woman, under the ownership of men.

When we say history is written by the victors, we mean history is written by the patriarchy.

Women have always played a central role in building society, yet here we are, even today, our word and our testimony deemed unbelievable, our work undervalued. Even more so if you are an individual of color, nonbinary, queer, trans, an immigrant, Muslim, Hindu, Sikh, Jewish, et al intersections of identity. Because of millennia of this hegemony—of this racial and gender inequality, we don't just live in the patriarchy, the patriarchy lives in us. And if you believe, as I do, that a just and exemplary society is one free of discrimination, where each human being is treated equally, we must—all of us—deliberately, consciously work toward that goal. A very simple step in that direction is this: recognizing that for too long the spotlight has shined on too few and too many stories are relegated to the margins.

One doesn't need to dig too deep—indeed you can simply scratch the surface of history—to reveal the stories of countless women that remain untold, their names and achievements unrecognized. I wrote this story to help change that. That's what Khayyam seeks to do when she first comes across the intriguing possibility of Leila: unearth a treasure that deserves its moment to shine. And while she advocates for Leila's story, she finds that she's fighting for her own story, too.

Leila and Khayyam may be figments of imagination, but Byron and Delacroix and Dumas are very real men whose lives and works we know. We've read their letters, reveled in their art and genius, too easily excused their shortcomings.

In writing *Mad, Bad & Dangerous to Know*—about two fictional women whose lives intersect—I felt a profound sadness for all the real genius we failed to celebrate. For all the art we will never see and the stories we will never read because their creators were not history's conquerors, because their lives were deemed unworthy.

History doesn't need to be an exclusionary tale. Our lives and worlds are richer for the diversity inclusion brings. The present always holds the power to write history. Let's write the truth. There is room enough on our shelves, and if you find you've run out of space, construct a new bookcase. Build another library. Dig deep to reveal the wrongs of the past, so we can write this world as it should be. So we can right this world. Period.

#WriteHerStory

ACKNOWLEDGMENTS

A decade ago, publishing my third book was barely a hope at the blurry edges of my dreams. Yet, here we are and I am deeply indebted to every person who has made my work possible in this world.

My gratitude to Daniel Ehrenhaft, Bronwen Hruska, Alexa Wejko, Rachel Kowal, Janine Agro, David Lanaspa, and the entire Soho Teen squad. So proud to have another book with you!

Big love to my fabulous agent, Joanna Volpe, and the amazing team at New Leaf, especially Jordan Hill and Abbie Donoghue. You helped me bring this story home. That means the world to me.

I am grateful beyond words to friends and family, early readers and joyful cheerleaders, who lifted me up, listened, and helped bring life to my writing. Merci beaucoup: Pierre Jonas, Marie-France Jonas, Elise Warren, Shveta Thakrar, Rachel Strolle, Amy Vidlak Girmscheid, Julia Torres, Gloria Chao, Eric Smith, Sangu Mandanna, Patrice Caldwell, Alia Thomas, Sona Charaipotra, Kim Liggett, Farah Naz Rishi, Dhonielle Clayton, Lizzie Cooke, Ronni Davis, Kat Cho, Rena

Barron, Anna Waggener, Amy Adams, Claribel Ortega, Sarvenaz Tash, Raeshma Razvi, Nathan Small Claus. To the twelve+, whether I see you at Thanksgiving or not, those fry-filled late nights at the Herrington with Hal fueled many a story. And to Professor Jim Chandler, for teaching a class so thought-provoking it led to this book.

Heartfelt thanks to my parents, Hamid and Mazher, and my sisters, Asra and Sara, for their enduring support and love. Bulldogs forever!

Lena and Noah, you are my inspirations, my reasons for everything. I love you up to the moon and back, plus two to three weeks (at least).

Thomas, if time is a flat circle, my story returns, eternally, to you.

RESOURCES

1. pp. 108–109, 143–144 translated and paraphrased from "Le Club des Hachichins," published in the *Revue des Deux Mondes* February 1846.

2. p. 173 George Gordon, Lord Byron. "She Walks in Beauty," London, 1814. https://poets.org/poem/she-walks-beauty

3. p. 231 George Gordon, Lord Byron Letter to the Countess Teresa Guiccioli: https://englishhistory.net/byron/selected-letters/countess-teresa-guiccioli/

4. pp. 259, 299 ". . . happiness is like the enchanted palaces we read of in our childhood, where fierce, fiery dragons defend the entrance and approach." Dumas, Alexandre. *The Count of Monte-Cristo*, 1844–1846. (Serialization in *Journal des débats*.)

5. p. 273 "There are women who inspire you with the desire to conquer them and to take your pleasure of them; but this one fills you only with the desire to die slowly beneath her gaze." Baudelaire, Charles. *Spleen de Paris* (petits poems en prose), Paris, 1869.

Selected additional sources:

Books:
Butler, Marilyn. *Romantics, Rebels and Reactionaries*.
Oxford: Oxford University Press, 1981.

Byron, George Gordon. *The Giaour in Byron*, edited
by Jerome J. McGann, pp. 207-247. Oxford: Oxford
University Press, 1991.

Dumas, Alexandre. *The Count of Monte-Cristo*. New York:
Bantam Dell, 2003.

Gautier, Théophile. *Romans et Contes*, "Le Club des
Haschischins." Paris: Charpentier et Cie, Libraires-éditeurs,
1863.

Johnson, Lee. *The Paintings of Eugène Delacroix: A Critical
Catalogue, Volumes 1 & 2*. Oxford: Oxford University
Press, 1981.

Robaut, Alfred. *L'Oeuvre Complet de Eugène Delacroix:
Peintures, Dessins, Gravures*. Paris: Charavay Frères
Editeurs, 1885.

Said, Edward W. *Orientalism*. New York: Vintage Books,
1979.

Shelley, Mary. *Frankenstein*. Chicago: University of Chicago
Press, 1982.

Websites:

The Art Institute of Chicago: https://www.artic.edu/artworks/110663/the-combat-of-the-giaour-and-hassan

The Château de Monte Cristo: https://www.chateau-monte-cristo.com/main/

Le Petit Palais: http://www.petitpalais.paris.fr/en/oeuvre/combat-giaour-and-pasha

The Metropolitan Museum of Art: https://www.metmuseum.org/art/collection/search/336577

Musée National Eugène Delacroix: http://musee-delacroix.fr/en/

The Telegraph: https://www.telegraph.co.uk/culture/books/3672150/Alexandre-Dumas-the-lost-adventure.html